JO-JO AND THE FIENDISH LOT

JO-JO AND THE
FIENDISH LOT

Andrew Auseon

HARPER TEEN
An Imprint of HarperCollins Publishers

HarperTeen is an imprint of HarperCollins Publishers.

Jo-Jo and the Fiendish Lot
Copyright © 2009 by Andrew Auseon
Library of Congress Cataloging-in-Publication Data
Auseon, Andrew.
Jo-Jo and the Fiendish Lot / Andrew Auseon. — 1st ed.
p. cm.
Summary: Just as seventeen-year-old Baltimore resident Jo-Jo Dyas is
about to kill himself, he meets Max, a dead girl who plays drums for a
rock band, and he travels with the band as they play shows all over the
Afterlife.
ISBN 978-0-06-113923-9 (trade bdg.)
[1. Death—Fiction. 2. Future life—Fiction. 3. Rock music—Fiction.]
I. Title.
PZ7.A9194Jo 2009   2008011721
[Fic]—dc22   CIP
                                                          AC
Typography by Hilary Zarycky
1 2 3 4 5 6 7 8 9 10

First Edition

For Sarah and Samara—you both burn so brightly

ACKNOWLEDGMENTS

For Those Who Helped Me Rock (I Salute You)

As I finish up my farewell tour, I want to thank my editor, Michael Stearns, for inspiring me, for believing in me, and simply for being a good friend. I will miss working with him. I'd also like to thank everyone else at Harper for their support and kindness, especially Farrin Jacobs, Ruta Rimas, and Gretchen Hirsch. My agent, Barry Goldblatt, also deserves a shout for talking me down from numerous ledges and for getting excited about my work even when I feel like setting it on fire. Most of the time he's successful.

I'd like to offer a special thank-you to my wife, Sarah, for continuing to put up with me, even on the nights when we hardly speak because I'm too involved with people who don't exist. And to my younger brother, Anthony, who is always a good judge of story and character and who is the one person I can ring when I want to call someone "Butter Lips" or "Dr. Ass."

Writing is tough, and it's always easier to spread your agony across a large group of individuals, which I've done liberally since 2001, when the work on this novel began. Without the help and encouragement of the following people, I probably wouldn't have ever embarked on—let alone survived—such a foolhardy task: the Auseon and Zogby families, Hannah Barnaby, Carmen Brock and Ben Homola, Margaret Carruthers, Cecil Castellucci, Ike and Kelsey Ellis, Eddie Gamarra, Fran Hodgkins, Joe and Amanda Kurtz, Kara Lareau, Scott Neumyer, Dominic and Kate Smith, Team Barry, my dear friends and classmates of Vermont College's Creative Writing for Children and Young Adults program, John-Paul Walton, and Sara Zarr.

TRACK 1:
THE END OF THE WORLD
AS I KNEW IT

BALTIMORE

That day down by the stream, I wanted to kill myself. Dead. Gone. Finished. And I would have done it, too, but the girl in the water stopped me.

With me I had the old .45 and a joint—everything I really needed, except a reason to go on living. My pop made a joke once, telling me never to take the old .45 out of his underwear drawer unless it was for a good reason. I had me a damn good one.

When you get the idea of killing yourself into your head, you can't think of a better reason to do anything else. The crazy idea sits there in the middle of your mind, like a big truck parked on some train tracks, and after a while the idea begins to seem less crazy and eventually even makes a bit of sense. Making yourself dead is a good reason to get up in the morning, if only so you don't ever have to get up again. Me, I did not want to get up one more morning without Violet.

The morning I got up to die was the prettiest day we'd had in months. I pulled on some sweats and this ratty Nirvana T-shirt I wore the night before and walked to Pop's old room to get the .45, which was heavier than I remembered. On the way, I checked on my nephew—my slut sister's baby—and made sure he was sleeping peaceful. Leaving the house, I took the change off the kitchen table like I was just running an errand down to the deli—maybe for bread or a slushie—like I'd be back.

I sat on the stoop for a few minutes, like everybody in Woodberry does, all of us nobodies sitting around on their flat concrete porches not doing anything. Our line of row houses goes all the way to the end of the block, and there ain't one of them looks livable—but then you turn around and see you've been living in one.

After a few minutes, Billie from next door walked out onto her stoop, cigarette dangling from one lip, her momma's baby drooped over one skinny arm. Billie was twelve years old but well on her way to being like my sister, who had a baby of her very own to dangle.

"Hey, Jo-Jo," Billie said between puffs. "What's up?"

"I'm gonna go blow my brains out," I said.

"Good luck with that," Billie said.

"Later, then," I said, and got up. I walked down Morton Avenue. I had spent seventeen years walking up and down that hill, and would probably have spent the next seventeen doing the same. That morning it took me only thirty seconds to reach the corner one last time. A whole life hiked in thirty seconds. If that's not a good enough reason to do yourself in, nothing is.

At the end of the block ran Druid Park Drive, a busier street, and I stood and waited as early traffic buzzed by before hustling across the road into the gravel parking lot of the old mattress warehouse across the street. I took one last look behind me at my neighborhood. A few houses up, Fat Emily stood in droopy stockings, unrolling a bleached old American flag above her front railing. In the street, Ray Hodges worked on his car, which bled a trickle of oil. Every time he gunned the engine, I smelled the gas in the air, the heat. Oil flowed all the way down the hill, pooling at my feet around a stuffed rabbit that had been ground into the roadside gutter. I'd had enough of all this, forever.

I slipped into the thick brush by the side of the parking lot and stumbled down a ravine to a stream where water bubbled over jagged rocks and broken liquor bottles. That was all it took, a few steps down into stubborn tangles of weeds and thick bushes, and everything changed. Deep forest green replaced concrete gray and asphalt black. Around me, trees seemed to tremble with bug noise. The hot asphalt stink was gone, leaving a heavy green nature smell, which was the only way I could describe it since I didn't know one jagged, curvy, three-leafed, spotted whatever from another. All I knew was that I liked it down there, and I think it was because the place felt alive.

I sat down by the edge of the water, not much caring about getting mud on my sweats or the way my high-tops just sort of sank into the cold water and soaked it up. The stream bubbled along its muddy bank and through an arched concrete tunnel under the roadway into darkness. Trees overhead formed a roof of branches and sunlight; the cars roaring past above sounded like one big breath of wind when I closed my eyes. This was where people would find me, if anyone even bothered to look.

I tried to think about things I would miss. There were a few: like the day soon when Pop got out of the hospital and would or would not be normal again, and maybe we'd go see an Orioles game like he'd been telling me we'd do for years, or that day in the future when the baby got old enough to say my name without any coaxing or my stupid sister, Carrie, butting in to say it for him. Or even just the everyday shits-and-giggles with my friends at school, even though most of the kids at school hated my ass and wanted to bash my jaw against a gutter. One of them had actually told me that, the same kid who always called me Snowflake.

A guy shouldn't have to work so hard to miss things.

But after a while, like always, the rest of the world just floated away, and I ended up thinking about Violet. I thought about her shot dead in front of her house on the east side, lying on the front steps, one arm stretched out toward the door like she'd been in the middle of delivering mail. The kid who done it got away, of course. People said he and Violet got in some fight before it happened—about me, no big surprise. The thing was, I was white and Violet was black. Most people don't care about that stuff anymore, but some people still do. I'd been beaten up for it before, but never Violet—she was a flower, and nobody stomps a flower on purpose. They just shoot them, I guess.

When I'd had enough of thinking, I took the .45 out of my pocket. I had to strain my wrist muscle just to keep the damn thing up. I had been sweating, nervous, shitting-my-pants nervous. But a weird thing happened when I held up that chunk of metal in my hand. It calmed me down.

I wanted to see Violet again so bad. But I didn't believe in God, so no heaven neither, which means I wasn't expecting to find Violet in some beautiful after-life where we wouldn't be what we really were, just two poor, loser kids with no one but each other. I was dumb, but not that dumb.

After checking the clip, I looked up at that pretty tree roof where the light came in, and then down at the moving water, and that's when I saw the girl.

The first thing I noticed was how she was real good-looking, like one of those girls at school, the ones who don't talk to you, who don't talk to anyone. She was under the shallow water, her hair floating up in a million dark curls like tiny little pencil scribbles. Under the water the girl's skin looked a creepy gray color. That was all I noticed at first: this pale chick, her face ringed by a halo of swamp crud and litter.

Like the idiot I am, I didn't realize right away that she was dead.

When I did, I barfed in the bushes. Then I leaned against a tree and coughed the puke flavor out of my mouth, because I didn't want to kill myself and have that taste in my mouth for all eternity. Around me the spring air hung ripe with that smell of green. My legs were wobbly, so I picked my way through the brush and took a seat on a busted log by the side of the stream. I sat there and waited, for her to blink, maybe.

The girl in the water looked Hawaiian, or kind of Asian, and she was beautiful all right—"cute as a button," Violet's Grandma Rafferty might have said—with round, almost chubby cheekbones that gave her a sort of babyish face. Her lips were deep black under the cold water, and were the kind of lips you imagine put those lip prints in dirty greeting cards. She was naked, too, which made the whole scene even sadder, and I did my best to look away, because that's not how I wanted to see any girl naked. Looking at a girl like that was just about the worst thing a guy could do. I saw her legs out of the corner of my eye, bumping into rocks in the weak current. Hand shaking, I lit up and tried to concentrate on the last joint I'd ever smoke, which, I could tell right away, was not worth the price I paid for it. One more disappointment.

I still held the .45 in one hand—but damn it, that girl! She had to go and ruin everything being all naked and dead. All I wanted was to end my life alone.

Angry—at what, I wasn't sure—I threw the burning butt into the water and then stood up and sloshed into the stream, making clouds of brown sludge burp up from the bottom and swirl around the girl's dark curls. But even in all that mixing brown her cute, sleeping face glowed gray under the water, like a coin in a dirty puddle. I looked down at that dead girl and thought about Violet, wondering what to do. I was only seventeen and I had seen two dead girls in my life, and two dead girls is two girls dead too many.

I squatted there in the cool water, my head all hazy, wanting the girl to be alive again more than anything. I had felt the same thing that day I looked down on Violet in her polished casket. I'd wanted to reach out and touch her perfect face and maybe bring her back to life if I could, as if we were both growing up in a world where that sort of thing happened. I wanted to bring back my reason for living.

So I touched the dead girl.

I bent down and leaned over, reaching out a finger to feel her forehead as if I were testing her for a fever, something my mom used to do to me when I was a kid. But this girl wasn't warm, she was cold. She could have been made out of ice.

That's when her eyes opened.

Before I knew it, I had stumbled backward and fallen on my ass in the middle of that bubbly brown stream. "Jesus," I said, and I just stared.

The girl sat up in the murky water, and I watched, stoned, as she moved to wring out her hair only to bust out laughing once she realized it wasn't even wet.

She wasn't even wet.

"Hey," she said, with a breath like the wispy fog that comes off ice cubes, "if you're going to stare at me, you could at least give me something to wear."

MAX

Right about then I wondered if the pot I'd been smoking might have been laced with something, something that made dead girls seem alive again . . . but even I hadn't heard of a drug that could do that.

And this chick was alive—alive enough to slosh over on hands and knees and grab my ears in her bone-white fingers and kiss me, right on the lips. I closed my eyes, smelling her smell, which was nothing but the stink of all that warmed-over mud and moss, and I tried to enjoy it. I hadn't kissed anyone since Violet, just like I had never kissed anyone *before* Violet. There I was, ending my life with a clumsy kiss, just like I had started it that afternoon when I first met Violet in Sherwood Gardens.

So I told myself I was kissing my dead girlfriend, but I knew I wasn't, even with my eyes closed and my brain playing pretend. This kiss was real different. The girl was ice-cold and smooth as a chilled beer bottle.

"Thank you," whispered the girl. Her hug was strong, and she kept on talking. "The smells. They're so damn bad, but are so, so good! I can taste them in the air. So strong I can taste it, the air!" Then she got real quiet again. "The wind, I always forget how much I love the wind."

Even worse, when I opened my eyes again to find her nose an inch from mine, I saw the chick wasn't gray from death, or from some weirdness of the light underwater—she was black-and-white, like old-movie black-and-white, with weird shades of gray thrown in. *Black-and-white, black-and-white*—the words moved through my mind, and I didn't know what they meant, but they scared me shitless. So I kicked her off me, hard.

"I want to eat, something with taste, something chocolate," the girl was in the middle of saying when my kick cut her off. Grunting, she keeled over sideways with a splash.

She fell with one leg cocked up, still naked, and giving me a perfect view of female things I shouldn't have seen but that I still sneaked a peek at. The instant I looked, I felt bad about it.

"Asshole," said the girl. Her voice was really high-pitched, like some kind of Christmas elf. Nothing about her so far seemed too real.

This girl wasn't my problem. So I didn't move, not when the girl got up, and not when she staggered out of the stream and up the slope toward the road. Only when she got to the top of the ravine did I go after her, as she pushed through the brush that opened up to Druid Park Drive and morning traffic. Snapping out of it, I ran up the muddy hill and caught one of her wrists before she could escape through the bushes. She spun around and began shouting right in my face.

"You want me to break your nose?" she said.

"You want me to break yours?" I asked, and it was a weird thing to say because I would have never in a million years hit a girl.

"I will," she said.

"So will I?" I said back.

Then she flinched, and I moved to cover my nose, and in that instant she kneed me right in the nuts. I went down cussing, the air rushing out of my lungs.

Doubled over, I watched her stand in the softly lit

gap between two big bushes. Behind her I could see uphill to the sidewalk of Morton Avenue, and I could hear the rackety clink of a semi bumping through a stoplight. She stood out all weird against the different colors of the street, her black-and-white body sort of like an unfinished part of a big painting. A minute ago she'd been dead in the stream, moving only because the water moved, but now she was up on two legs and about to go scampering through my neighborhood buck-naked.

"Stop," I wheezed.

She turned, but I couldn't see her face in the sunlight glittering through the leaves. "What do you want, mama?" the girl said.

Who was she? *What* was she? I was not a smart kid. I had been flunking out of one of worst damn high schools in Baltimore for two years. I lived on a block where reading a book meant starting the crossword puzzle in *TV Guide* and not even finishing the thing. I was stupid, but even stupid people know magic when they see it.

"Stop," I said again.

The girl looked at me all funny. "Don't you know who I am?"

I couldn't tell if she was joking or not. "Sorry, no," I said, getting to my feet, balls aching. "Should I?"

"Oh, right," she said, realizing she didn't make any damn sense. "You wouldn't know."

"You're naked," I said, trying to get the conversation back on track.

"Congratulations," she said. "You're a fucking genius."

I liked her attitude, but was sort of afraid of it, too. Shivering, she crossed her arms over her boobs and hugged her body, making her tiny dark curls shake. She was short and wide, a little soft, with impressive girly muscles on her arms and a pair of matching tattoos on each shoulder—fists with lightning bolts clamped in them. Her facial features were just sharp black lines. Every time she talked, it was like watching a cartoon moving in a kid's flip book.

"Are you cold?" I asked as she shivered.

"No, I'm not cold," she said. "I'm hungry. I'm so hungry I could eat your face."

I took a step closer. "You go out there all naked and black-and-white and shit, then the whole block will freak out."

"Then give me your pants," she said back to me, like it was no big thing.

"No," I said. "Find your own pants."

"Your shirt, then," and she took a step toward me, reaching out. "I forgot how bright the color gets," she said, her voice dreamy. "Give me your nice blue shirt, bunny. I even love the word *blue*. I could say it all day long. Blue, blue, blue." She was acting like my sister's baby when he saw something he wanted, sort of hypnotized.

"I'm not giving you my shirt," I said.

Even as I said no, she touched me, running her hands along the front of my T-shirt. One of her fingers slipped and touched my belly, so cold, and an ice-cream-headache feeling rushed through my whole body.

"What were you doing down there?" I asked. Her hands stayed on my waist.

"I'll tell you if you give me your pants," she said.

"Maybe," I said, starting to cave.

The girl's eyes grew wide. They were more like perfectly round black holes than eyes. "What about you?" she asked. "What were *you* doing down there?" Her gaze shifted down into the dark pocket of trees.

I didn't answer right away, trying to remember exactly what I had been doing, fighting through the fog in my brain.

The girl looked down at the .45 hanging in my hand. I'd completely forgotten about it dangling there in a grip so tight it ached, and it took me a few seconds to unclench my fingers and let the muscles loose. "Suicide?" asked the girl, shaking her head, maybe even a bit pissed. I didn't say nothing.

"Death is overrated, moron," she said, leaning over to grab my wrist. Then she moved my hand with the .45 in it—and I let her—and pushed it into my sweatpants pocket until the gun was out of sight. "Now quit fooling around. We have important things to do."

There was a lot to be scared about with this chick. What scared me most was that I didn't know if she had some kind of sway over me, or if I had wanted to put the gun away all along and she had given me a good reason to actually do it.

"Like what do we have to do?" I asked.

"Food-like," she said. "I'm hungry. Do you still have slushies on Earth?"

When I answered, "What flavor?" I knew that she

had for sure gained some weird puppet master hold over me, and she didn't even need any magic to do it.

"Who are you?" I heard myself ask.

"My name is Max," she said.

"*What* are you?" I asked.

"I'm a musician," she said. "Now give me your clothes."

Probably ninety seconds later I stood in the middle of traffic getting honked at by a Mercedes with windows so black you couldn't even see the guy behind the wheel. I was out of my head, straddling the white line with cars brushing by on either side. It was already hot out, and I could feel the sweat sliding down my cheeks. I was used to sweating, sure, but not like that, not because my heart was beating fast, not because I was shaking. I felt like I had run a marathon, yet I hadn't done anything but have a conversation with a dead girl.

The girl, Max, had almost gotten me naked. I was halfway out of my T-shirt when I realized what I was doing and pulled my clothes back on. She'd showed up naked, which meant she could wear nude as long as she needed. Besides, she was acting like a real nutcase, which made me want to act less like a gentleman than I probably would have if I found some other, more polite naked black-and-white zombie girl in the bottom of a stream.

My brain moved me across the street toward the deli at the corner of Morton and Druid Park Drive because it didn't know what else to do with me. I glanced over my shoulder and looked hard into the bushes but couldn't spot her. Not even a shaking branch or a splotch of gray. Had she really been there? Was she really dead? Did she really want a slushie? There were too many questions. If I had stopped and thought about any of them for even a second, I probably would have gone crazy—that or stepped in front of a car. So I went to get a slushie. That seemed easy enough. I had done it before. I knew how to do it. I couldn't screw it up too bad.

"Hey, Doris," I said, stepping inside the deli. I remembered to grab the door before it could slam and make the little bells ring too loud.

"Morning, hon," Doris said, and didn't even look up. She was busy squishing sausage on the stove, her small head just barely reaching the stove top. Grease popped and fizzled.

The Radar Deli was all about Elvis and America. It was littered with cardboard cutouts of the King from all different stages of his career. Jumpsuit Elvis, Blue Suede Shoes Elvis, Black Leather Elvis, even Jailhouse Rock Elvis—all stood around the small room like over-size paper dolls. There was a counter with five padded stools on the right. A couple of old freezers stood against the wall on the left, below a large American flag that was tacked to the cracked plaster.

The place was mostly empty when I walked in. An old dude—Ron the furnace-installer guy—sat at one of the small tables in back reading a newspaper. He swirled the last of his coffee in the bottom of a Styrofoam cup. He gave me this look when I came in. It was the usual "Get a job, fool" look that all the dirty old dudes around here seemed to give us teenagers. What did he know? He had his head plugged up a furnace all day.

I still had the money I took from the kitchen table back home, and I counted through it. Doris waited, annoyed, one hand on her hip, sausage squasher in the other.

"What can I get you, hon?" she said, knowing full well I wasn't done counting.

"How much are them slushies?" I said.

"For breakfast, hon?" she asked, hand still on her hip.

"Sure," I said. Then I put down a handful of change that would have pissed off any waitress. Doris sighed and adjusted her glasses so she could count the coins. Her wrinkly little face looked straight off one of those munchkins from *The Wizard of Oz*, if it were in a retirement home, maybe.

"What flavor?" she said, sliding the change off the counter.

This was a question I had asked the girl but had forgotten the answer to. Maybe I just put it out of my mind, thinking it was too weird to have even asked the question in the first place. So I stood at that sticky deli counter wondering what flavor a girl like that would want, which was like puzzling over some messed-up math problem that you knew had no answer.

I was so twisted up by the choice of Blue or Cherry that I hardly heard the door chime.

But I heard it real clear when Ron the furnace-installer guy said, "Holy Jesus." Behind the counter, Doris dropped what she was carrying, a spoon or a spatula or whatever, and it crashed to the floor. Then she started praying under her breath.

The girl—Max—filled most of the doorway with her naked body and didn't give a damn about it. I must have been in shock because I just stood there watching as she checked the place out real patiently, like she was reading prices at the supermarket and trying to make a choice. In the gray, smoky light of the deli she looked less black-and-white than before, but even an idiot could see that she wasn't normal, wasn't right.

She smiled at me, and I recognized that kind of smile—Violet used to flash it all the time, when she followed me when I told her not to, or when she ate what was mine when I told her not to, or when she put her clothes back on when I wasn't done looking at her, touching her, holding her. It was a kiss-off smile. It was someone playfully giving you the finger as they're smiling and saying, "I told you so," at the same time.

"I said I was hungry," Max said. "I said to hurry."

"I'm getting you a slushie," I said. I said it quietly, mostly because my voice shook when it came out. "You want Cherry or Blue?"

"Blue's a color," Max said. "What's it taste like?"

"I don't know," I said.

Even as she talked, her eyes darted around the room—the gleaming counter, the American flag, the Elvises—stopping on something I couldn't see because it was behind me. Before I could turn, she moved—fast, like an animal—and she scared Ron so bad he skidded back in his chair, losing his Orioles cap. Max yanked open the door of the freezer and just began grabbing food right off the shelves like she'd paid for an all-you-can-eat buffet and was getting her money's worth.

She scarfed pieces of cake I know for a fact had been in there for months, and then started opening soda cans and chugging the stuff. But none of it seemed to be what she wanted. Doris, Ron, and I watched like dummies as Max came over and grabbed the jug of red slushie syrup, tipped it back, and took it in the face, mouth wide open.

That's when old Doris started screaming.

That was it. I grabbed Max around the waist and pulled her away from the counter, making her drop that slushie jug. Syrup splattered everywhere. Max was laughing and laughing, her face sticky with red sugar. She looked like a vampire that had hit the mother lode.

Doris, poor Doris, was coming after us now carrying one of those cardboard Elvis standees and swinging it like a weapon. I almost started laughing too.

Max was deadweight, probably because she wasn't helping, and we hit the floor by the bar stools, her on top of me. I wiggled out just in time to get Elvis's big-ass cardboard pompadour in my left eye.

"Damn!" I yelled.

I looked down at Max with my one good eye, and she was still naked—like that would have changed in thirty seconds. I didn't know what to do. We couldn't go out in the street with nothing on and get chased around by an old lady with a two-dimensional life-size Elvis.

As Doris charged at me, I hopped on one of the stools and ripped that American flag right off the wall. I think Doris would have been more offended if she had the time, but she kept right on with that standee, stabbing at me like I was a mouse and her Elvis a broom—once in the neck, once in the chest, an upturned collar in the ear.

Then I did something I would never do again. I climbed down off that stool and grabbed Max by her curly hair, and then I pulled her to her feet, and that, let me tell you, made that dead chick scream Almighty. Wrapping her in the flag, I shoved her out the door to the sidewalk and slammed the door behind us.

Nobody followed. That was for sure.

"Just calm the hell down."

I pushed Max out into the street and into an alley, a long strip of concrete with small redbrick garages on either side. I was pissed off, really pissed, and I shoved her hard, mostly because she didn't seem to feel it or care. She curled the flag around her like a kid wrapped in a warm towel. When we turned the corner into the alley, I walked up to the closest trash cans and kicked them over—all five, one after another, sending them smashing against one of the wooden garage doors. The alley was empty except for a gray-and-white cat scraping at a hamburger wrapper that was stuck to a spot of dried bubble gum. She took off when I got all crazy on the trash cans.

Max spread her arms out wide, holding on to the flag. She looked like a naked superhero. I thought about trying to make her stop, to make her put her arms down and cover herself up, but I already knew better. There was nothing I could do. Everything felt like a dream—a long, bad, and never-ending dream that sucked.

It was so hot out. The air felt heavy, more like water. Sun in my eyes, I leaned up against one of the garages and sat down on the ground. It felt good to get off my feet.

"Do you smell that?" she asked, spinning around barefoot on the glass-covered concrete, not feeling a thing.

"I smell roadkill, maybe," I said angrily, because I did. I felt like screaming. My muscles were tired, even my mind felt tired. Is the brain a muscle? I didn't know, but it felt stretched and pulled and all worn-out.

"It's a fresh smell, an alive smell," she said. "And it makes me want a cigarette real bad-like. I'm going to find a cigarette and smoke it so I can actually taste the tobacco. You want one too?" She used a corner of the flag to wipe all that red syrup from her face.

"Sure," I said. "Get me a cigarette, whatever."

I pressed my palms into my eyes and felt that good pressure. Something was catching up to me just then, something bad I'd been running from—panic, maybe, horrible reality, maybe—spurting up like a dirty oil well in my insides.

I took a deep breath and then did something stupid, and that was cry. That was what I did when I got so mad I wanted to break something or die. Then I did another stupid thing. I punched myself in the head really damn hard. It hurt so bad that I wanted to start giggling. Violet used to hate it when I did that—she said it was the only thing that turned her off about me, which is why I did it so often after she died—because there was no reason to quit doing it, no one to turn off.

"I can't do this anymore," I said to no one. I didn't mean Max; I meant all of it—Violet's murder, the gray smog of Baltimore, the shriveled munchkin at the deli, the Elvis in the eyeball, and the crazy chick standing next to me wrapped in a flag. I was done.

I felt a frozen touch on my shoulder. Three fingers, I could feel them right through my shirt. Max. "You don't have a choice," she said. "Nobody does." I don't know if she knew that I'd lost somebody, but it sure seemed like that's what she meant.

Violet's touch, I remembered it so well. Sitting there with my hands over my eyes, I thought back to how we met, how I found her sitting cross-legged on a big brown-and-white-striped blanket beside a wall of tall flowers with thick green stalks and curly purple petals. The whole world had smelled wet, sort of clean, like bagged mulch that had just been thrown. I'd walked over to pick something up for her, a Frisbee she'd tossed for her dog but forgotten about, I think, and when I'd turned to go, she'd touched my shoulder to ask a question.

I remembered and wanted to uncover my eyes and see Violet instead of Max, because that's the way things should have been. When Violet died, the universe tilted like a table with dishes on it, and everything that had been sitting on top slid off and broke on the floor.

The fingers on my shoulder pushed me roughly. I didn't respond, but I opened my eyes. Max stood in front of me cocooned in the Stars and Stripes. "What's your name, bunny?" she asked.

"Jo-Jo," I said. "Jo-Jo Dyas."

"Where you from?" she asked.

"Here," I said. Then I hesitated, sniffing. "Where you from?"

"You don't want to know," she said. She took another deep breath, smiling bigger than I'd seen anyone smiling in a while, and then crouched down in front of me so we were eye to eye. I turned away because I was crying. "Fine," I heard her say. "I'm from Akron. That's in Ohio."

She was up close, her colorless face bright in the sunlight. "Are you a ghost?" I asked. I wanted to believe in ghosts just then.

Max grunted and then put her hand on my cheek. "You wish," she said. Then, running her black-and-white fingers across my skin, she said, "Are you scared of me?"

I closed my eyes. Yes, she scared me. Yes, I wanted to go home and get back in bed. Yes, I wished I could have just blown my brains out all over the weeds and liquor bottles as planned.

But when I opened my eyes and looked at her again, the fear was gone. Max was scared too. I could see it in how the muscles at the corners of her mouth turned down, how she'd gone from touching my hand to squeezing it. I remembered that same look on my sister, Carrie, before she had her kid. There was terror there, even in her effort to stay calm. On Max's chin was a tiny grass stain. It looked like someone had scratched a piece of plain white paper with a crayon.

Neither of us said anything. I couldn't be sure, but I think she gripped me so tight because she didn't want me going anywhere.

"You're the only person I know," she said, "and I need your help."

"With what?" I said, wiping my nose. "You can't take my pants."

With that, she smiled and tapped me on the nose, once, twice, three times, saying one word with each tap. "I . . . *tap* . . . need . . . *tap* . . . wheels . . . *tap*, mama." Then she whacked me in the forehead once with the palm of her hand. I didn't even blink. I was used to getting beat on, having grown up with an older sister who was one serious world-champion wench.

"You mean a car?" I asked, and I wiped my nose with one hand and then cleaned the hand on my pants.

"That's right, a car, four wheels," she said. "Immediately."

I thought about Violet, and how scary it gets when you find yourself all alone. "I'll help," I said. "I'll do it, but not for you. *You've* been a pain in the ass."

Max stood up and stretched so her tattoos of fists

and lightning seemed to ripple, suddenly full of energy. "Perfect," she said. "So who are you doing it for, then? You doing it for your mama?"

"I'm doing it for Violet," I said. I wanted it to sound real important. "She would want me to help."

"Okay!" Max said happily. She turned on one heel and walked off toward the end of the alley where the busy street cut in. She never looked where she was going, just kept walking out into the open, not checking to see if she was about to be flattened in traffic. Crazy chick. That flag swept out behind her body like she was Merlin or something. Her feet crunched over broken beer bottles.

"Don't you want to know who Violet is?" I called after her.

"I don't care!" she shouted over a shoulder, her chin resting on the red stripe of Old Glory, curls darkening half of her face. One eye sparkled in a dead-pale socket. "All I want to do is find my friends, get loaded, and play."

When I heard that, I started to get interested in where all this was headed. For the first time that morning I followed Max down the street out of curiosity and not . . .

fear, I guess. Something big was about to go down, and I wanted to be there when it happened. If I could keep dreaming this dream long enough, maybe I'd never have to wake and face what had happened to my life.

"Where are we going?" I shouted.

"Cemetery," Max called back.

Or not.

BALTIMORE

My friend Bart had himself a job, which meant he had a car. Thing is, his work and his wheels kind of went together, and not in a good way, neither. Both a job and a car are mostly good for getting chicks, but Bart was the ice-cream man, and Bart drove the ice-cream truck. His biggest fans were of the grade-school variety. So when it came to scoring, Bart usually came up cold.

Bart and I had gone to school together until Bart dropped out to sit around and smoke pot and sometimes break into people's cars to snatch purses. So when the ice-cream gig fell into his lap, it was like winning some lottery except instead of millions he was swimming in dairy.

Bart's usual sales route had him heading down Rockrose Avenue around one o'clock. That afternoon, he was right on time, and when his big white truck came swinging around the corner, I was there waiting. *We* were there waiting.

He slowed down, the truck speaker blasting "Ring Around the Rosie." His Playboy air freshener twirled from the rearview mirror, twisting and untwisting on its string.

Before Bart could say a thing, I opened the driver's door and jumped in so he was close enough to hear me when I said, "Hey, buddy, keep on driving now." But my good old pal wasn't interested in chatting. His eyes were glued on Max.

She stood out in front of the ice-cream truck, her thick, white legs sticking out from under those fifty stars, her arms crossed over her chest. I half expected her to shout, "Up, up, and away!" and go flying off somewhere.

"Slow down but keep on going," I said to Bart, real cool, and then waved to Max, who climbed up on the runner of the truck and slid through the open door. She walked behind me into the back, where Bart stored the ice cream in a long freezer. When Bart had customers and set up shop, one part of the truck opened to make a window where he swapped kids' money for goodies. The inside of the truck was plastered with pictures he'd ripped from porno magazines.

Max stared at the naked girls, mouth hanging open, like she'd been hit over the head with a hammer. "Wow," she said. A plastic bag dangled from one wrist. It was full of some of my sister's old clothes that I'd dug out of a closet.

"Put some damn pants on, will you?" I told her, which knocked her out of that upright coma and got her rifling through the bag.

"Morning, Jo," said Bart, steering around a corner. The truck's tires squealed against the road.

"Yeah," I said. "Morning."

"So, um, what are you into here?" he said to me, jerking his head toward the back of the truck where Max was changing. He smiled out of the right side of his mouth, like always. When he was ten, Bart's mom had bashed a wine bottle against the guy's head and left him with a wiggly white scar that messed up the side of his face.

"I don't know, man," I said. Was I as clueless as I sounded? It sure felt that way. "We need a ride, man. You help us out?"

"Always," said Bart, putting on his turn signal. "I'd

do anything for a lady. Besides, she's hot."

I stared at him. "Man, she's *black-and-white.*"

Bart flashed half his teeth under his shredded pair of lips. "Black, white, purple, I don't give a crap," he said, gunning the motor. "It's all the same when you're south of the border." I waited for him to tell me he was joking, but he didn't and just went on being excited to have a naked chick in his truck. It didn't matter to him that the girl was the color of a day-old newspaper.

I checked on Max and saw her trying to tighten a stained pair of my sister's shorts. They hung loose on her. Max was a solid girl, but not tons of fun like Carrie, who seemed to think that because you had a baby, you didn't have to move your ass more than ten feet a day, that it was everyone else's job to fetch your shit for you. Max pulled one of my sister's hot-pink short-sleeved shirts down over her head and turned from side to side, modeling for a mirror that wasn't there. Then she noticed the ice cream in the freezer and dove in headfirst.

I couldn't believe I was still there, with her, going where?

"Where you need the taxi service?" Bart asked,

squealing up to a stop sign.

"Cemetery," I said, and when he looked at me funny, I shrugged.

"You have got to be kidding."

"You know which one?" I called to Max.

"Not just any!" shouted Max from inside the freezer. "Try Green Mount! Is that right? Green Mount Cemetery?"

With that, Bart's squiggly white smile jumped, and he nodded, making his greasy brown hair bounce all around on his head. "Weird thing is I *do* know Green Mount," he said. "I also know better than to do other than what a lady tells me. Next stop, the grave, sugar cone."

We drove east on 41st Street, across the bridge over Highway 83, and kept going deeper into Baltimore City. The roads were almost completely empty. We rumbled alone through every green light. It was a quiet Sunday drive, with Max muttering to herself in back and Bart glancing at her in the rearview mirror every so often, not saying much. We cruised to the music playing real soft over the truck speakers, sounding sort of like rain plinking on the thin metal roof.

My Bonnie lies over the ocean, my Bonnie lies over the sea . . .

It was kind of depressing sitting in the truck like that, the song playing through the deserted streets, not a soul to be seen. It was a sad song, and it made everything around it seem sad too.

My Bonnie lies over the ocean, so bring back my Bonnie to me . . .

I hardly ever went downtown. People there were one of two things. They were white folks with too much money, the kind who looked at you like there was some sort of invisible line that separated your whiteness from their whiteness, a line that you were stepping over every time you left your side of town and came over to their side, where everything was nicer, the water clearer, the skies bluer. And then there were black city folks, who didn't want white trash anywhere near their streets, and whenever we passed through a hood, they spotted us coming a mile away and puffed up with attitude, ready to fight before you even got a chance to park the car.

Violet had been born and raised on the east side, and I had crossed all those invisible lines to be with her. I hadn't liked downtown before Violet and I met, and after she got killed . . . well, I liked it even less. The city was a place where good dreams didn't fly but ended up running down the gutter into the sewers. Welcome to Baltimore.

"Jo-Jo!" Max called from the back of the truck. I flicked the Playboy air freshener to make it spin and then got up and walked to where she leaned against the ice-cream freezer eating a Drumstick. Inside the freezer were five gray tubs of different-flavored ice cream— mint chocolate chip, peach, vanilla, chocolate, pralines and cream—and a collection of Bomb Pops, Push-Ups, Klondike bars, and Drumsticks. Bart may have been a burnout, but at least he was a good ice-cream man, and every neighborhood needs a good ice-cream man.

"What's up?" I asked.

"There are a few things we need," she said.

"Like what?" I asked, bracing my arms against the side of the truck as it turned a corner and made the ice-cream buckets jump. "And *for* what?"

She raised a finger, motioning me to wait. "This is so damn good-like!" she said, taking big hunks off the ice cream with her front choppers. "I was going to say that we need some shovels."

"Shovels."

"I'm meeting some friends of mine."

"What friends?"

"The ones I'm meeting."

"At the cemetery? With shovels?"

"At *a* cemetery," she said. "I'm pretty sure this is the one, but this shit isn't exactly a science, you know?"

I didn't.

She gobbled the rest of the Drumstick, sucking down its cone and some stray nuts with a few last bites and a smile. Burping, she looked up like she wanted me to be all happy with her, but then she saw the expression on my face and her dumb-ass smile drooped. "What, don't you trust me?"

"I don't *know* you," I said, and then I started getting real mad. "If I'm going to help you, I need to know stuff."

"What stuff-like?"

"Who you are, maybe, and what you're doing here?"

The word *here* flew out of my mouth like some half-eaten chunk of food. As soon as I said it, I wished I hadn't. Max and I looked at each other, silent, rocking to and fro in the back of the truck. I had done it. I had made it clear that I was from "here" and she was from "there," wherever the hell "there" was. I was afraid to find out. I almost wanted to tell Bart to turn around, speed us back to Woodberry, where we could hit that bong I knew was waiting for us and break out the Play-Station, business as usual.

Max must have read my mind because she scooped a glob of ice cream from the chocolate tub and stuck it in her mouth. "All right," she said. "We'll do it like I'm a genie. You get three questions, like three wishes, okay?"

I couldn't tell if Max was making fun of me or not, but it didn't matter. An hour before, I'd been sitting in the mud with a gun. Now I was on my way to a cemetery with a dead girl who wanted shovels.

"Okay," I said. "Why are you here?" Then I thought of something. "Do you even know where *here* is?"

"Whoever said I was *here*?" she said. "Maybe you're *there*. You ever think about that? You're the one toting a gun, mama."

I hadn't thought of that, and then what she was saying hit me. "Am I dead? Is that what you're saying?"

She laughed and turned away to root around in the

stuff scattered across the cramped ice-cream counter. "I'm just jerking you around," she said, picking up a bundle of silver scoops that were held together with a green rubber band. She slipped off the rubber band and put it on her wrist. "Listen to me, Jo-Jo. I know what's going on. This is the city of Baltimore, state of Maryland, God bless America, on good old planet Earth. I've done my research, I'm here, and you're here, so let's all just move on-like. Okay?"

I looked down and saw my hand gripping the freezer lid handle, my knuckles white. I had almost believed her, almost believed I was dead. Just like I'd wanted for so long. Dead. I trusted people too much, just like Violet had always said.

"You know where you are," I said, to change the subject. "But *why* are you here?"

"First of all, I'm here because I need a damn vacation," she said. "But on the business side of things, we needed to go polish our act someplace where nobody knows who we are." She shrugged. "And damn it, we're so big right now that it was pretty tough-like to find a small enough venue. Luckily Baltimore isn't exactly on the cutting edge. I mean, you guys ever hear of trash cans?"

It didn't make sense, but I moved on. "Why do you look like that?" I asked. The truck sped up as it tilted down a steep hill.

"Like what?" she said, turning to me, perfect black eye sockets like bullet holes, horror-movie eyes.

"You know," I said.

"No, I don't," she said.

"You're black-and-white, dude!"

"Oh, that," she said, and let out a sigh of frustration. "That's just me." When she saw my straight face, she didn't say anything at first and then threw back her hair, putting it in a ponytail and fixing it with the green rubber band off her wrist. "Are you really going to waste one of your questions on that? What are you going to ask me next, why I have two arms and two legs, or two eyes and a nose? That the best you got, Jo-Jo?"

The truck scraped up a driveway from the street. "Let's finish up," Max said to me. "Because I can tell we're getting close-like, and no doubt my boys are pissed."

She moved toward the front, but I stepped in front of her. "I get one more question," I said.

"Just one."

"Yeah."

"Ask. You know you want to."

She was right. I was sweating, because I had to know.

I had to know.

"Where are you from?" I said.

The truck turned a sharp corner, but neither of us moved, having found our balance. There was a squeal and a crunch and the wheels hit gravel. The engine died.

Max looked at me square in the face. "I'm from the Afterlife," she said.

She waited, letting it sink in real good.

"The afterlife?" I said. Sort of sounded like a punch line.

We were in an ice-cream truck. It was supposed to be cold. Cold, nothing. I was dizzy and boiling. "The afterlife," I said again, but this time not like a question.

"No." Max shook her head. "You're thinking of the other one. I'm from the Afterlife. It's capitalized. People are always messing that up."

"Heaven?" I asked, hand cold, head hot, space closing in on me.

Max laughed and slipped three of Bart's ice-cream scoops into the belt loops of her shorts. "Wrong again, bunny. You're thinking of the place where all good people go when they die, and I hate to break it to you, but there's no such place." The metal scoops along her waist rang against each other. "There is a *the* Afterlife, and a lot of people go there, except most of them aren't so good."

She left me there. I watched her climb down out of the truck with Bart, who trailed after her like he was following a girl who'd just picked up a six-pack and was going home all by her lonesome. Feeling sort of sick, I climbed into the front passenger seat and sat there hunched over. My head hurt. I wanted to hit it again, to pound it until I didn't feel anything anymore. But that could wait.

We'd parked in front of a pair of big metal gates with brown stone towers on either side, like a castle. A wall ran along the sidewalk, cutting off the living from the dead. Past the walls and between the skinny black bars were low hills dotted with specks of gravestones, like them big Irish crosses, and tiny boxes that looked like houses but were really just tombs of rich-guy assholes who were still rich even when they were dead. Across town a church tower poked up from the city skyline, a sharp shadow on the sky.

Max and Bart said a few words to each other, but I couldn't make them out in the loud whoosh of traffic drifting off Greenmount Avenue, which lay just past the trees. Stepping up to the gates, Max yanked them open with a ghost-story squeak.

Behind her, Bart whistled. "We robbing graves now?" he asked, grinning his half grin. He didn't seem fazed by any of this. Not a bit.

"What do you think, mama?" Max said, and she pulled one of the silver ice-cream scoops from a belt loop. "You can scoop, can't you?"

"Scoop?" Bart said, and then his messed-up face went totally blank. It took both of us a second to catch on, and another second to wish we hadn't.

Max winked. "Let's dig," she said, and walked into the cemetery.

A half hour later, my wrist hurt, my sweatpants were mud-stained, and sweat dripped off my chin, because I was digging. I used my hands sometimes, and I dug.

I don't know why I did it. Yes, I do.

For weeks after Violet's murder, I had wanted to. Dig her up, I mean. It was sick, but I'd wanted to do it. I hadn't been ready to say good-bye, and I didn't really believe she was dead. You never want to believe that shit, and at first, you don't. It takes a real long time for the truth to sink in, that it's over. You want to cling as long as you can, no matter how much it hurts.

I had dreamed of digging her up. Now I was knee deep in dirt.

I don't know how no one saw us or stopped us. It was daytime, the sun was high and bright, and we were digging up graves in a busy cemetery. After every few minutes Max would sink both arms deep into the dirt, like one of them pioneers panning for gold, sticking his arms into a stream hoping to strike it lucky.

We knew when we were done. I heard shouting from under the ground, a deep muffled roar. Then a scrawny black arm punched out of the earth, spraying dirt and a few wooden splinters. There was a lightning bolt tattooed on each of the four big knuckles. As soon as that happened, Max had us start on the other grave, the one next to the first, digging as that one arm waved around in its hole, looking for something to grab on to. I tried to ignore it. I was too busy scooping. All I did was dig, dig and hum, hum to myself.

My Bonnie lies over the ocean, my Bonnie lies over the sea . . .

Those two graves had belonged to an old couple that had been buried together, their names everlasting on the limestone: "Javier Sanchez (1912–1986) and Roberta Sanchez (1915–1994): Forever in Love."

My Bonnie lies over the ocean, so bring back my Bonnie to me.

When we finished digging, it wasn't an old Hispanic couple that climbed up out of the open graves.

It was a couple of twins.

WES AND EDGAR

You sit in the front pew of a church you have never been in before. You are surrounded by a group of people you have never seen before. You sit beside two parents you have met once, maybe twice, and spoken hardly ten words to in two years' time. You listen to heartbreaking music, music that sounds so sad it could chip away the mortar around the bricks in the wall, music that makes the whole building shake like a person trying not to cry. You can actually smell the cold, a stale basement odor, air that has been sitting around with itself for a long time. You hear only crying. It's the sound of people trying to cover their grief with handkerchiefs and sleeves. They're trying not to sound sad, which is a strange, special sound all its own.

You sit between her parents, surrounded by her friends and family, in her black church that you'd never go to, in an unfamiliar neighborhood where you don't feel comfortable, and you wonder: Why did a street pig called White Knife Johnson stalk a sixteen-year-old girl with her whole life in front of her and then up and shoot her for no reason? But as you sit there in that hard-backed pew, you know that *you* are the reason—and so does everyone else. You are the reason she is dead.

They bring in the casket draped in black, piled high with violets, and you feel the whole place quiet down. The stillness of the body inside makes everything else still too. But it ain't the same as peace. A girl murdered so young and with so much left to do in her life may be silent forever, but that sure as hell don't mean she's resting. No way in hell.

We had dug open two graves in Green Mount Cemetery and no one had even shouted "Boo!" Not a soul. I turned away from the first casket and rolled onto my back in the pile of dumped mud, out of breath, cooking in the heat. I'd dug a hole for my Violet. My wrist ached for her. My shirt was soaked for her. I had mud up and down my arms for her.

I wasn't sure how I'd ended up there again, by an open grave. The pain felt just the same. Except this

51

time somebody was coming out of the ground instead of going in.

Bart had stopped digging a while ago. He crouched with his hands on his knees peering down at the two teenagers who were standing up in the graves. He whistled. I'd been keeping count. The dumb ass had whistled fourteen times since we started our little trip, and he was still finding stuff to whistle at. Me, I was done being wowed. A few fingers on my right hand bled, but I couldn't feel them. I was back in that church downtown staring at a casket covered with violets, flowers that were about six hours away from a slow, crumply death.

The two teenagers climbed out of the graves. They were two big dudes.

The first one was tall, crooked-nosed, and black—inky black, not African American—black like Max's eyes, an abandoned well black. His bent nose was sharp at the tip, and his eyes were sort of close together and small. The dude was buck-naked, like Max when I found her. His long hair was the same light gray as my sweatpants. It had been shaved at the sides and plastered flat across his head to the back of his neck. He looked pretty pissed, which I'd sort of expect from a dead guy.

The other kid looked the same in a lot of ways—the nose, the eyes, the lack of color. But he was bigger, fat, which made his nose stubbier and his eyes even closer together under all the extra skin. His hair was done up in the straightest do I'd ever seen, and I'd seen some serious hairstyles on Baltimore's west side. It was as if the dude had been standing upside down and then got turned right-side up again, his hair staying the way it was. He was nude but more aware of it than the other guy was, and cupped his hands over his thing so no one would see. I knew right away that he was the sort of kid who would have cupped his thing even if he'd come out of the grave and the whole damn place had been deserted.

They were brothers. That was obvious. Both guys had fists tatooed on their chests and little lightning bolts on every knuckle. They looked like two big bundles of trouble.

And they weren't even dirty. Not a smear. Bart whistled again. This was right about the time most folks would have flipped out, but not me. People always wonder what they'd do if something unexplainable happened, but the truth is, you handle it like every-thing else. You understand the stuff you can and wait for explanations for the rest of it.

I could hardly move my right arm, and I sort of cradled it in my left hand. I could taste cemetery dirt, and I wondered if I was going to hell for what I had just done, if there even was such a place.

The twins stood there supremely naked, looking relieved.

"You took your time," the thin, crooked-nosed guy said, glaring at Max.

Max gritted her teeth, holding her sore scooping arm. "Like I knew you'd show up six feet under," she said.

"You think I liked waking up in a coffin?" he said. "It's morbid."

Max dropped her ice-cream scoop, wincing. "You are aware that I need-like my wrist to drum?"

"Ever heard of a shovel, *Max*?" the tall guy said, and he cracked his neck loudly.

"Ever heard of singing in key, *Ed*?" she snapped back.

She tossed something at their feet: two of Bart's white ice-cream-man aprons. "Now come on, we need to go get Penny."

"I'm surprised you didn't get Penny first," said the guy—Ed—reaching down and snatching the aprons off the ground. He threw one at his brother and it hit the chubby dude right in the face because he wouldn't lift his hands away from his thing to catch it. "Wouldn't have been the first time you two ditched us."

"Yeah, well, I'm here now, digging up your sorry ass with ice-cream scoops," Max said. "So show a little respect."

Ed harrumphed. "We have a ride?" he asked.

"What do you think that is?" Max said, tilting a thumb toward the truck, which sat parked a few graves away, just behind the gate.

"I see," Ed said, scratching his belly and nodding. He looked real pleased. "My dear, this single act may just make up for your years of unnecessary torment." He hurried off in the direction of the truck, wrapping the apron around his waist. The guy hadn't even looked at me or Bart, just charged off like he owned the cemetery and every last headstone in the place. "That's no ride, mama!" he called back. "It's a movable feast!"

Tubby walked up. "Hey," he said, and he knocked his shoulder up against Max's. "Thanks for the helping hands, mama. You got no idea how bad it was starting to stink down there with those stiffs. I forgot that things smell here. The bad stuff gets all stuck-like up in your nose."

"That smell was you, fat ass!" shouted Ed from the passenger seat of the truck. Bart stared at him, his eyes half shut like they were when we got high, and I think he was a little wigged out by having some jerk sitting in his truck with nothing on but an apron. Bart wasn't whistling no more.

"The guy in the truck, that's Edgar," Max told me. "We keep him around for comic relief, but he never turns out to be very funny."

For a second, the three of us watched him mess around in the glove compartment of the truck, throwing maps over his shoulder and shaking old Pepsi cans, a few of which he actually lifted up near his face and licked. Then he vanished into the back.

When this got boring, the tubby guy blinked and turned to where I sat by the side of the open grave with crud all over me. "Hey," he said. "I like your soul, mama. It's nice. Weak, but nice."

"Um," I said back, totally confused, "thanks."

"Wes, this is Jo-Jo," Max said to the tub. "Jo-Jo, Wes," she said to me.

"Hey," I said.

"Hey," he said back.

"Jo-Jo's with me," said Max.

"What is he, like a stalker or a groupie or something?" Wes asked.

Max looked at me funny, and then she stepped closer. I stood totally still as she picked a few blobs of mud out of my hair and dropped them on the ground. "I don't know what he is," she said. "He just, I don't know, *is*."

It was the best I could hope for, I guess.

Wiping her eyes with the back of one hand, Max walked over to a statue of a dancing angel, a headstone near our two open graves. The angel had been worn down so much by weather that its face had been beaten smooth, only two shallow divots left for eyes. Its triangle wings had shrunken into two gray fortune cookies. It had probably been there for something like a hundred years, through rain and wind, fading away like a memory. But it was still dancing. At the angel's small, stony feet sat a bouquet of flowers. And I noticed they were violet, bright violets.

Max bent down and took one from the pile. She pulled it out from the stack and snapped off the stem, and then slipped it behind her ear.

"Anyone need a flower?" And I swear she looked at me when she said it.

The horn honked. Edgar was leaning way over into the driver's side of the truck in his apron, giving us an eyeful of business none of us wanted to see. Of everything I'd seen so far, *that* was what would probably give me nightmares.

I caught Wes staring, but not at his brother. He was looking at the truck and scratching his chin. "A car," he said to no one in particular. "I love cars." Then he smiled at me. "I had a car once, a Chevy Nova. It was the best."

"Wow," I said, trying to be nice. "Those are pretty cool."

"No," said Wes. "It was *really* cool."

I bent down and picked up the muddy ice-cream scoops. I had become a zombie, waiting for Max's next order. She could have asked me to do anything, and I would have done it, because I had nothing better to do. Except maybe die, I guess.

"That's my truck," Bart said, the first thing he'd said in a while. He grinned like a moron, that waxy white squiggle taking up most of his face.

Wes stuck his thumb out toward him. "Who's this guy?" he said, saying it to Max, right in front of Bart as if Bart weren't even there.

"Can't you tell?" Max said, placing that violet bouquet in the arms of the dancing angel, real gentle. She looked into its faraway eyes. "He's the ice-cream man."

BALTIMORE

"Where to next," Bart called from the front as we passed under 83, "the morgue?"

No one answered.

I sat staring out the truck's small square back window. We bumped over potholes and past a man with a hook for an arm. He stood in the median and held up a creased cardboard sign that said: "Gulf War Vet, Need Money or Food, God Bless You." He was there and then not in a split second. Under the highway overpass, homemade tents made from blankets and shopping carts were huddled up against the walls. When you see something like that, you don't know why anyone thinks this world is a good one. For every guy living in a nice house, there are a hundred like that vet stashed under some bridge like mice under floorboards.

The truck got air every time we hit a bump. I was

sitting on a fold-down bench that Bart usually used for naps but sometimes used when he brought the girl he was seeing on a "ride." That was the reason I was sitting on the bench with only one butt cheek. I wasn't really sure where that bench had been.

"I said, where we going, folks?" Bart shouted back between the front headrests.

"Where we going?" I asked Max. She sat beside me, rotating her right wrist and frowning. Her twisty black curls were all in her face.

"Downtown," she said. "The thousand block of Charles Street, near the intersection at Eager Street, I think. We looked on a map." Then she glanced at me, eyebrows up. "It was from the year 1919. Do you think that matters?"

Before I could say, "Probably, yeah," Wes spoke up, yelling, "That's it, 1010, or maybe 1014!" across the truck. He was going through the ice-cream freezer, opening each kind of Popsicle to taste it before moving on to the next. The floor was covered with sticky white paper wrappers.

"I wouldn't take Wes's word for it," said the tall guy, Edgar, or Ed, or whatever. "The big guy can barely count past eleven. Once I saw him get to twelve, but he used notes."

Ed wouldn't sit. Why? I wasn't sure, but probably because he felt like being a pain. He stood with his long arms stretched across the back of the truck holding the rubber straps on each wall. And he stared at me, *glared* at me. I glared back.

"The thousand block, Charles Street!" I called to Bart in front, and he gave me a thumbs-up to show he heard. He went up a hill, and Max and I slid together on the bench, thighs kissing.

Ed let go of the two rubber straps and clapped his hands together. His arms were so skinny he looked a bit like a bird without any of its feathers. "Quick question," he said, scanning the truck and ending up with his white eyes back on me. "Who in the hell is this guy? Is he our manager now or something, a personal hygiene assistant for my lovely brother perhaps?"

"That's Jo-Jo, mama," Wes said as he licked a fresh Bomb Pop. He licked real slow and with the very tip of his tongue.

"Jo-Jo's the reason you're not still sleeping with a corpse," Max said. Her eyes were slits when she looked at him, and her voice had dropped all grumpy. In the heat, the violet behind her ear had already started to droop. "If it weren't for him, you'd be stuck in a shallow grave. So just sit down and shut up."

"Fine," Ed said, smiling, but not a good smile. "Let's do that. Let's take a look at our hero. Well, for starters he's funny-looking, and I mean ugly. Not average-like or mediocre or acceptable, but genuinely disgusting. He's got bad skin, an Adam's apple that sticks out like a golf ball, and the worst unshaven mini-mustache I have ever seen, in this life or the last. And that's me being nice-like. Shall I go on?"

That's all I could take. It was bad enough knowing you were a loser, but having some dickhead read off a checklist was something else. That .45 sat like a big old rock in my pocket. "Listen," I started, but was completely cut off by Max as she reached over and socked the tall guy in the leg. It was all knuckles, and he grabbed at the spot, grunting and closing his eyes.

"Yow!" he shouted. "I still feel enough pain for that to hurt."

"What is your problem?" Max barked. "Jo-Jo saved me, mama. I could have had a couple of kids poking

63

my dead body with a stick, like last time. Not exactly fun-like. I'm kissing his feet now, and you should too. Now quit being so *you*."

"Or *I* could have had a dog try to hump my leg," Wes said quietly.

"Or Wes could have had his leg humped again!" Max repeated. "You want that?"

"I would love that," Ed said, grinning. "I wish I saw it the first time."

"You are the biggest moron who ever died," Max said. "Your poor brother got screwed when he got stuck with you, mama."

"That's funny," Ed said. "I could say the same thing about your brother."

He had just finished and closed his mouth when Max attacked. I saw her white fingers flash out before he did, heading right for the opening under that ice-cream apron. The moment she had him, his face seemed to cave in around the middle, and he sort of shrieked—it was a girly noise. I loved it.

Gasping, Ed doubled over, holding them two rubber straps on either side of the truck. He just hung there.

"Quit bugging me," Max said. Her voice was as cold

as she was. "We've got work to do, so let's play nice-like. Okay?"

"We've got to work together," Wes piped up. "We're supposed to be a band, a family, like the Partridges. Besides, we probably only got forty-eight hours, so quit messing around."

"Okay, okay," Edgar whispered, nodding fast.

Max let him go, and he dropped to the bench with his arms wrapped around his body, curled up in a ball. "Fine," he said. "Got it, got it. Live a little, will you?"

Max dusted off her hands and then folded her arms and looked at me. "So, is Jo-Jo short for something?"

She wasn't going to be changing the subject so fast, not without throwing me another bone. "Wait," I said, squinting at her. "Are you really a musician? You guys are like, really a band?"

"Of course," said Max, grunting. "We're the Fiendish Lot."

When I didn't react, her jaw dropped. "Hello? The hugest band of all time, ever?" I still said nothing.

"Come on, Jo-Jo, we're bigger than the Beatles." She shrugged. "And they were bigger than Jesus."

* * *

By six o'clock, downtown was closed off and packed to the gills with fags. It was gay-pride day, or weekend, or something, and there were big sparkly floats parked around on the sides of the streets covered in pink and purple streamers. Half the chicks on the street were probably guys, but they still looked damn good, and I felt sort of weird thinking so. The ice-cream truck rumbled north over the cobblestone streets and past Baltimore's George Washington Monument into gay-pride traffic. Sidewalks overflowed with guys in tiny shorts, mesh shirts, crazy costumes, and butch dykes with flattops and boots walking dogs, all of them weaving in and out of the street holding up the flow of cars and not seeming to give two shits about it. Every time any of them saw the ice-cream truck coming, they began to cheer and beat the sides with their fists. "Ice cream" must mean something different to those folks.

Bart managed to find a gap in the crowd and pulled up near the curb at the intersection of Charles and Eager streets. He kept the engine running. The four of us climbed up through the front seats and down the steps to the sidewalk.

Bart didn't follow. "This is as far as I go," he said to

me across the passenger seat. "I ain't joining the dance of the fairies. Not today, brother. You're on your own."

He broke the bad news with a smile, his awful scar almost screwing it up completely. Then he pulled away and left us on the corner surrounded by a small group of oily guys in studded leather harnesses. Bart was okay. I'd forgotten that. Maybe I'd look him up at the end of the week. Maybe we'd be friends again. We'd smoke a bowl. Maybe talk about old times or our crazy day in that ice-cream truck.

The road was packed with overflow from a big old bar called the Hippo and another called Grand Central. Everybody buzzed around those two doorways like bees on sugar. We walked down a few row houses and found a tall brownstone that had a stained-glass window above the front door—a green-glass tree with leaves twisted to make the number *1010*. Max walked up the wide porch steps first, to a door that had a brass door knocker. The rest of us followed.

"Your friend's in *here*?" I asked her. "How the hell you know that?"

"Because he used the key," she said, but that didn't make much sense to me.

Behind us a group of guys in drag walked by wearing big brown wigs and eyelashes, and when they saw Edgar and Wes standing on the stoop in nothing but those white aprons, they began to hoot and whistle. Nobody seemed to care that they were black-and-white, not on a day like that with so many freaks about.

"How'd your friend get the key?" I asked.

Max pushed the doorbell, but it didn't make no sound. "To get from *there* to *here* you have to have something, an object," she explained, making motions with her arms to show how far apart *here* and *there* really were. It looked pretty far. "When people die, they instantly become part of that other place, where we're from. They're pulled to it, like they're caught-like in an undertow. Whatever they got on them at the time, it gets dragged right along with them to the other side. But none of it's supposed to be there. What they're wearing, what they're carrying, it's all still native to Earth. So it will always be kind of tugging to come back here."

"Like a homing pigeon," I said.

"Sure, I guess," said Max. She tapped her foot, trying to stay patient as she waited for the door to open, and she kept talking, a bit distracted. "All that stuff ends up over there when the dead do." She peered through the window. "Some people know how to use individual objects to jump back to where a person died, because they'll always be tugging to go back where they belong."

I thought about this. I wondered what would have been in my hands if I'd gone ahead with the suicide. I guess there was only one object I would have taken with me—that damn gun, maybe my Nirvana T-shirt, a pocketful of change.

"So your friend has the key to *this* apartment?" I said. "Someone died in there?"

"People die just about everywhere doing just about everything," she said. "The guy in this apartment died holding a rubber ducky in one hand and a beer bottle in the other. That's all I know."

"And you could use that key, or that bottle, to come jumping back to his bathtub?" I asked.

"That's about it," she said. "We call it life-tripping."

"Like it's a drug or something," I said.

She shook her head and groaned. "Trust me. It's no day in the park. You don't even want to imagine the migraine I got right now."

"So you really *can* take it with you," I said. "*Stuff.*"

"Everything has a purpose, a connection to something bigger." As she said it, she poked me in the chest with a finger. "Even you."

She tried the doorbell again, but it still didn't ring. Someone behind us cleared his throat.

We turned and found four guys standing on the steps. At the front was the leader, some short throwback grunge dick with a blue goatee and a purple T-shirt for some ancient band, Temple of the Dog. The whole group looked like they'd stepped off a 1990s album cover. "We're dropping off the sound system for the party," the guy in front said. Under one arm he carried a big speaker, a black box with wires piled up on top of it. The other guys carried guitars with the straps thrown over their shoulders.

They looked at one another, confused, until Wes stepped out of the way and said, "It's about time."

The guy with the blue goatee hurried up the stairs, only stopping for a second to open the door, which was unlocked. His friends came after, dragging pieces of the drum set and microphone stands up the steps and into the apartment. As the last one passed—some fool with a ponytail and a soul patch—he flashed Max a grin and said, "I like your makeup, very emo."

When all four of them had vanished inside, Wes looked at me and raised his eyebrows, and then a big grin took up his whole fat face.

"You've still got it, Max," Ed said, laughing. "Although I've never quite figured out what *it* is." That's when Wes started laughing.

"Yeah, yeah, yeah," Max said. "I'm just waiting for him to throw it in." Wes kept right on laughing. "Now come on, let's do this," she said.

She led us through that doorway into some stranger's house, and we followed like we belonged there.

There was nothing in the giant living room but a cheap coffee table holding photo albums and an empty yogurt container. Trippy colored pottery hung all over the walls. I could smell burnt eggs through the kitchen doorway. The sound guys started setting up on a low stage in the back of the room, wires everywhere.

We checked the dining room next. A glass table stacked with laundry, bras and panties mostly. A bowl of stale corn chips sat on the floor by a stack of CDs. Someone had spilled booze on the floorboards.

In the three bedrooms were just a few acoustic guitars

and a hell of a lot of books. The door to the fourth room was locked, and behind it we heard a girl's voice talking on the phone.

Finally, we reached the bathroom in the back. There was something different in that one—a boy, naked, dead in the bathtub.

PENNY

All it took was a kiss.

Getting down on her hands and knees, Max crawled over the edge of the tub, angling her head to get at his. One of those fancy loofah sponges hung from the shower-head above them, sort of like mistletoe. Max planted one on him real gentle, and then he shook from head to toe and opened his eyes. It might have been sort of romantic if she hadn't been wearing my sister's clothes and he hadn't been naked in some stranger's bathtub during a gay-pride festival.

Penny was different. Where Max was all bright white and the twins were jet black, Penny was sort of shiny, like silver, like, well . . . like loose change, to make the bad joke. If the sun had been streaming in that bath-room window, Penny would have glowed, honest. As he uncurled in the old claw-foot bathtub, his jittery jerks and slow unfolding reminded me of the day my nephew was born, how he seemed to be giving his body a test drive. And like him, Penny was almost hairless except for this tiny bit of bristly peach fuzz that covered his head. Unlike Edgar and Wes, Penny was small, even smaller than Max, his body built like a bunch of tight rubber bands tied together. He sat up, groggy, clunking around in the tub, and then lifted his head and blinked. A giant fist had been tattooed on his scrawny back: a big fist shaking a lightning bolt, the letters TFL arched over the top.

I could tell right away that Max only had eyes for Penny. I didn't know how I felt about that or why I would care. But I did.

Cracking his neck in either direction, Penny looked up. I was the first person he saw, and he stared right at me. His eyes were all black with an outline of white, like the sun this one time I'd watched a solar eclipse with my class on the school playground. His breath was a fog. It made me nervous. *He* made me nervous.

"Say something, Penny," said Wes. "You okay?"

It was Penny's face that got to me, because it was just a baby face. He looked like a kid. Dude could have been my little brother.

But he didn't say something. He sang something in a growl.

"Let's light it up. Let's glow. World may be endin', but we got places to go."

The rest of them laughed.

Ed looked at my blank face and whispered, "It's the Painted Ladies, bunny." He said it in a way that made me feel like a moron for not having heard of this band.

"Hey," Max whispered to Penny, pulling him to his feet. "Go easy. It takes a second to get your balance." The twins gathered around.

"You good, Penny?" Wes asked.

"Sure, sure," Penny said. His voice was deep. It didn't match his body, his face.

Ed palmed Penny's small buzzed head. "Good to see you, mama," he said. "I was hoping you'd show up with your head in the toilet."

"Or under a truck," Penny said, and they chuckled.

He looked at me, making the rest of them all look at me too. "What's the bunny's story?" he asked.

"Who? Him?" Wes said, thinking. "That's Jo-Jo. He just is."

Max kicked me and smiled. "That's right," she said.

They helped Penny out of the bathroom. You could still hear that girl on the phone behind the closed door at the end of the hall. The band in the front room was still moving their stuff around, thumping and calling back and forth. "We need to go," Max said to Penny as he put his weight against the wall. "I don't even know where we are, exactly. Somebody's apartment, don't know who."

"Yeah," Penny said. "We got work to do." He pushed away from them gently and walked off toward the front door, his naked thing just hanging right there for every-body's viewing pleasure. I was starting to get a bit sick of all this running around in aprons and hand-me-downs, so I said something before he could reach the front room.

"Maybe we should get some clothes," I said. "Since we're here and all."

When none of them disagreed, I felt better. I knew I was there for some reason, even if it was just to find pants for a naked midget zombie.

We moved into one of the empty bedrooms and closed the door. The walls were empty, and the bed was stripped of sheets. A dusty old computer sat on the desk, and beside it on the floor was a milk crate stuffed with trophies. Against the wall sat two zipped suitcases, their sides bulging out from too much stuff, and next to them a big wooden chest of drawers. I flipped over one of the travel tags on the suitcase and looked at the name. It said "Tim." No address, no phone number, nothing.

Penny opened the top drawer on the chest and rifled through it. He grunted and then shut it, sliding out the next one. This time he pulled out two pairs of beat-up blue jeans and tossed them over one shoulder to Wes and Ed. The twins untied the ice-cream aprons they'd been wearing and got dressed. Penny pulled out another pair and did the same. The jeans were so big that the leg fabric piled up around his bare feet. There were plenty of shoes, a whole bagful under the bed. Getting down on all fours, Penny dug around in the last few drawers until he reached the bottom, and when he opened that drawer, he said, "Oh." I hadn't seen a tricky grin like that since the day my nephew peed on me when I was changing his diaper.

"We have wardrobe," said Penny, and he held up a T-shirt. It was all black with white stencils across the front that said: "THE CLASH." He put it on. It fit him perfectly, like he'd been buried in it.

He tossed shirts to the rest of them, even one to Max, who changed out of Carrie's hot-pink number and into a faded green army top that had some of them sergeant's bars sewn onto one shoulder. She swapped her drawstring shorts for a pair of cargo pants ripped off at the knees. After all that, the combat boots seemed a natural choice.

"I like Tim's taste," she said, tying her laces. Then she looked around the room. "We all set to go, then?"

"Hold on," Penny said. "Take that shirt off," he said to me. "It's got pit stains." Then he hurled something at me, and I bent over to catch it.

When I unrolled the white wad, I saw it was an old T-shirt, full of holes, a huge skull grinning across the front.

"Now *that* I can live with," he said.

After we ditched the house, Penny woke up more and more, and once he hit his stride, he seemed to know the city better than I did. He marched away from the crowds on Charles Street and into a part of town I had only heard about but never seen. It was east. It was down hills and through potholed streets with fog coming up from the sewer lids. It was called East Baltimore Street and was the setting for every dirty story I'd ever heard.

Anybody who had once had a brother that got arrested for selling drugs, or a friend who had picked up a girl for one night, or had a few extra one-dollar bills to get rid of, had spent some time on East Baltimore Street. It was like the Land of Oz if that wizard guy had been a down-and-out porn star.

Penny moved like a hound dog sniffing out a clue, weaving around them bums on the street corners panhandling for change, and he didn't look back for anything. The rest of us stayed quiet and just followed, because we somehow knew better than to draw even more attention to ourselves.

Neon washed the evening streets with light. There weren't no stars in the sky anymore, just a scattering of signs: "XXX" and "Girls" and "All Nude." A well-dressed dude stood out front of every lit doorway handing out flyers and coupons, grabbing at people's arms to convince them to come inside and see the girls. The lights were so bright they looked smeared, like late at night when you're tired. The street was packed with people. I ain't ever seen so many cops sharing that small a space with so many scumbags, everyone just sort of hanging around talking, the music beating from cars, girls wearing tiny tops and black-leather knee-high heels.

Max's eyes were huge as she stared at all the flashing colors. "Every time," she said—to me, I think. "Every time I come back, it's like, I don't know, a carnival. You can hear the electricity pop-like. There's so much of it."

"Getting mugged is fun and all," said Ed, "but do we really have to come all the way down here for a cutter?"

"Closest one," answered Penny, and kept walking.

"Can I have sex with someone, someone alive?" Wes said. "That would be such a special thing." No one even acknowledged that question.

Each one of them seemed lost in their own world. Me, I was busy thinking as we walked down those hilly trash-covered streets. I was thinking about homing pigeons. If it was true that people could die and come back to life, then go back to being dead again, then what was stopping any of us from doing it over and over? It sounded like a season ticket to some real morbid amusement park.

I kept wondering, what if?

Right before we hit the worst of East Baltimore Street, where a couple of strippers were taking a break to buy hot dogs from a vendor with a scarred silver cart, Penny turned down Gay Street. He stopped at a doorway. The lightbulb above it was gone, and only sharp pieces of glass were left in the socket. On the wall next to it hung a poster that said, "3 DVDs for $9.99." There was a picture of a naked chick with a belt on and not much else.

"Here?" Max turned to Penny. "I don't know about you guys, but back in the day, I never would have been caught dead in a place like this." She knocked. When no one answered, she knocked again, harder.

After a few more tries, we finally heard someone far back in the building somewhere. Whoever was inside did a lot of moaning through a string of curse words.

The door flew open, and in the doorway stood a dude who looked about 75 percent hair. He wore black plastic sunglasses, his head covered in long tangles that didn't stop at the front of his face but tumbled down to his chest in a sloppy brown beard. In one hand he held both a can of beer and a TV remote. Sticking out of the front pocket of his leather biker's vest was a carrot. He wasn't wearing anything below that except a pair of light-blue boxers.

He took one look at Penny and said, "Crap."

"Is this a bad time?" Penny asked.

The big biker saw the rest of us. "Double crap. What do you want?" he said, answering the question with a question.

"What do you think?" Penny said, stepping into the house. The dude didn't even try to stop him, just backed out of the way. The rest of us followed, Max and me bringing up the rear. I closed the door behind me and locked the bolt, because I had been taught all my life to do it, just in case some weirdos tried to break down your door in the middle of the night. Weirdos like us.

"Triple crap," the big biker said, and he pulled at the tip of his beard. Then, nodding, he started walking. "Okay, okay, come on," he said with a wave of his hand.

He took us down his skinny hallway. We passed a room where the TV was blasting an old movie full of gunshots and then through a doorway to the left, into a big room with a high ceiling. The windows had been sloppily covered up with newspaper, but orange street-lights and some of them XXX shop signs were bleeding in through gaps. An outdated AC unit rattled up in the ceiling.

Then the dude turned on the overhead lights.

It was a tattoo place, a sweet old seventies-era parlor with a chessboard floor. That famous old poster of hot Farrah Fawcett hung above the cash register. The two big chairs were green and cushy, and they looked like what I imagined dentist chairs looked like, because I had only had my teeth cleaned once and that had been at the dentist's kitchen table. That's what happens when you don't have insurance.

I wanted to sit right down and give that big biker my arm. Ever since I was ten years old, I had wanted a tattoo, but my stupid sister always said she'd waste me if I got one—because Ma "wouldn't have approved." If nothing else went right that night, I was going to get me a tattoo, what I wanted, where I wanted it, and as big as a damned football.

But as I stood there thinking about it, picturing all the cool tats I could get, something really weird came into my mind: What good was a tattoo if I was going to kill myself? I stood there with the skinny hall behind me, the hiccuping fluorescent light of the parlor ahead, and I kind of wrestled with the thought.

The bearded dude and Penny were talking over by the cash register, and Edgar and Wes were touching everything like a couple of little kids going through Christmas presents, picking things up, listening to them, smelling them, and putting them back.

Then there was Max. She just sat there on a rust-colored couch with cushions so squashed in, they made the middle of the couch look like it was smiling. She sat slumped, arms down between her knees, rubbing the flats of her hands together. She looked giddy.

It was crazy to think that I had known her less than a day. It was even crazier to think that she was the reason I hadn't done myself in yet.

"What are we doing here?" I asked Wes, who was shaking a bottle of prescription pills next to his ear to catch the rattle.

"We're getting colored," he said. "Can't look like this if we want to party."

The big biker walked over, yanking the bottle out of Wes's hands. He stuck it in a cabinet below the cash register, one that had a baby-proof latch. "You don't want those," he said.

"Maybe I do," Wes said.

I wondered what the leathery guy was thinking when he saw me, a regular Joe, chilling with a bunch of black-and-whites in raggedy clothes. If he did find it messed up, he wasn't showing it. He pulled a pack of smokes from his vest pocket, the one that wasn't carrying a carrot. "What's your name?" I asked him.

"Harlan," he said, "Harlan Hogg."

"I'm Jo-Jo," I told him.

"Like I care," he said.

Then he turned to Wes again and lit a cigarette. "The little guy says you've got something for me?"

It seemed to take a second for Wes to understand what he was talking about, but then it looked like a light went on in his brain, and he held up one stubby finger. "Give me a minute," he said.

Wes moved away behind the cash register and then turned his back to us. With a real juicy sound, he cleared his throat. Arching his back once, twice, three times, he started to gurgle like he was drowning—a sound that led to some really hard-to-listen-to heaving.

An instant later he straightened onto his tiptoes, like a rod had been shoved right up his butt. Then all that fat came crashing down again. It was over.

Wes turned around with a little tube in his hand. It was slimy, and I knew why.

Dude had just barfed up a jar. The colored stuff swirling inside, maybe paint or ink, glowed like some kind of radioactive slime.

Slamming it onto the counter, Wes looked at Harlan and asked, "Do you have a bathroom around here, mama? I need to wash up some."

With a frown, Harlan pointed off in the direction of the hallway.

"Now you've got it," Penny said from the couch, "so let's do this thing."

I felt bad for Harlan Hogg. He looked pretty tired as he wiped his forehead and walked across the tattoo parlor to the wall by the register. He didn't seem too pissed, but it was hard to tell under all that hair. Maybe folks who walk around wearing leather vests and boxers have a whole different philosophy on life. That would explain the carrot.

Standing in front of the wall behind the cushy

chairs, he reached out and touched a big crucifix. It was a fancy painted-wood one, colorful, with Jesus pegged up on it looking real awful. Harlan rotated that cross, uncovering a round hole that had been punched in the wall plaster. Inside the hole was a dirty, regular old light switch. "Damn, damn, damn," he said as he flipped it.

The second that switch moved from "OFF" to "ON," the wall began to groan. A few autographed photos of rock stars shook but didn't fall. From behind the wall came the sound of gears turning and the smell of engine smoke. Harlan didn't move none. He just stood with his arms crossed and watched.

Real slow, the wall moved to one side, opening like one of them sliding minivan doors. It opened up into another room, a tiny one tucked back behind the apartment wall. When all that bumping and grinding was done, the tattoo parlor had doubled in size.

The new room was clean. White sheets covered everything. Covering those were plastic zip-up protectors that looked just like the ones my grandma used to keep over her sofas. In the middle of the room sat a huge chair, like the two in the parlor, only ten times more complicated. There were special rests for both the arms and legs, and all these scary-looking straps and buckles. At the top near the headrest was a big metal neck brace. It was connected to a winch, like it could be cranked real tight. Above the chair was a second sexy Farrah Fawcett poster, same as the first.

Next to the chair stood a metal rack that held four big tanks of colored liquid. The ink inside had the same dazzling flash of the stuff in the jar Wes had yakked up. The tanks were connected to clear tubes that wound down in curly loops to something that looked like a glue gun. The whole business reminded me of IV deals you see in hospitals, a bag of junk dangling from a metal pole, a coatrack on wheels.

Max got up from the couch and walked into the room, flinging her borrowed clothes every which way. "Any objections to hitting me first?" she asked, climbing into the big chair.

Harlan Hogg strapped her in—wrists, ankles, waist, chest, and finally her head, cranking the winch until Max couldn't move her neck one bit, her eyes bugging out. He turned on a bunch of tiny lamps set into the ceiling and walked around the chair real slow. He tipped his sunglasses down to get a better look.

I didn't need a better look. I was as close as I wanted to be. From where I stood, it looked like Max was trapped in some electric chair. I stood watching, not knowing what else to do but jam my hands into my pockets to keep them from shoving that big biker out of the way and busting Max loose.

Harlan hummed, knocked ash off his cigarette, and then sat down on a tiny wheelie stool. Yanking that weird gunlike thing from its clip on the rolling cart, he pushed a button. A needle came out one end of it. It was real long. With the pull of a trigger, that needle became a blur and made a mad squeal like an electric toothbrush.

He started with Max's face. She whimpered a bit as the color flowed over her cheeks like ripples across a pond. It was for damn sure the coolest thing I'd ever seen.

Harlan stopped, smacking his free hand up against his face.

"Shit. I'm so out of it. What color did you want again?"

By the time Max was halfway done, an hour later, I was sitting on another wheelie stool right next to her, watching that needle fly. One side of her face looked like an empty paint by number, and the other side looked as real as mine. Harlan was some kind of artist, no buts about it. Every one of his movements was perfect. We talked as he worked. He said it made him more comfortable.

"What is that?" I asked, meaning the color. It didn't go only where he put the needle. It seemed almost to bloom across Max's empty white palms.

"Living ink," said Harlan. He pulled back the needle, checking his work. "Some of it is just normal tattoo pigment, but I mix it with that stuff they bring me from . . . from someplace else, hell, I don't know where, but not *here*, if you get my drift. That's what's in the capsule that Chubs barfed up. Don't ask me how or why it's got that glow. All I know is that some exclusive customers will pay a lot of cash for one of these tattoos, folks who want a little something extra."

"Extra?" I asked.

"Of course, when you're cadavers like these assholes, the color never lasts. They're never able to keep it. Like leaving a steak out overnight and expecting it not to stink."

I wondered what he meant by "these assholes."

"You know them?" I asked.

"Who? These kids?" He laughed, still moving that needle gun through the air like it was a reflex, a bodily function that came so easily he didn't need to think much about it. "I never seen these little shits before in my life," he said. "But there's always someone knocking on my door naked, and for some damn reason they're always doing it at three in the morning, like for some reason dead dudes can't come get cut over coffee.

"Guys like me have been messing around with this bunch ever since they started showing up through that door they have. It's a trade-off. We help them out when they come stumbling in all monochromatic, and they supply us with the ink." He grinned with teeth that were all brown and ugly, adjusting the controls on the gun at the same time.

"You must be freaking out," he said, chuckling, but I hardly heard him. I followed his hand as it guided that needle right inside the soft white of Max's eyeball. As he drew, Max made a high-pitched hiss through her teeth.

Over the next few hours the others took their turns

in the chair. Harlan gave them all exactly what they ordered. Max came off the presses kind of dark-skinned, with very blue eyes and lips that seemed permanently made up—sort of a hooker look. Ed and Wes chose matching brown skin, a dark brown that was almost their old black and just barely believable. Palest of all was Penny. He could have been some guy who'd spent the last ten years locked in his basement playing video games and eating microwavable lunch pockets. He asked for red eyes, even after Harlan kept telling him no one would buy it. But Penny, man, he wouldn't back down an inch.

When it was all done, the four of them sat in a big mess on the couch drinking bottles of Natty Bo that Wes had found in Harlan's fridge. They talked and laughed, their bodies all mixed together, and even though they looked more like me now than they had all day, like real people, I felt more than ever that I didn't belong. They could have been one big living thing, a love blob. That kind of stuff is always nice to see, but always a little hard to watch when you ain't included.

Harlan was smoking and cleaning his strange coloring machine. As he rinsed the needle gun with something from one of the hanging tanks, he glanced at me and grunted. "What in the hell are you doing here, kid?"

"I don't know," I said.

"Well, you'd better figure it out, right quick," Harlan said. His hands trembled. They hadn't been shaking before, not when he worked the needle.

"You should walk out that door right now and go home to your mama," he said. He looked at me hard, and then lowered his sunglasses so I could see the wrinkled bags under his eyes. "These kids look like you, but they ain't like you."

He was a nice guy, Harlan Hogg. Instead of going on about worlds and magic and all that, he picked up the strange gunlike needle and held it up for me to see. "Let me cut you, kid," he said. "For your trouble. You may not last the night the way you're going, but it's good to strike while the iron is hot. Whatever you want, it's on the house."

I looked around the room at the stained white walls, where sheets of paper hung in plastic sleeves. There were snakes, and crosses, and naked chicks in high heels, and horny coyotes wearing Confederate flags, but nothing caught my eye. Not until I turned toward the doorway, where different-colored flyers were plastered over the windows that faced out onto the busy street. Above the doorway I saw what I wanted.

In a tiny line above a drawing of the comic character Calvin peeing on Osama bin Laden and below sketches of butterflies was flowers. Little flowers. They looked all planted together in a perfect row: daisies, daffodils, tulips, and others. So I picked one and climbed into Harlan's horror chair.

I barely felt a thing. When he finished, I looked down at my violet.

It moved, like a mini-cartoon playing over and over again on the inside of my right wrist. Below it, I could still see the green of my veins, the blue of the blood under the skin. The flower's petals seemed to vibrate, as if caught in some gentle breeze that sure wasn't there. And I felt alive again.

BALTIMORE

Baltimore would never see another party like the one that went down that June night. The group of us walked back across town just as the action was getting started. It seemed like all of Baltimore was oozing in that direction, an APB for all the homos in their sequined masks, preppies done up in brand-name khaki, even the gangsters from both the east side and the west side pushing center. Everybody was coming together. We ended up back on busy Charles Street, which cut down the middle of things like a clogged artery. Nobody, and I mean *nobody*, stayed home that night.

We found the brownstone again with no trouble. Most everybody else in downtown had too. The doorway was packed, and the drinkers trailed down the front steps and along the sidewalk. Max and I followed Ed, Wes, and Penny back up the stairs and into the stranger's house again.

Ed and Wes went to go hunt down kegs—"One for each of us," Ed explained to me. For some reason, I was his buddy now.

Penny wandered off without any explanation, leaving Max and me alone—like the start. I was glad.

The band played over everything, filling the place with noise. You could tell they had spent more money on alt-rock haircuts than on guitar lessons. They were total wannabes but still had groupies—hot ones—with small shirts and pigtails. The blue goatee dude we'd met earlier drummed and probably spent more time raising his fist into the air than beating on anything.

Off the front hallway, a wall of beautiful people blocked our way. They were not my favorite kind of folks, and I wasn't really theirs. I wore sweatpants and was sticky from the blazing afternoon. Grabbing my arm, Max shoved a couple of pretty boys out of the way and pushed us through. When they looked like they might push back, Max raised her head and stared them down. They backed off real fast.

I found us a seat in front of the big bay windows, a couple of squashed pillows sitting on a wooden ledge.

Candles burned in two plastic dishes crusty with red and black wax.

"Could this band possibly be as weak-like as it sounds?" Max shouted.

"If 'weak-like' means they're crap, then yeah," I shouted back.

"I'm going to get a drink," she said, and then slipped off behind a group of girls who were drinking martinis in expensive glasses. The girls were laughing. At first I thought they were laughing at me, because I'm ugly, and zitty, and trash. I'd sort of forgotten those things until Edgar reminded me and everybody else in the ice-cream truck. It hurts when you finally hear how other people see you. It hurts worse when you'd always known but just forgotten.

Max plopped back down next to me on a pillow, a beer in each hand. "Now this is more like it, mama," she said. The band took a break, walking off the stage, and then a DJ started up.

"Why do you call everybody 'mama'?" I asked, reaching for one of the beers.

Shaking her head, Max pulled the plastic cups away, working hard not to spill any of the foam. "Hold on there, Grabby," she said. "These beers have 'I'm with the band' written all over them. And you're not with the band."

"I get it," I said, feeling stupid, but I felt good.

"Fine, here," she said, and then handed me one of the cups. "'Mama' is the most common first word a person says when he wakes up dead," she said, drinking. "I bet you didn't know that, did you?"

I shook my head. It felt like it could have rolled off my neck, across the floor, and out the door. What she was saying was insane. "I didn't."

"And that's the same in every language," Max said. "We use it when we're picking on somebody who's newly dead, you know, who doesn't know what the hell is going on."

"Jesus," I said. "What about 'bunny,' same thing?"

"Kind of," she said. "A 'bunny' is a wimp, *lâche*, soft, the kind of person other people need to take care of."

It dawned on me that this was what the four of them had been calling me all day. I took a long drink of beer. "Is that the next most common thing folks say when they die?" I asked.

"No," Max said, finishing her beer with a loud slurp.

"That's 'shit.'" Then she raised her eyebrows and gave me a sly smile.

"So if there really is an afterlife, does that mean there are tons of other worlds too?" I asked.

She thought real hard. "I'm not sure," she started, "but I have a theory. You know about Disneyland, right?"

"Duh."

"Well, at Disneyland they have these different parts of the park. They call them lands. First, they got this Frontierland, where everybody's wearing these animal skins and riding around on log flumes and shit. Then there's Tomorrowland, where they show you what Earth's going to be like someday—underwater cities and robot housekeepers. The works! There are other lands too, like Adventureland or something, I don't really remember."

"Okay," I said, getting confused.

"Well, my theory is that the universe is probably like Disneyland," she said. "Think about it. The universe is huge-like and cluttered, like Disneyland, filled with all sorts of overblown freaks in costumes and way too many gift shops to be healthy." She held up one hand, like a "Stop! In the Name of Love" hand, to keep me from talking.

"Places like Earth and the Afterlife, and probably others, all kind of fit together to form my big cosmic Disneyland. Each place is unique-like, different, but part of a whole. Frontierland and Tomorrowland are way different, but both have restrooms and blobs of gum stuck to everything."

"That's it?" I asked.

"Well, that's all I've got for now," she said, coughing. "Boy. That was a mouthful. Can I have a sip of your beer?"

I gave her the cup.

"If you're supposed to be dead, then what are you doing *here*?" I asked.

"Testing new material," she said after she swallowed. "When you are as famous as we are, it's pretty tough-like to get honest feedback. You fart and people call it Mozart. To get the truth, you got to go where you're just like everyone else, and then nobody holds back."

I grunted. "Hate to break it to you, but you're nothing like everyone else."

"We're more alike than you think," she said with

a grin. "Oh, and we also come for the alcohol. It's so much stronger than what we got. Drinking this stuff is like getting hit-like by a bumper car."

She drank my beer, and I sat watching the candle flames wiggle around and I thought about death. The mass of dancers moved up and down together to the music, and through the cigarette smoke they looked like one big body breathing. Every so often I felt a drop of sweat hit me, but it didn't hurt, and I didn't give a damn—it could have been rain for all I cared. I looked at my wrist, where the veins crisscrossed, and down at my purple flower moving in its breeze.

Max finished my drink. "So who's Violet?" she asked.

When I didn't answer, she asked, "She your girlfriend?"

Eyes down, I nodded. "She was sort of my girlfriend."

"What do you mean, 'was sort of my girlfriend'?" Max said, finishing my drink and looking around. She found a half-empty cup that had been left behind by someone else, and she started downing that too. "Did the two of you split up?"

I liked how she described it—*split*—it sounded painful, just like it had felt when I found Violet dead on the steps, as if we were one person torn right down the middle. "No," I said. "She died. Someone shot her."

"And you think you can find her?" Max said.

"Yeah, sure." I laughed. I was a terrible faker, always had been.

"You suck-like at lying," she said, growing serious. "Just because I told you there's life after death doesn't mean everyone ends up where you'd expect. Trust me, *I* know."

Then she leaned her body into mine, like she had leaned into Penny on that couch in the tattoo parlor, and it felt right and wrong at the same time, and I wanted to kill myself and cry. I don't know why it felt so good to have her there. Tears came to my eyes, real baby tears again, but I didn't care. Even though Max was freezing cold, I didn't want that moment to end. I pictured her in that stream when I hadn't known her, and even though I still didn't know anything about her, I wanted her to stay right there and never leave. She was the sweet cold against me.

"I had someone die on me once, too," she said. "You

can go back, Jo-Jo, but that doesn't mean things will be the same. Sometimes you just have to let them fade away."

"I know," I said.

"Don't worry," she whispered. "You'll survive. You've got a good soul."

"Yeah, how do you know?"

"I can see it," she said. And when I looked her in the face, I knew she wasn't screwing with me.

I felt like such a wimp, sniffing like that, rubbing my eyes. But she didn't get up and didn't walk away. "You know, some people know how to read tea leaves," I said. "They look at them and can see the future. I wish I could do that."

"Why?" she asked.

"Because, before, when she was around, I knew where I was going," I said. "But now I don't got no future I can see. Nothing's out there. It's a big blank without her."

Max stared at me in this weird way. Harlan had messed up her right eye, and to one side of the pupil he had left a dark black cloudy spot in that perfect sky of blue. "You got to quit looking into your drinks for answers," she said, and finished that second half-empty beer. "You're supposed to drink them, stupid."

I laughed.

A cymbal crashed across the room. We looked up and saw Wes trying to squeeze his way by the microphone stands on the stage. Behind him, Ed hopped onto the platform and began going through the sound equipment. Some of the other people in the room noticed too, but just for a few seconds and then went back to their talking. When Penny showed up, I knew something was going on. He walked through the crowd and they stepped away to give him room. They probably had no idea why but did it anyway because he seemed the kind of guy you did that for.

Climbing onto the stage, he snatched the guitar from the stand nearest the front and looked at it with his red devil eyes.

"I'm up," Max said, and slapped me on the knee. A second later she was there next to her friends, taking her place behind the drum kit.

Folks in the crowd seemed real confused at first, especially the groupies. They searched the room for members of the band. I'd bet a million bucks that those guys had gone upstairs in a couple of the bedrooms to get laid and had no idea what was happening with their stuff downstairs. The sound of the DJ got softer and then clicked off, leaving a room full of people wondering what the hell was going on. I was one of them.

Then my friends began to play.

Wes started low, thumbing a bass string. His chubby body wobbled along with his own beat.

Then Max joined in with nothing but a snare drum, and it became like an army march, her fist and lightning-bolt tattoos jumping under her shoulder muscles. They flexed with every click.

Penny began to scratch his guitar to the beat and then dropped in an extra scratch on the offbeat.

The crowd forgot they weren't watching the band they'd come to see. They got into it, moving, slowly, turning with that heavy rhythm sound.

As the crowd twisted, Wes sped up his thunder, so secretly that you almost didn't notice him do it. My heart sped up with his slow plucking too, like it had been plugged into that beat.

Out of nowhere, I heard a scream. We all did. Right about then the artsy-fartsy sculptures fell off the walls and exploded over the floorboards. People looked to the ceiling, the heavens, like the whole damn city was under an air raid. As the scream grew louder, it got real clear, a siren, and I knew before long that it was Ed.

His guitar held one horrible, distorted note over the rumble of everything else. It was a bolt of lightning that was about to blast from a storm that'd been brewing for days without release—a storm that was readying to blow.

Members of the other band had come down from upstairs, but they stood there on the steps looking pretty floored, shirts unbuttoned, hair all over the place. The crowd moved up and down around them, like pistons.

When Edgar's screaming note came to a head, Penny opened his mouth—and from that baby face shot a voice that didn't match one bit. It jumped right out of his mouth as a devil leaps from a man who's been exorcised.

He sang.

It was unlike any song I had ever heard before, that any of us at that party had ever heard in our nothing little lives. It washed over us like a tide.

I sat on the pillow by the window listening to every single word as if Penny was shooting them across the room and right into my brain, written for me and me alone. Everything he was saying was the truth. I knew that. Nobody in apartment 2A on the thousand block of Charles Street that night would go home the same. It would have been impossible. We'd been baptized in Penny, and after years of bullshit, the way of things suddenly made sense, painful sense. I was alive, damn it. I'd been reminded down deep in the farthest place of me, and my insides glowed.

When it was over, silence. An empty space was left where the music had been.

Standing up, Max waved to me happily. Then she climbed out from behind that wall of drums, hopped off the stage, and walked over. She grinned, face shiny. The muscles on her arms looked bigger than normal and trembled. Every single thing about her looked good to me. I had never seen someone so full of life—and this chick was officially dead. I wanted to tell her, tell them all what they'd done for me, how they'd maybe saved my soul just then. So I got up off my seat to do it.

We crossed the crowded room toward each other.

I was so focused on her that I almost missed the flash to my left, a movement by the front door. A face

I recognized. I didn't know a lot of people, but I knew those beady eyes and that upturned nose. That face floated by the open door for just a second, checking the living room before heading outside. I would never forget him, because I'd fixed that face to the body to the arm to the gun that killed my Violet.

White Knife Johnson was there.

All of the hope, the good things I'd found in those five minutes, that had filled me up and touched every idiot in the room, popped like a balloon. I was me again—fat, ugly, stupid, and alone as they come. Something must have happened, because Max saw it clear as day in my eyes, and her smile vanished.

I moved faster than I ever had before, turning and pushing through the crowd. I scattered college guys and chicks and reached the doorway before White Knife had even reached the steps to the sidewalk.

I hit him from the back. It happened so fast. I don't think he even knew who I was or why I was hitting his ugly self. We fell into the street, and the mob cleared a way for us. I got in a couple of good punches, if I remember right. His head was in my hands. Then his head was hitting the street. Then his thumbs were in my eyes. We were so close together I could smell his cheap cologne and the salt of his sweat.

One hand in my pocket, one hand on his shirt, I went for the .45. Then it was in my right hand. People screamed. I think they ran away, maybe. But I was on top of him where I *wanted* to be. His hand was on my hand, and we fought for the gun. And I think I heard Max screaming words, but damn it if they weren't as clear as Penny's had been.

We fought for the .45, slapping, sweating. And—it was so weird—I started to lose, real bad, real fast.

Then it was like a kick in the guts, and there was a slow, spreading, burning feeling. The report seemed to come whole seconds later, and it scared me how long it took to break through all that shouting, but when it came, everybody noticed. They fell back. All of them. They checked to see who it was, if it was them.

It was me.

I was at the bottom of the huddle, caught in legs and arms, but soon enough the crowd vanished. They left me alone in the middle of a circle. I didn't want to be in the middle, not alone.

Something warm and wet ran down the inside of my

left arm and to the ends of my fingers. Blood. My T-shirt turned darker than black, and as I watched, I started to cry. I reached out to turn my body, to get out of the street so I wasn't alone, but my arm wouldn't work. So I used my other one. I goofily turned in a circle, like a spider with a leg torn off. No one was even helping me, they were just watching, even White Knife. His eyes got big and glassy, and he could have been a mirror, because I felt as scared as he looked.

I didn't want to die.

"Jo-Jo!" Who was it? Then I knew it was Max. Max.

Everyone got quiet then. I didn't understand why no one was talking. They all just watched, even though they knew what was going to happen.

"It's okay, Jo-Jo," Max said, and she slid along the concrete on her hip, on her side, like she was sliding into second. Her eyes—those weird, soft, empty eyes—looked right through me.

"Max," I said.

"Think about Violet," she said. "Do that and you'll be okay."

So I lay there on that hard sidewalk, my hands covered in stickiness, and thought about Violet. I pictured her pretty face, a happy face with different-colored braids and lips that looked like a perfect, unbroken skin of ripe fruit. I remembered her laugh. It sounded fake, a polite laugh, what someone does to be nice to old people who tell bad jokes. But it wasn't. That was Violet's real laugh. Then something made sense to me for the first time. Maybe all along Violet was just being polite, because I told bad jokes and she didn't want to hurt my feelings. Right away I knew that was the way it had been all along, and it made me miss her even more.

Ed and Wes came running up, and I watched their faces change, and before I knew it, Ed had ripped his way through all those people standing there and dropped down next to us on the concrete, his face real close to mine. "Breathe," he told me. "Breathe, you idiot." So I did. I breathed big, and I cried. Penny was nowhere I could see.

My hands were black with blood. It was warm, but I felt cold, cold like Max. She sat by me holding my hand. She rubbed the middle of my palm and whispered, "It's okay." She whispered it again.

From the start it had been all wrong. I should have

never gotten out of bed that morning. If I had stayed in bed, I wouldn't have died, and none of the rest of it would have ever happened. This wasn't how it was supposed to be.

DYAS, Jonathan Joseph. June 18. Beloved son of Frederick and the late April Dyas; loving brother of Carrie Dyas; uncle of Peter Francis. Memorial Service will be held at the DELINE FUNERAL HOME on Reisterstown Road, Friday 3 to 5 and 7 to 9 P.M. Service of Christian Burial Thursday 11 A.M. at Church on the Mount, Woodberry.

Published in *The Baltimore Sun*.

TRACK 2:
DEATH'S A BITCH

1

When folks first wake up after dying, they usually say one of four things:

1. "Mama"
2. "Shit"
3. The name of God
4. The name of a loved one

Or so they told me.

When I woke up after dying, I said, "Violet."

One second I was on the street, and the next second I was gone, but where? I reached out for Violet in the darkness, and I was positive we brushed fingers. I swear it. Her face swam in a fog echoing with voices, with screams. Violet. I couldn't think of nothing else. And then with her name on my lips, I blacked out.

When feeling returned, it came back in tiny, bite-size bits, a tingle. It was enough of a shock to start my arms and legs flopping all around. My fingers brushed my leg and felt nothing but skin—*my* skin—so that's when I figured out I was naked. Or I was on my way to being so, as a pair of hands worked me over, peeling my clothes off me like they was peeling a banana. Once that was done, I got dumped to one side and left behind.

Lying there unable to move, I worked out the details. My eyes wouldn't open. My fingers wouldn't curl no matter how hard I tried. My privates and everything else just sort of hung out there in the chill for the whole world to see. None of this was good.

Slowly, I began to feel the others. Bodies, dozens of them, wiggled around me, to my sides, some on top, even some below, crushed underneath me. They groaned and howled with sore-throat voices. Spidery fingers groped in my armpits and between my legs, and everything slipped and slid around in a cool chunky goop that splattered everywhere in all that action.

It was like sleeping on a pile of fish with all that slickness and chill, a rubbery noise like boots on a linoleum floor. I wanted to cry, but I couldn't open my eyes, and when tears should have come, no tears came. I couldn't even do that. I was dry. So I began to howl too; suddenly

I could do that along with everyone else.

A knee (it had to have been a knee) whacked me in the gut and a woman[1] began to scream, "Help! Oh, help! Jesus, help me!" in this English accent, and that kind of woke everyone else up because voices started cracking like fireworks. Only then did I get an idea of how many folks were there with me. Must have been thousands, everyone in the place freaked out, yelling in languages I couldn't understand, their voices weak and muffled, like little kids screaming under the covers.

I lay there listening since I really had no choice, and cried my no-tears, and I heard my voice mixing in with all the others, screaming for my mommy. I hadn't seen my ma since I was a little kid, and I didn't remember her much, but I guess that's what happens when you're as alone as you'll ever be, and scared.

An arm slid around my gut and squeezed real tight, and if the breath hadn't already been trapped in my throat, I would have lost it. A buzz of feeling had returned to my shoulders and back, so I thrashed

---

[1] Victoria West, 1932–2005: died in her bed from a respiratory-tract infection, her daughter by her side.

with all I was worth, which wasn't much. The person[2] holding me began screeching in Chinese and kicked around wild. Then he began to drop down, sinking into the bodies below. He was trying to save himself by holding onto me, and greased up as I was, I started slipping too.

And even though I didn't really know if I believed in him, I begged God for help. This is what I said: "Get me out of here, man. If you do, I promise I'll change. I won't sit on my ass and let life fly by. I'll make a difference this time. Even if it kills me, again."

I didn't expect anything. I'd learned not to. I spent most of my childhood wanting to believe. Having faith is like dropping seeds that may or may not grow, getting down on your knees and digging, getting dirty even if you're not sure anything will ever come of it. Me, I never even had one bloom. All I had was a couple of dirty knees from all that digging.

At least that's what I thought before I heard the voice.

"We got a couple of sinkers!"

---

[2] Li Zhuang, 1950–2005: took his own life with a razor, in his car, on an empty street, in an unfamiliar town.

It was *not* the voice of God—unless God sounded like some Australian guy who'd stuffed corks up his nose, like that guy from that old eighties movie *Crocodile* whatever. But it was *a* voice, the sound of a person[3] speaking a bunch of words I actually understood, which felt like a great big hug in that huge mess of panic.

Out of the dark and the cold came a feeling of hope, if such a thing were possible. Maybe everything was going to be okay after all. Then an elbow caught me across the head and sent me back to the blackness, a smile on my ugly face.

I woke up on a table, a bright white light in my face. I kept my eyes closed. I still couldn't move, but this time it was because I was all trussed up like a turkey.

"Just listen to the music," said a low voice. It wasn't mean or nasty, just kind of bored. "And whatever you do, don't fight."

I couldn't move. I still couldn't cry. I couldn't do anything but lie there strapped down and naked and take what was coming. So in my mind, I opened up

_____
[3] Hugh Macarthur, 1940–1982: severed artery while fleecing rest-stop vending machine; bled to death.

an invisible mouth I didn't even know I had, and I screamed at the top of my lungs until it felt like my heart would pop.

And I noticed.

I didn't have a heartbeat.

Heavy boots scraped away from the table and across a room. A drawer opened, followed by the constant turning of a metal crank. There was a click and then an ongoing crackle of fuzz. It was an old vinyl record. It skipped as it turned, and the sound was total shit, even worse than normal for a crummy old turntable, but it was a noise I knew, no matter how faint and dusty.

Classical music rose into the air, strings, like something Grandma Rafferty would have listened to on her old messed-up eight-track player that made the songs sound like they were being played underwater.

The footsteps came back. Then huge gloved hands touched me again, curling around my jaw and pinching it to make my mouth open and my tongue roll out. This big guy[4] didn't need to poke me, seeing as how I

_____

[4] Darryl Johnson, 1957–2002: suffered heart attack during first-ever slow dance on first-ever date, to "One More Night," by Genesis.

couldn't move a muscle—but he did anyway. Fingers pinned down my tongue. A clamp was lodged between my upper and lower teeth. Then, humming along to the music in a low voice that was surprisingly pretty, the big guy stuck a tube down my throat.

It felt about as big around as my garden hose and had a fat nozzle at one end. I didn't know about the nozzle until the guy banged it against my front teeth, trying to squeeze it past my lips and into my mouth. The tube was cold, and it slithered down my throat like some kind of snake nesting in my lungs. I gagged at first, real hard, and a wet noise exploded out of me. I bucked, but the straps held me. The tube slid down. It took up my whole windpipe.

"Give it up," the man said. "Give me that last breath and it'll all be over."

The man stepped away again, long enough to push a button or flip a switch, because I heard a click that started a machine chugging. The tube stiffened. If there had been any room in my throat before that, there wasn't now. I felt the nozzle start sucking. It was a vacuum. Maybe it was my imagination, but I swear I felt my lungs deflating like a couple of slit balloons.

I was in hell, and I knew it. The only way out was to die or black out, and since I was already dead, I didn't have much choice in the matter.

I lay in darkness, either on a table or in a dream—I couldn't be sure which. I heard a clock ticking. I wanted it to be real so badly. I knew what a clock sounded like. I had one back home, in my room, by my bed. You take little stuff like that for granted. I'd have clung to my house keys if I had them, or hugged one of my sister's filthy scrunchies to my face, anything that reminded me of life. A clock worked pretty good. Clocks are *everywhere*, always counting down to something.

And as I listened to all that ticking, I felt Violet come in the room.

She was right there, only inches from my arm, I would have bet my life on it. She wore a dress with flowers. I could see it even with my eyes glued shut. She must have gone out and spent some money to look nice for me, gone and bought a dress blasted with little flowers that looked like they were twirling from a bridge and then someone had taken a picture with all of them caught in air, frozen like that. With a dress like that on, everything seemed right with the world. I wondered if she'd come to say her last good-byes, that this was *that* time—the end.

Then Violet opened her mouth and with a smile said, "Do we have him?"

"Looks it," said a second voice, a man's. It was a different voice from the guy before. This one had no accent. "He's clinging pretty hard, but he's about done."

As he talked, I could feel Violet slipping away, back out the door and down the hall, to someplace where I couldn't see or hear her anymore. Our last moment had come and gone, and instead of bringing me peace, it felt a lot more like a tease.

"Oh hell, he's crying," the girl[5] said as Violet left for good. "I hate when they cry. It's just depressing, all that squeezing with nothing coming out."

"Really? It bothers you?" said the man[6], between heavy breaths. I didn't want to believe that Violet hadn't been there at all, that there were just strangers over me.

---

[5] Rebecca Gaylord, 1980–2003: struck by a stray artillery shell while suntanning on the beaches of a war-torn country.

[6] Dr. Tyler Perrelli, 1945–1986: died from complications after a colleague left a pair of forceps inside him during surgery.

"Well, you'll get used to it."

"I never will," said the woman-who-was-not-my-girlfriend.

"Okay, let's try," the man said. Freezing fingers grasped my face and pried my eyes open. *"¡Hola!"* he shouted into my face as he bent over me, but my vision didn't take, because all I saw were shadows, maybe a shiny speck in the distance. *"Nin hao!"* he shouted into my face next, and I felt his spit turn foamy and fly all over.

"Bonjour! Konichiwa! Marhaba!"

But only one person could bring me out of that funk, and she was gone. I found that current of sleep I'd been sailing on and caught it . . .

2

After a long tunnel of darkness and dreams, the fog began to lift. I caught glimpses of stuff: a table, a movie screen, a door. I heard some guy clear his throat and a sniff—normal sounds. The greasy bodies, the table, the hose, the strangers' voices—all of what came before seemed like a nightmare, because when I was finally able to open my eyes, the scene in front of me looked pretty damned ordinary.

I sat in a wheelchair, at a table, in front of a real fancy paper place card with my name printed on it. Except the last name was spelled all wrong, "Dias" with an *i*. I was all done up in a soft, almost toilet-papery jumpsuit with a pocket on the front. Below the pocket the letters "MIA" were stamped in black. On the table next to the place card sat a clipboard, a pen, and a small stack of crinkly papers, the kind you push down real hard on to make your writing copy through.

The room was dim and filled with scrawny-legged chairs and folding tables like you'd find in some beaten-up school classroom. A sign on the door to my right said, "English 3-R."

I wasn't alone, either. Folks sat slumped in chairs, stuffed wherever they could fit. They had the look of people nodding off on a couch after Thanksgiving dinner. One old guy was snoring. The whole scene felt so normal—like I was about to break out the microwave popcorn and watch some shoplifted DVDs with my cousins who worked the Target returns department.

The other guy[7] at my table had a bushy mustache, which brushed the tabletop every time his head bobbed down with sleep and jerked back up again. What really had my attention wasn't his sweet upper lip, or the fact that he was flirting with a bloody nose, but the fact that the dude was glowing. It was as if he'd sat on a light socket and the bulb had gone right up his ass. His chest gave off light like a dying fire, red and quivering.

Once you realize something like that, a fact that had been there all along without you noticing, you start

---

[7] Adolf Ulrich, 1920–2005: run down by a school bus as he picked up his morning newspaper.

to see it everywhere. And damn it if everybody wasn't glowing.

I leaned over. "Dude, you're glowing, man," I said, surprised at my slurred speech.

Mustache guy glared at me under his puffy eyelids. "Yeah, well, so are you, jerk." He wasn't handling having died all that good.

I heard the click of a film reel and looked up. Film clattered through a projector. Everything stayed quiet, dark, until a white square exploded across the wall, like a window opening onto a snowstorm in the North Pole. With a crackle, we were suddenly watching this creepy montage of all the different ways a person could bite it. The music was silly, or supposed to be, an accordion chugging along filled with wacky cartoon sound effects. A bear mauled a guy. A woman accidentally electrocuted herself while shaving. A couple smooching in a paddleboat shaped like a duck sank. A motorcyclist twirled head over heels across the pavement. A steamroller flattened a kid's lemonade stand. An old man keeled over in the front row of a strip joint, one-dollar bills spilling from his fingers. Then stillness.

The words *Begin Again* filled the screen.

The emptiness faded up to black-and-white footage of this guy[8] sitting on a desk in a classy office in what was probably the penthouse suite. He wore a swanky gray suit as he smiled into the camera—at me, like I was the most important person ever. He had more teeth than looked natural, or maybe they were just real small and packed real close together. Before he started gabbing, a title popped onto the screen in big type: *Fred Edwards, President and CEO.*

"Hello," he said. "Welcome to the first day of the rest of your afterlife. My name is Fred Edwards, and I am the president and chief executive officer of the ATP, or Afterlife Territorial Provinces. I will act as your guide as you acquaint yourself with the strange new world that awaits you."

He stood up and circled the desk, moving his hands all infomercial-style. "You are probably wondering where you are and how you got here. You are probably also wondering what to do next, and what this new stage in existence holds for you. Well, I can help you with some of these questions, but as in your previous

---

[8] Fred Edwards, 1957–1990: burned alive after falling asleep with a lit cigarette.

life, the future . . . is in *your* hands."

He walked out of his office, and with a shudder of the background he was suddenly standing in front of some busy train station or something just like it. People pushed past him as he raised his arms like a preacher. "Here in Avernus Terminal, human beings from all across the globe come together after living every kind of life imaginable, from the joyous to the tragic, from the long to the very, very brief. They all meet here, in this singular place, as have billions before them throughout human history. They have come together as you come together today, to begin again.

"You are probably asking yourself, 'What happens now, Fred? Are all of my best years behind me?' Well, let me assure you that here in the Afterlife, we believe the best years of your life lie ahead." Out came that glittery smile again, teeth too white to have ever been used for chewing. "The existence we offer is as rich and full an existence as you will find anywhere else. Because here in the Afterlife, life isn't *what* you live, it's *how* you live."

With a flash, he was suddenly sitting at the head of a table. A group of cheery folks clustered around him looking giggly. They included everybody you'd expect—a black dude, some Asian guy, a Latino, and a chick with a buzz cut who was probably into other girls. "To help people better acclimate, we have seen to the creation of government agencies and programs meant to provide help to those in need, such as . . ."

The filmstrip flashed to a man hugging a spacey-looking old lady: "Surrogate family placement."

A guy dressed in body armor and a helmet gave a thumbs-up: "Security."

A wrinkly old dude with a necktie shook a young desk jockey's hand: "Employment opportunities."

With a flash, Fred was perched on his desk again, legs crossed, arms folded. "And many others. As it was in life, there is never any shortage of questions. So if you ever need help, do not hesitate to contact the appropriate representatives, or to consult some of the helpful information provided." Squeaky music began to fade up in the background as he walked around the desk to an office chair that looked so leathery it must have killed a whole herd of cows. "We will do our best to serve you," he said. "That's why we're here, and always will be. Yesterday. Today. Tomorrow."

A logo appeared at the bottom of the screen as the music rose to a crackly blast. "For all of us here at the MIA, the DED, and the ASH, I'd like to say thank you for coming. We look forward to seeing what you do with *your* second chance at life. Remember. It's a *good* morning." The credits rolled.

Some ripped Viking woman[9] with arms like a man wheeled me into a room full of office cubicles, then down an aisle teeming with people who seemed to be in a hurry, and then parked me in a gloomy alcove where a guy[10] with a long ponytail sat filling out paperwork with the tiny nub of a pencil. His gut actually sat on top of the table, like it was just another piece of work he'd get to eventually. I wasn't feeling too good at that point. I was already done and over having died. I was starting to wonder when I'd get to go back home. When the joke would be over and I could wake up again in my wrinkled and overripe Spider-Man sheets.

---

[9] Greta Speer, 1918–1964: experienced cardiac arrest after an allergic reaction to a gift of perfume.

[10] Uri Zuhkov, 1960–1990: boxer in an underground bare-knuckles circuit until he suffered brain damage, paralysis, death; choked on own vomit.

"How are you feeling?" the guy asked without looking up. He had an accent, kind of Russian, like a villain in one of Schwarzenegger's old action movies, back before he became a governor. "You look a little dazed."

"Why are everybody's insides glowing?" I asked.

He laughed, glancing up even as he kept scribbling. "That's your *sol*, pal," he said. His accent changed as he said that one word, like he was trying to sound more American. "It shows how well you're living. Yours looks okay. A little below average."

So what Max had said about my soul had been true. I'd been so crazy over how she and her friends had looked to me that I didn't really think about how I looked to them. Apparently I'd been glittering from the inside the whole time.

"My name's Uri," the man said, throwing one big arm over the desk so he and I could shake hands. "I've been appointed as your caseworker. So if there is ever anything I can do to make your afterlife easier, let me know." He handed me a business card. It was real classy. But what the hell was I going to do with a business card?

Shuffling through his pile of stuff, Uri banged it one

time into a clean, neat stack and dropped it in front of me. "Everybody here needs to have the proper pieces of identification; we call them the Afterlife Papers. Once we get your information in order, you can take it to be processed and notarized. Whatever you do after that is your business." Then he winked. "So if you can find the patience to bear with me for a few more minutes, I can get the ball rolling. Okay?"

He *had* said to ask him questions. "The hose?" I said. "What was the hose?"

"You mean exam room A?"

The hell if I knew. "The hose," I said again. It wasn't hard to understand.

Nodding, he tapped his stubby pencil on the desktop and scratched his nose. "Most of the people who come through our facility still have their last breath left in them. It gets lodged in their lungs, kind of sits there like a meal that just won't go away." I didn't understand why that made him smile.

"Okay," I said.

"A last breath is a potent source of energy."

"That so?"

"It would be like lighting a cigarette near a gas

leak," said Uri. "Bang."

"Bang," I said dully.

He lifted his arms and gestured to the room around him, the cubicles and the desks, the coughing machines that were covered in some black grease. "Everything brought over from life retains that kind of energy. How do you think we have these wonderful electric lights, or the use of these amazing technological devices?"

"I don't know, man."

"We burn almost every item that arrives," he said, "piles, all of it taken to the rendering plants to be used in our combustion-powered turbines. It's enough to allow for a tenuous but powerful current. Did you know that a spool of dental floss can generate enough electricity to power a single lightbulb for up to twelve hours?"

"No, I didn't," I said, caring little to not much at all. I didn't see any "amazing technological devices," as he called them, just a bunch of clunky crap that made the whole room look like the tail end of a really sad garage sale.

"We've got to get to that energy before the Afterlife does," he said, laughing. "Am I right?"

"Whatever."

"Full name?" he asked, starting to fill out my papers.

"Jonathan Joseph Dyas."

"Date of birth?"

"June 18, 1987."

"Date of death, if you know it?"

"June 18, 2005."

Uri looked up at me. "Cute," he said. "So English is your first language."

"Yes, sir," I said.

"You're American, right? Where from?"

"Baltimore, Maryland."

He licked the tip of his lead and scribbled in a few of the boxes. "Done, done, done." Sitting up, he cracked his back and put on a real fake-ass smile.

"So why are you here?"

"I don't know. You tell me."

"No, I mean how did you bite it, buy the farm, croak, as they say?"

"I shot myself, on accident," I said. I suddenly remembered lying on the cold, wet street, how the eyes of everybody around me got so damn white and wide when they figured out that I'd be dead in a few minutes.

"What do you plan to do during your stay?" Uri asked. The lights in the dingy room flickered, dimmed, and then brightened back to life with a zap. "How do you plan to make the most of your time here?"

This question didn't make any sense to me. "Aren't I dead, dude?"

"You shouldn't take your situation lightly, Mr. Dyas," Uri said. "Everyone has a reason for being, a true purpose. It's what fulfills you. I'm sure you understand." There was an uncomfortable silence as he waited. As we both did. "There must be something you would like to improve upon or change from your last life. A mistake, a missed opportunity, a dream unfulfilled. Otherwise you wouldn't be here." We did a little bit more of the uncomfortable silence thing before he clapped his hands together. "So then, how would you label your purpose? Business? Recreational? Spiritual? Artistic?"

"I don't know."

He gave me a real good once-over then, something he hadn't bothered to do yet. "I'll just put 'Undecided,'" he said, and scratched something down.

Then gathering up all the crap, Uri clipped a few papers together, stamped the cover sheet, made me sign every page in triplicate, and then handed the whole damn mess over. "Now don't lose these," he said. "Take them downstairs to the MIA booth within the next twenty-four hours to receive your permanent identification. That stands for Ministry of Immigration and Acquisition. And that's all there is to it." Again, he flung that log of an arm over his desk to shake my floppy hand.

But I didn't leave. I stared at him even after he'd done his part and tried to send me packing. Clutter covered the top of his desk. A stained coffee mug with the words "I Only Breathe Out of Habit" sat on top of an in-box stuffed with forms. One of those squishy stress balls poked out of a half-open drawer.

"You said I could ask you anything, right?" I asked.

"Of course," said Uri, easing back in his chair as he realized he wasn't getting rid of me so easy.

I stood there feeling pretty pooped, the clump of paperwork in my arms weighing me down like a cinder block. I'd gotten used to sitting there chatting like normal folks do. I didn't know where I was supposed to go. "What if I want to find somebody?" I asked. "A person who came here, you know, *earlier*?"

He nodded and pointed. "A common question," he said. "Perhaps even the most common." Leaning back in his chair, one foot creeping up on the cubicle wall, he raised his eyebrows in curiosity. "Hoping to find someone special?"

"Violet Rafferty," I said. "She's my girlfriend." It had been a long time since I thought of her in the present tense. There wasn't a better feeling.

Still lounging, Uri scrawled down her name on a sticky note and grinned up at me with soft, charcoal eyes. "Well, when a newly dead person is expected to arrive, the government sends out death announcements to notify next of kin and friends. So whoever you hope to find will most likely be outside waiting for you."

He waited for me to respond, but I wasn't interested in talking.

I cupped one hand over my eyes and started to laugh, and just like the woman back in the examination room had pointed out, no matter how my eyes scrunched up, I couldn't pinch out a single tear. But I didn't care. I was so damn happy, happier than I'd been in forever. I was going to see Violet.

No one came.

I sat hunched in my wheelchair with a blanket over my knees, abandoned in the middle of a lobby bustling with people. A steady drip of chilly water dropped on me from one of the weak, trembling light fixtures, but I was too tired to move. What would have been the point? Where would I even go? I felt a million years old and cold. Most of all, I felt alone.

People moved everywhere, swerving to avoid me as they passed. Most of them looked grayish, like the cast of some old movie that had strolled right out onto the street from the big screen. The rest, the new ones like me, jacked in wheelchairs or getting shakily led across the floors by men in white jackets, dazzled in full color. All of us glowed like we'd eaten a bag full of plutonium popcorn, but some brighter than others.

In the center of the station sat a circular counter with a sign that said "Information" dangling over one side and a sign that said "MIA" dangling over the other. Above those, a big sign like a scoreboard had been attached to the wall. I'd seen signs like that before in train and bus stations. They showed when rides were coming and going out, and where they were headed. Only, this sign wasn't listing places. All those little letters hanging on black shingles came together to make people's names. Mine was up there, right under Horace Mack and above Imelda Santos.

But no one had been waiting for it.

As I watched, the big board whirred once, and then all the letters began to flip and change—*click, click, click, click, click, click, BUZZ.* With that big buzz, the letters stopped clicking and fell still, making new names. Everyone in the station stopped what they were doing to search. Most of them were women—moms, probably. They held their hands against their hearts with worry, like moms do, and they took that board apart with their eyes, looking for a son, a daughter, a husband, parents, anybody really. Even I got a bit of a thrill when one of those ladies let loose with a crazy scream of joy. She'd recognized somebody. A person she'd been waiting for had finally shown up, after God knows how long. One person was all it took.

My head slid sideways across the back of the headrest

and landed on the shoulder of this wrinkly guy[11] with one eye that a wheelchair pilot had parked right next to me. If I hadn't been sitting in a big room full of dead folks, I'd have guessed the old man was a corpse, had gone and died there waiting for his ride to fetch him. He was just asleep. He breathed in and out even though there was no air moving. Nothing kills your confidence like an eyeless grandpa guy who's been ditched in the middle of a station like it's the lost and found.

"Jo-Jo?"

My name, I recognized my name. Looking up, I tried to focus through the tired. When I did, I saw a pair of eyes that I knew.

A girl stood in front of me. One of her hands touched the arm of my paper suit—five little fingers blending into the white.

"You," I said. Then I took her hand and rubbed it all over, pressing it against my face and feeling its smoothness on my chin, closing my eyes and pretending I was somewhere else.

---

[11] Vladimir Kruglov, 1924–1989: trained whole life to bring down government but when time came, someone else beat him to it; fell off Berlin Wall during celebration of its demise.

She bent down next to the wheelchair. Whatever it was, that glow burning behind the walls of my ribs brightened up when that girl came calling. She moved in real close and whispered things to me, none of which I remembered. Our foreheads touched and her hair hung around us like a curtain, shutting out the world. She kept right on talking, telling me it was all okay, telling me I wasn't alone, even when I started crying and gripped the back of her jacket, holding on tighter than I'd ever held on to anything, like I was falling and she was my parachute.

"You're not alone, Jo," she said. "I'm here." That was the gist of it.

"Violet?" I said, even though I knew damn well it wasn't Violet and had from the very second I saw her.

It was Max.

3

We left the terminal through the large front doors, Max[12] wheeling me past a line of concrete barriers and out into the day.

Max broke into a run, and I zoomed ahead of her along the sidewalk. I gripped the metal armrests tight as we bumped down a ramp and into an empty street, flying right by the sign that said: "THANK YOU FOR RETURNING ALL WHEELCHAIRS, CARRIAGES, AND HANDCARTS TO THE TER-MINAL BEFORE DEPARTING."

I wish I could say that we came out of that dark station into the sun, but then I'd be lying, because there was no sun in the Afterlife. In fact, there was no real light at all, just a steady white haze, like a fog bank rolling in

---

[12] Maxine Tabitha Insco, 1964–1980: perished in car accident while driving under the influence, retracing the route where her brother was killed.

from the bay and cozying over you like a blanket. The city rose up around us; every building looked like it had been colored with a blunt lump of charcoal, like it had been sitting in a storm cloud, under a blanket of bad weather that had never broken up and blown away.

The lamps that burned real weak along the streets seemed to sense me coming, and as we rolled down the ramp, they blinked, fizzled, and then went out altogether. After that, everything was shadows.

"Stupid, shitty power," grumbled Max.

"Put me back," I muttered as she wheeled us away from the building.

"Ha!" Max said. "You wish. The farther you get from there, the better."

"But I need to get my Afterlife Papers," I moaned.

"We got your stupid papers," she said. "You nodded off-like. I had to sign for you since none of your family was there to do it. You're my responsibility now. So don't go pissing me off, mama, or I'll disown your ass."

"What about Violet?" I whined.

She smacked me upside the head. "You're right. It was very nice of me. You're welcome."

"Ouch," I whined, stirring in my seat.

"Don't even try to get up," Max said. "If you do, you'll be kissing street. Sit back and let me drive."

I didn't fight her on that. I just slouched in my seat and watched the bright white sidewalk tiles roll by underneath me. We swerved around potholes, big old office buildings sprouting up on all sides like petrified redwood trees. Above the rooftops hung this web of cables that dangled in low swoops over the whole city. A few real creaky-looking cable cars hung from the wires, squeaking slow over the filthy streets. They reminded me of those crispy shells of dead bugs you sometimes see hanging in spiderwebs, sucked dry and fragile.

"What is this place?" I asked.

"This is Avernus," said Max. "It's the capital city, and it's a hellhole. I mean that almost, but not quite, literally. Don't ever go downtown, if you can help it. Full of weirdos."

"How did you know I'd be there?"

Max snapped the wheelchair to the right and we shot into an alley. It was so dark I could just barely make out the gloomy pinhole of light at the far end, and we sloshed through invisible puddles of something. "I watched you die, remember?"

147

"How could I forget?" I said. "Guess I was lucky, then."

"Sure are," she said. "People get lost all the time. They have this book they use, called *The Last Minutes*. It tells how everybody on Earth dies a few minutes before they actually do, like breaking news, only before it happens. They put their names up on the boards above the arrivals gate so relatives know who's coming down the pipe."

"So you knew I was going to die and you came to get me," I said. This was by far one of the nicest things anybody had ever done for me, right up there with the time Violet helped me pass my algebra final and the time Bart saved me from that pit bull on uppers.

"I didn't come to get you," said Max, growing annoyed. "I just happened to see your name, so I waited around for a while. It was boring."

"Well, I didn't ask you to," I said, even though I was secretly glad she had. I didn't want to imagine what I would have done if she hadn't.

"It was the least I could do," she said. "I felt, well . . ." And her voice trailed off. "I felt responsible for you getting killed, even though it wasn't my fault. At all."

"It was all me," I said. "I screwed up."

"That's an understatement."

I got all choked up inside, words on the tip of my tongue. "Thanks."

"Sure."

"So did I really die?" I asked.

"You have to ask?" she said.

I looked around at the busted windows and crumbling sidewalks. If Avernus was some kind of capital, then where the hell were all the people? It seemed too still.

As we rattled around a corner, we passed this dude[13] sitting on the curb. Normally, I wouldn't have looked, because it's rude to stare at people who are different, but I couldn't ignore this guy. He sat all hunched, elbows on his knees, wearing a giant costume clown head that came down all the way to his shoulders. With that skinny body and that big planet head, he sort of looked like a living candy apple. His mask had laughing green lips and a big red ball of a nose and even a top hat that shot out crooked from his skull like a cannon. This

---

[13] John Gray, 1980–2004: crushed by falling church bells during freak blizzard.

poor fool didn't seem to be doing much of anything, maybe just sitting and thinking about the fact that he was wearing a giant clown head. A wooden sign was hung around his neck. It was fastened with a lock. The sign said: "Only Clowns Repeat Their Mistakes."

About halfway down the next block, Max picked up her feet and rode the rickety wheelchair all the way down the street. I didn't really like how she seemed to be having a grand old time while I was dead and wearing a paper suit, feeling like I'd been hit by a bus.

She must have noticed me drooping, because she stuck one hand into her pants pocket and whipped out a small gray flask. "Take a shot of this." I tipped back what she was handing out, whatever it was.

The stuff in the flask was like a barely drinkable mix of lighter fluid and those red-and-white peppermints you get at some takeout places. "What is it?" I sputtered. Even though the liquid burned when I drank it, it only flashed, like a match that fires up but don't stay lit. After two swigs, I felt a little more alive than before.

"Does it matter?" she said, pushing with her foot to keep us rattling along.

The flask looked pretty pricey, maybe yuppie gear

from some swanky catalog. The letters "USG" had been engraved in the silver. "So what's USG?" I asked.

"Ulysses S. Grant," she said. "He liked his cough syrup spicy-like."

I held that flask up so I could see it better.

"Is this really General Grant's?" I asked.

"It could be another U. S. Grant's, but I doubt it," Max explained.

"That's nuts," I said.

"That's nothing," she said. "Sometimes I wear Marilyn Monroe's underwear."

We coasted up to a sign. It stood by the side of the road, above a bold black stripe that had been painted across the street like the starting line to some race.

"YOU ARE NOW ENTERING LITTLE ANGLO. KEEP YOUR AFTERLIFE PAPERS ON YOU AT ALL TIMES. UPON REENTERING AVERNUS CITY CENTRAL, PLEASE READ THE INCLUDED RESTRICTIONS REGARDING YOUR RIGHTS AS CITIZENS AND EXPECTED SAFETY AND CONDUCT." An arrow pointed down at a small plastic tube hanging from the bottom of the sign. I sort of expected to see some pamphlets or something, but the tube was empty—so much for my rights as a citizen. With a shove from Max, we kept on rolling.

Every street looked the same. I guess it's hard for stuff to really jump out at you when everything is black or white or some shade in between. The homes looked like they'd been built in maybe the 1940s or 1950s, a neighborhood of tall, narrow row houses with bay windows and chimneys, like you'd see in DC, or Philly, or even East Baltimore. A lot of properties were only half there, walls missing, windows boarded up. Piles of rubble blocked the streets. Old furniture made up those heaps, and kids' dolls, and toeless boots and cracked wooden wheels, and in one spot I saw a deflated football sticking out from underneath a rocking chair.

Max pushed the wheelchair down an uneven sidewalk that was a lot like the one on my old street, Morton Avenue. Graffiti was splashed over anything that could be covered. "Life: Waste Not, Want Not" said one tag in blocky letters. Another looked down on us from what looked like a used-up old water tower. The initials TFL were tattooed on a big black fist grabbing a lightning bolt. It looked familiar.

I was just getting sort of comfortable, knocked awake from General Grant's stash of death hootch, when Max stopped short and almost sent me toppling. I looked up to see what she was staring at and got an eyeful. A huge billboard had been glued to one of the long, corner-row-house walls. It was a picture of that dude in the snazzy business suit I'd seen in the film. I'd remember those five hundred teeth anywhere. He had one arm outstretched like his big poster self wanted to shake my dinky hand.

Problem was, it didn't look friendly at all. It was freaky. He reminded me of a local news anchor, or Satan.

Below the giant open hand, the poster said: "FRED EDWARDS WANTS TO BRING FAMILIES TO-GETHER."

Max glared at it. "You are so lucky," she said to me.

"Me? Lucky? Why?"

"Because if I had a dick, I'd totally pee on that right now," she said.

I was too tired to pee on anything, but we did give the giant talking head a double dose of the middle finger before rolling on.

* * *

Max's house was small, like all the others, with a saggy front porch and a skinny gray set of stairs leading from the sidewalk to the front door. In a hanging planter where I'd normally expect to see freshly picked flowers bobbing, there was just a pot of dust. Max parked the wheelchair in front of the house alongside a bunch of abandoned junk—a stray boot, a wagon wheel, a sink.

My muscles had started to ache. It was a hot, hollow pain starting at my toes and sizzling upward. By my tenth step, I had to sit down and take a breather. "Come on," said Max, tugging at my paper shirt. "It's to the basement with you, to sleep it off."

With one of my arms slung around her shoulders, Max dragged me around to the side of the house. My hand bumped up against her boob, but I couldn't be bothered to care much. I fell against the basement door, which had a small window shaped like a crescent moon. Like an outhouse in some old Western.

Max opened the door into a darkness that was close to solid, felt around in that blackness, and grabbed hold of something. Then she started to crank, round and round. There was a pop and a hot stink. A real tiny lantern flared and began to burn. I stumbled in, grazing my head on the low beams of the ceiling, but I hardly noticed. I was exhausted, dizzy. I'd never felt so out of it.

In the middle of the room was a dirty mattress covered in blankets. I made a beeline for it and dropped onto the lumpy bed like I'd been shot again. A huge puff of dust flew up into the air.

"Thanks for finding me," I mumbled. The room was spinning wild. "I didn't want to be all alone."

"I wouldn't let that happen, bunny," said Max. "You'll be fine-like once you get your shit straight."

Then, standing over me, she unzipped my paper jumpsuit, and it slipped right off like I was a snake shedding my skin. I sighed, head on a hard pillow, staring at the ceiling as Max took off my clothes. She finished with my paper booties.

Then, to my surprise, she started to undress too. First the hairnet that she'd had under her wig. She peeled it off and threw it in a corner. Then the leather jacket, which she tossed on a pile of crumpled tarps. She grabbed a grubby white towel from one of the rafters and wiped off her makeup, and then, with a shrug, rolled up her T-shirt and whipped it away. I got a quick glimpse of bra before she pulled down a fresh tank top. Last came the pants.

Max walked hunched around the room dressed only in a tank top and white panties that could have been Norma Jean's.

I wanted to see her naked, and I didn't even know why, especially since I'd already seen her that way down by the stream in Woodberry. Back then I thought she was a corpse, which was a total turnoff. Maybe I was seeing her in a new way now, as more alive, which didn't make a whole lot of sense since we were both dead.

As if she could hear me staring, Max glanced over a shoulder. "Go ahead and look," she said.

"Sorry," I said, but didn't look away.

"Hey, you can't help it. I got a nice ass. Look all you want." She sat on the edge of the mattress, picking clumps of eye shadow from her lashes.

"Why were you all dressed up?" I asked.

"The wig?" she said, clawing her matted hair with her sharp fingernails to mess it up. "It was a disguise-like. The cops aren't big fans of the band."

"It's not a very good disguise," I said dreamily. "There's no color here. All wigs sort of look the same, unless you've got one of those big afro ones."

Max raised her eyebrows. "I'm starting to understand why you wanted to kill yourself," she said.

I yawned. "Max, am I dying again?" I asked. "Because it really feels like I'm dying." I reached out and put my hand on hers.

"No, you're not dying," she said. "That's just the pull of this place hitting you. Feels a little like you're leaking, doesn't it? Like you're a balloon with a hole in it?"

She had the nicest black eyes, like marbles. It was hard to look away, especially as a shadow crept into the corners of my vision and just kind of took over. "Can you even die here?" I asked. "I mean, if you're already dead?"

She paused. "I'll send you a postcard when I find out."

The room was perfectly still. After a few minutes, the tiny lantern began to fade, slowly at first, then all at once. The whir of electricity died and the black of the basement flooded over us. We would have lain in total darkness, if not for our bodies.

We glowed from the inside out, like jack-o'-lanterns.

4

Something woke me up. A slam. Then footsteps clomping overhead, feeling more like they were clomping against my skull. And a shout. "Yeah, well, at least I *wear* pants!" More damn footsteps. Then the door scraped open and slammed again.

I lay there waiting to fall back asleep, a sure sign I was wide-awake, like it or not.

Dim white light lit the other side of my eyelids, so I felt around for a pillow to smash against my face. The one I found smelled faintly of ass. I couldn't really recall much about the day before—a filmstrip, a wheelchair, a wig, and a girl's rear end snapped into white cotton underpants. I squeezed my eyes shut tighter, waking myself up even more. It didn't help that I had to pee real bad.

Like a kid, I hoped that if I kept my eyes closed, then what was happening on the other side of them wouldn't be real, that I was safe, tucked away warm on the inside of myself. I was pretty stupid, but I've always believed in the stupidest things. *The monster disappears once you turn on the lights. The world is the same at night as it is during the day. Your mother had a fighting chance. Your father can change if he wants to.*

She died quickly. She didn't feel any pain.

Violet.

I heard the basement door squeak open. I cracked an eye. Someone turned the crank and the lantern came on. A few seconds later a pair of legs stepped over my sprawl on the floor. From my point of view, I was pretty sure the person wasn't Max—there wasn't a hint of hips, and that girl had some serious hips on her. This was a kid[14], older than me but runty, with a small little nose like a candy corn, and hair that had been greased to one side like he was trying to impress some girls from 1952.

I shifted in the sheets, and when Slick heard the movement, he stared down at me in the darkness.

"So, have you seen my toolbox?" he said, as if we'd been in the middle of a conversation.

---

[14] Kevin James Insco, 1949–1968: brain cancer.

"What?" I propped myself up on one elbow, annoyed.

"My toolbox," he repeated. "Can you help me find it? The generator's broken."

I did not feel like helping him. My head pounded like it'd been punted, and my throat felt dry and scratchy.

"You must be Alan," said the kid.

This made me roll over, one eye open. "No."

"Todd?"

"No."

Stopping his search, he looked at me, arms folded across his chest. "Really? Wait, so *who* are you?"

"I'm Jo-Jo," I said.

"Jesus," said the kid. "I guess I lost track after Bruno. If you're wondering, he's the reason the sheets still smell like that. Dear Maxine can be a bit like animal control sometimes, trying to save every stray she finds." He took one more look at me and shook his head. "She'll bring home *anything*."

"Real funny," I said, trying to sit. The second I got up, I wanted to be back down again. I climbed into my papery jumpsuit, which was starting to show some wear.

My eyes were starting to adjust to the dim, and I

could see the kid picking through stuff on a metal shelf by the wall. He had wiry, muscular arms that were visible in the shadows like the bleached bare limbs of a maple tree in winter. I noticed him watching me as he tried to get a bead on his precious toolbox. "You'll get used to it," he said, "that tired feeling, that pulling."

"Awesome," I said.

"The Afterlife will leech the energy right out of you," he said. "It's gradual, but you really notice it when you first get here. Man, I'd hate to be you right now." As he talked, an orange glow shined from a spot below his collar, like a lighthouse beam.

"Well, same to you, dude," I said, rubbing my eyes. "How long have I been sleeping?"

"You've been in our basement for probably a week," the kid said. He dropped to his knees and reached under the bottom shelf, which was piled with creaky metal tools that could have been farm implements or torture devices, depending on what you were willing to see. "Got it!" he said, dragging out a black toolbox caked with dust.

"Hooray for you," I muttered.

"Thanks for all your help," said the kid. Then he turned and left, leaving the basement door wide open.

If I'd had the energy, I'd have kicked his ass. But I didn't. Instead, my attention was wholly taken up by the pain in my gut. It felt like I was getting stabbed a few inches below my belly button. I guess that's what happens when you haven't peed in a week.

Rushing outside into the cool, hazy air, I dropped the front of my jumpsuit and let it rip. It was one of those moments when you can't freaking believe your body can hold that much stuff, where you count and wait and start to wonder where all the piss keeps coming from. I could have stood there reading the newspaper for half an hour, but since there wasn't one handy, I arched my back and put my hands on my hips, looking out over the junk piles clogging the streets.

"If you're going to make water, the least you could do is water my garden," said a voice.

The comment made me jump, knocking a kink into my stream. I glanced over my shoulder and saw an old man[15] with a beard standing up on the front porch behind me. He was pretty small, like a miniature walrus wearing a bathrobe, and was drooped over a twisted wooden cane. The light around him burned brightly.

"How do you have a garden?" I asked, more into my business than his. "I figured nothing would grow around here."

"You're right," said the old man. "But I'm performing a little experiment, so do me a favor and aim here." As he said it, he poked with his walking stick, which made a conversation that I didn't think could get any weirder more so. "I planted some apple seeds a few inches down."

"You're old, so you're the boss," I said, turning my arc toward a black X that had been painted on the dusty ground by a jumble of mashed chicken wire.

The old man didn't respond right away, but when he did, it was with a smile. I could tell just by the edge in his voice. "See, you still got some life left in you."

I hadn't noticed before, but my pee came out bright yellow, like radioactive lemonade. I mean, who really

---

[15] Benjamin Dean Insco, 1887–1950: drowned in a toilet, drunk and pleased with himself.

pays attention to their pee, anyway?

I started laughing and that made the stream wobble, a colorful beam slicing through a black-and-white background. This must have been what it was like when the first prospector discovered gold: After all that hacking through layers of mud, he struck a vein of pure sunlight.

I turned to see if the old man was seeing what I was, but he'd up and vanished, making me wonder if I'd imagined the whole creepy conversation.

I went back into the basement crawl space and tossed the place, searching for something to wear other than that giant zip-up napkin they'd given me at the terminal. Behind a shelf of broken flowerpots, I found a bag of ratty hand-me-downs. In a short-sleeved collared workman's shirt with a huge black stain on the heart and a pair of gray jeans, I headed back outside to the front of the house and then up the stairs to the door.

The small entryway opened up into a big front parlor with bay windows overlooking the porch outside. A square dining-room wooden table sat in the center of the room. Above it hung a metal chandelier on a thick black chain. In one corner stood a weird little piece of furniture, like a wooden podium, with a metal arm sticking from its side. The crank ended in a handle that had been worn down from a lot of use.

Pictures spotted the walls—*full-color* pictures. Once they'd caught my eye, I couldn't look away.

They'd been stuck into thick black frames and carefully arranged in rows. They dazzled, so much that they hurt to look at straight on. I recognized a few of the shots, like a famous one of an A-bomb blowing up, but most of them were pretty ordinary. One showed a kid's birthday party with candles that burned as yellow as egg yolks. All in a line like that, the photos felt like little windows out onto all different kinds of scenery.

"Those are Ben's."

I spun around to find that runty kid who'd been digging around for his toolbox. He held a hammer and a length of wire, his cheeks smudgy and black.

"Who's Ben?" I said.

"You're standing in his house."

I turned back to the frames. "Did he take these?"

The kid wandered past me into the big room and up to that antique wooden booth thing. He cranked the handle, listened, and cranked it again. "No. He just collects them."

"How come they're color when everything else around here isn't?" Everything else was so drained and gray-looking, but the candles on that birthday cake looked like they would have burned me if I brushed them.

"They're not the only thing that's color," said the kid. He walked up to me and dropped his arm down next to mine, the hammer still bobbing in his fist.

Next to his ropy gray arm, my own looked bright pink, but a little less so than I remembered, like laundry that has been washed again and again until the color fades. The kid watched me real close, eyes unblinking. "Don't flip out," he said calmly. "The color's the first thing to go. It's purely cosmetic. Happens fast and means nothing. The picture frames are made from a metal that holds in the energy, slows the fade."

I continued to gawk at my arm. "Why don't they do that with people, then?"

A smile crept up into the corners of his mouth. "What, you mean store them in little boxes for all of eternity? I think those are called coffins."

A door slammed. Voices echoed down a long hall. The kid and I turned around to see the old man who'd watched me pee just ten minutes before wobble out of one of the rooms. He was followed by Max who was— big surprise—yelling. The old man trucked down the hall at a pretty impressive pace, with Max trying to push in front of him every chance she got. She wore a dark black suit coat that was way too big for her little doll shape, and its bunched sleeves drooped around her elbows.

Near the dining room, Max flung her body ahead of him, wedging it between the old man and the next door he was planning to open. She pressed her back up against the wood, sneering evil. Neither of them had noticed the kid and me standing there.

"You have no right to go down there!"

"I don't have a right to go down into my own basement?" said the old man.

Max returned his stony gaze. "I repeat. *There is no one down there.*"

"You don't exactly have the best record when it comes to lies," said the old man.

"Listen," said Max, pointing her finger in his face, "if

we're going to get along-like, we're going to need some trust around here, some honesty."

"A little honesty would be *so* refreshing," sighed the old man.

"Right," said Max. "So let's give it a try. There is no one down there!"

"Then let me see."

"I shouldn't have to. How many times do I have to tell you that *there is no strange boy in the basement?*"

The kid next to me cleared his throat. "I don't know about you, but I believe her," he said.

They turned and looked at him, and then at me, and then at the basement door.

"Crud," said Max.

Five minutes later, the four of us sat around the square wooden table in silence. To my right was Max, to my left was the kid, and across from me looking crustier than ever was the old man. If facial expressions could have talked out loud, here's what the faces around that table would have been saying:

Old man: "Max, you are one lying little bitch."

That kid: "Max, I totally screwed you over, so next

time you're going to dump some tall, pimply dead freak in our basement, check with me first."

Max: "I want to break something."

Me: "My head feels like a melting car battery."

The old man pushed back his chair and began to slowly circle the table. With every step, the walking stick tapped on the floorboards. Around and around he went, a game of Duck Duck Goose, only instead of tapping our heads to signal we were "it," he jabbed us with his corkscrew cane. The glow inside him seemed to grow and dim and twist, strong, like a small fire whipped around in a wind but not going out.

He started shooting questions, not giving Max time to think of lies to answer them.

"Who is *he*?"

"A friend."

"From where?"

"Gehenna."

"Does he look Indian? No! Where's he from?"

"Where do you think?"

"What's his name?"

"Rick."

"Does Rick have a last name?"

"Richardson." Max banged her fist on the table. "Damn."

The old man cocked one eyebrow. "Rick Richardson. That might be the worst name you've ever come up with."

"I agree," she said.

"Why is he in my house?"

"I met him at the club. I brought him home to, um, to do it."

"It what?"

"It, *it*."

Massaging his temples, the old man collapsed back into an empty chair. "You expect me to believe that you brought this boy home for sex?"

"Duh," said Max. "I have peculiar tastes."

"Listen to me, dear," he said, and leaned over to pat Max's hand. "You know I love you, but you are the absolute worst liar in the world. And now that you mention it," he said as his eyes passed over me, "you have terrible taste in boys. You always have."

I'd had it. Come at me with a baseball bat, that's cool. Take potshots at my bedroom window with a BB gun, hey, it's up to you. Hell, you could even spray-paint a big old knob on the hood of my dad's Pontiac, and I wouldn't say a word. But implying that I wasn't worth a girl's time, now that was something else. Violet proved that wrong, so saying it wasn't so much an insult to me as it was an insult to my girlfriend.

"I'm sitting right here, dude!" I shouted.

The old guy squinted at me, that goofy Muppet mustache twitching. He did his best to straighten up and look more menacing, but it only made him look fatter, like one of those puffer fish. He sighed. "You met him at the terminal, didn't you?"

"What? She didn't meet me at the terminal," I pointed out. "She came all the way to Baltimore. She showed up naked a couple blocks from my house."

I didn't see Max making "cut it out" signals with her hands until it was too late.

The old man's eyes bulged. "Is this true?" he roared.

If she could have, Max would have reached over and strangled me. "Yes. It's true," she said, wilting in her chair. Hardly a second later, she snapped up one arm and fingered the kid. "But Kevin helped us! He used his ID to get us into the building. He watched the whole thing."

171

Kevin popped up like a Whac-a-Mole. "I didn't have a choice! She blackmailed me!"

Max hissed at him, her eyes pinched into two slanty black lines. "Yeah, well, I'm not holding that secret anymore, mama. Kevin likes a girl named Jill, and she's a security officer at his office, and she's got huge fucking whale thighs."

Kevin tossed his chair across the room. "I'm going to kill you!"

I continued to sit, elbows on the table, chin in one hand as the whole place exploded around me. After so many years living with my pa and a series of his on-again, off-again girlfriends, I knew better than to get in the middle of two folks intent on killing each other.

Before Max and the kid could come to blows, the old man stepped between them, cane raised. "Shut up!" He beat the floor. When Kevin tried a last-second lunge, he got a swift jab to the crotch in return. That sent him squirming to one knee, whistling through his front teeth.

The old man turned to Max. "Listen to me," he said. "You have come so far. Don't use your time trying to rescue every person you meet on the street. Play your music. Shine your light. That is what matters."

"I don't help every person," said Max, "just the ones who really need it." Then her voice grew strong. "And you know damn well why I have to try."

"You have a problem, Max," he said.

"It's a hobby," she said.

"It's an *obsession*." The old man reached out, and I expected her to dodge out of his way, but she didn't. She stood perfectly still as he squeezed her shoulder. "*He* wouldn't have wanted you to do this."

"We don't know what he would have wanted, do we?" she said. Turning, she stormed out of the room and down the long hall, yelling as she went. "I don't understand you! *Now* you're interested in what I do?" A door squeaked. There was all sorts of thumping. "Suddenly you're interested in my music? You've never even come to one of my shows!" A drawer slammed. "You see me ten times a day and don't say a word-like, but when a strange corpse ends up in your basement, you suddenly want to have a conversation."

A minute later, Max reappeared. She had a black bag thrown over her back and was lugging a black cardboard guitar case. Stomping every step, she marched over to me and practically dragged me out of my seat. I really didn't want to move at that point. My insides felt like they'd gone a few rounds in a cocktail shaker. "And for the record," she went on, "I'll choose the guys I bring home to have sex with, thank you very much. You can sneak around here like a troll all you want, but just quit trying to become involved-like in my afterlife, because it's too little, too late."

"This is *my* house," said the old man, thumping his cane one last time.

"Don't I know it," said Max, moving us toward the exit. She opened the door, throwing a glance behind her, for effect, I guess.

"Don't you dare walk out of here until this conversation is finished!" yelled the old man, howling now.

"It's over," said Max, and slammed the door so hard the whole damn house shook.

I didn't recall really enjoying the sun all that much when I was alive, but I sure missed it now, as I stumbled out onto the front porch of Max's house into a gray day that would have made the happiest person blue. I was just starting to get it. There wasn't any day or night in the Afterlife. Dawn, noon, and dusk—they were all just states of mind.

Max moved fast down the street, tightrope-walking the curb, the guitar case knocking against her hip. Two white drumsticks stuck up like rabbit ears from her back pocket. I walked two steps behind. I was having trouble keeping up, what with my weary body and my cloudy head.

"He drives me *insane*," she shouted.

"Which one?" I asked.

"Ben," she said. "The old man."

"Who the hell is he?" I asked.

"He's my grandfather," she said, speeding up. "He's my mom's dad, and a real selfish prick. He died in the early fifties, before I was born, so I never knew him when we were alive."

"What about the runty kid, Kevin?"

"My cousin," she grumbled. "I remember when he died. It was pretty tragic. Of course, I didn't know what to think. I was four, and dumb. They pumped me full of candy to keep me from having a nervous breakdown."

Something was occurring to me as I listened to her tales of woe that weren't all that woeful. "You're lucky,"

I said, kicking stones out of our way as we walked. "A lot of folks don't have normal families, not when they're alive, not ever."

Without even looking at me, Max blew that idea out of the sky with one single harrumph. "Yeah, well, families are families. Most of the time they're more trouble than they're worth."

Max pulled ahead, leaving me in her wake. "Hey, slow down," I said.

"Sorry, Jo-Jo," she said, voice trailing off. "This is where we say adios!"

I tried to run but wasn't ready for that yet. "Why are you acting weird?" I called.

"Weird how?" she called back. "How am I acting weird?"

"Mean," I said, "you're acting mean."

She stopped and spun around, raising the guitar case to keep us apart. Her face was sharp, all business. "Well, you know something, Jo-Jo, the real me is pretty mean. In fact, some people think I'm kind of a bitch. So don't go making any big personality judgments based on one night in Baltimore."

That wasn't good enough for me. "I need help, Max!"

"You'll be fine."

"What am I going to eat?" I said. "Where am I going to sleep?"

For a moment, her tone got nice again, and she seemed to transform back into that chick who had listened to me yammer on about my girlfriend. I missed that Max. I'd thought it was the real her. "Eat if you feel like," she said. "You don't have to if you don't want to. As for sleeping, you don't have to do that either, but if you want to, you can always crash in the basement. But you'll have to get lost-like if I need to stash some other guy under there for a few days."

Those weren't the big questions, though. "What about Violet?"

"What about her? I'm pretty tired of talking about it."

"Max," I said, begging, "what am I supposed to do now? I don't know."

"And I don't care," she said, walking off. "Just do it and do it fast."

"What does that mean?"

Turning around, she walked backward, facing me, boots clunking over the broken slabs of cement. "Listen and listen real close-like, Jo-Jo. In case you haven't figured it out yet, this whole deal is about second chances. It's about making the most of what you got in case you didn't the first time. So a little advice—don't waste another minute standing here talking to me."

"I don't understand," I said.

"You need to find out why you're here," she said, snapping open a pair of sunglasses and sliding them on.

"Or what?"

"Or you won't be *here* anymore."

With that, Max was on her way. Hoisting the guitar under one arm, she hiked off toward the rooftops of Avernus. I could hear her humming. She might have looked like the freewheeling Bob Dylan, if Bob Dylan had been a bullheaded black-and-white Asian chick with a nice ass.

Not that I ever liked his music much anyway.

5

If I learned one helpful thing from my friend Bart in all our years growing up together, it was this: If a girl won't talk to you, follow her. It isn't glamorous, but it works. Tailing somebody doesn't necessarily make you a stalker. It's when you start carrying a camera and planning your bathroom breaks around hers that you got a problem. At least that's what happened to Bart.

Staying far enough away so she couldn't see me, I tracked Max through the city, back from where we'd come the week before, through the rubble-cluttered streets of Little Anglo into downtown. I didn't have a clue where I was going. I just followed. We passed burnt-out husks of shops, and hobos asleep in gutters, and one or two potholes so big it looked like they could have swallowed entire buildings at one time or another. One area was covered top to bottom in those slashy little Chinese symbols, a jumble in every storefront. If I'd had to guess, I would have said it was a whole neighborhood of takeout places and dry cleaners. I knew better, though. Hands jammed into the pockets of Kevin's gray jeans, I kept Max in sight as she lugged that guitar through the crowds, a stranger to everyone but me.

We'd reached a busy part of town, not like those ghostly slums surrounding the terminal. People streamed by— dead people who had gotten used to living again, even if they didn't really call it that. They wore all kinds of clothes. They carried bags and briefcases. They spoke a tangled knot of different languages, most of which I didn't understand. They hurried around like they had somewhere to go, though I couldn't figure out where, or to do what. Daily life in that dreary ghost town had a lot in common with your average American rush hour, with one big damn difference.

Everybody glowed.

Some say that the eyes are the window to the soul. I don't know where those folks picked up this little piece of information, but it's pretty obvious they ain't ever seen a dead person before. If you asked me now, I'd say the real window to the soul is the sternum, or maybe that flat space a little bit higher up, up there near the collarbone. You know you're staring deep into a person's purest being when they radiate from the inside out, trembling with a bloody light like a dying car fire.

Another thing—some people glowed a lot more than others. And some hardly glowed at all. The dimmest hadn't just lost that inner bright but seemed to have faded away a bit too, more like memories of people than the real thing. With their heads down low, they stuck to the edges of the crowds, alone, ignored. I walked right on by those ghostly non-people like everybody else did, and as I passed, a shiver ran up my spine.

Leaving Chinatown, Max made her way through a real seedy web of alleys. I'd never seen so many wig stores or pawnshops or vacant nothings. Small bulbs as big around as your thumb fizzled in metal cages on the street corners, and even though there was nothing really going on, the streets teemed with people. Dudes with pounds of face jewelry sat cross-legged on the sidewalks, begging, but I could never quite figure out for what. Tall chicks with knee-high boots bopped along the curbs, scanning the crowds. I steered clear.

But I must have drifted too close, because at one

point a woman[16] with caked black eye shadow called out to me. "Hey, baby, you look like you still got some punch in those pants!"

I didn't say nothing, but just kept on following Max, who suddenly turned into a narrow passage between two buildings that was more a skinny hallway than an alley.

When I rounded the corner, Max was gone.

It wasn't hard to figure out where she went. At the end of the alley was a fancy old building that towered above the overturned trash cans. It looked way out of place, like a UFO that had landed in the middle of the city and was doing a piss-poor job of blending in. Wide marble steps led up to a pair of half-moon doors that came together to form a black circle. The trembling neon white sign above the doorway read "The Tick-Tock Club" in faded, frosty-white light. Electricity crackled. Higher up on the face of the building, a giant clock ticked so loudly it made the ground under my feet shudder. It felt weird, but it felt good—a reminder that there was always something bigger than me.

---

[16] Elisheva Gubuernia, 1964–1997: commuted seven hours to work every day, slept three; fell asleep at the wheel.

A trio of punk dudes sat on the steps. I looked at them blankly, still stunned by the place behind them.

"What are you staring at, ND?" one of them[17] asked fast, turning away to drink something out of a flask. His pointy mohawk made him look like a pinwheel.

"What's the Tick-Tock Club?" I asked.

"The only place in town to see a live show," said the punk. He bobbed his head, spikes coming real close to making me a candidate for a glass eye. Then he froze and checked me out real close. "Wait. Are you some kind of ASH narc?"

"No, I'm just lost," I said.

"Right, a lost sol," he said with a smile. "Aren't we all?"

Pointing at the front of the club with one white, skeleton finger, he grinned. "If you're lost and looking for direction, then that's the place you're going to find it."

After getting my hand stamped by a bald bouncer wearing a dog collar and cowboy chaps, I walked into the

---

[17] Jebediah Masterson, 1982–2000: chose to live life and try everything, not wanting to miss out; dropped acid and jumped out a window but did not fly as expected.

fanciest joint I'd ever been in—dead or alive. It looked like how I imagined a museum might look. Except most museums probably don't have a girl passed out on the floor of the coatroom with a bucket on her head. The carpeted lobby was strangely still, but I could hear the white noise of people talking in a room nearby. On either side, two swooping stairways like mirror images of each other curved up to a balcony. A teenage couple stood at the railing overhead, arguing like crazy. When they saw me coming, they lowered their voices to whispers but kept at it.

Ahead of me, a short ramp rolled up to another pair of doors, this one sporting silver handles shaped like lightning bolts. I grabbed hold. A weird thrill shot through me, a static shock, and I threw open those doors and plunged headfirst into mayhem.

The Tick-Tock Club was huge, but it barely had enough standing room to fit all the punks and freaks and psychos that packed it. Most of the people—I couldn't tell if they were girls or dudes—wore enough makeup and hair junk for about ten Halloweens and a hundred proms. As I walked in, people turned. Heads tilted up. Eyes swept over me. Then it was back to talking.

You could tell just by looking that the Tick-Tock Club had once been a fancy old theater, one that had seen better days. The auditorium seats had been torn out and piled in one corner. Discarded bottles rolled along the slope of the floor. The dark curtain draped over the empty stage looked sick, chewed, like it had been stricken with some strange skin disease. At the front edge of the small stage, a rim of white footlights glowed.

Scattered around were some small tables that hadn't been wiped clean for a long while. Ashtrays overflowed with butts. Off to the left by the back wall, a six-pack of drunks lurked around a bar. It was shaped like a clock dial. Anybody could see that. Each of the twelve hours was marked with a rotating stool with a puffy seat.

I worked my way across the place to the bar.

Arms stretched over the counter, I waited for the bartender to notice me. She was a really pretty girl[18] but tough looking, too. Scribbly Middle Eastern writing was tattooed up both her arms and around her neck. I was from Baltimore, where most chicks had bangs heaped

---

[18] Ronnie Christina Puzo, 1984–2000: slipped on a banana peel and broke her neck.

up on their heads like mounds of crazy cake frosting. This girl had a boy's haircut, with the front cut in a perfectly straight line across her forehead. She had a nice dark body. Small but rock hard, like she might just ask you to sock her in the stomach to show off her six-pack abs. The girl gave off a light so bright you'd be able to find her even in the darkest of corners, a superpower every bartender should have, if you ask me.

"I'm looking for Max," I said.

"Max who?" she asked, wiping the counter. She gave off heat; it felt nice.

"Max from the band, the Fiendish Lot."

The girl tried to read me. "They're about to go on," she said. "Take a seat if you want." With that, she dropped a dark gray glass bottle in front of me.

"Thanks," I said.

Hurling some empties into a bin with a crash, the girl looked up at me, drying her hands with a rag. "You just died, didn't you? Newly Dead?"

"I guess," I said.

"So what do you think so far?" she asked.

I lifted my bottle. If not for about a thousand choice details, it was as if I was back at that party on Charles

Street. "It's okay," was all I came up with.

"Most people just think it's a pale imitation of what they had before," said the girl, and then waited several seconds before a smile spread across her face. "Get it, a *pale* imitation?"

"I get it," I said.

I took a sip. Whatever it was, it tasted like expired mosquito repellant, but it woke me up. It was the same stuff Max had stashed in her U. S. Grant flask I'd nursed off a week ago.

"It's on the house, bunny," the girl said, leaving to serve a guy[19] with a flattop.

I left the bar and crashed at one of the nearby tables. Everything felt almost normal, beer in hand, music blasting, head aching. I leaned back in my chair and looked up at the high ceiling overhead, only to find a sky full of angels gazing down. The club's roof had been decorated with plaster carvings of wavy-haired angels flitting every which way, arms reaching out like they were washing windows. It was hard not to laugh. That picture was the closest thing to paradise I'd seen yet.

---

[19] Ramesh Kumar Agrawal, 1939–1979: malaria.

It's funny how you can feel totally alone even with a bunch of people standing around you talking so loud they end up shouting to be heard. I looked around the club at all the different faces. I wasn't the only scared one. That was for sure. I wasn't the only young one, either. Everyone kind of looked the same in the shadows of the footlights—young and old, girls and guys, black and white and Chinese. If you squinted just right, all those bodies became a sea of sols, of golden lights flickering like cigarette lighters waving in the wind.

"Pretty, isn't it?" said a voice.

I looked up and saw the girl bartender next to my table. More accurately, I saw her dark gray hips sliding under her clothes.

"Yeah," I said. "It's like a lawn full of Christmas lights and shit."

"I'm Ronnie," said the bartender. "I'm friends with Max."

"I'm Jo-Jo," I said.

"Nice to know you, Jo-Jo," she said, pulling out a chair.

"Is Ronnie short for Veronica?"

"Nope," she said. "It's short for Ronald Reagan. My

parents were big conservatives, real tight asses. That's why the tattoos. Tried to freak them out-like."

"Did it work?"

She shrugged and took a drink from my bottle, swishing the stuff around in her mouth like she was fighting cavities. "I'm sure it was just a phase, but I died before I could find out. Broken neck. I slipped on a banana peel. Can you believe that?"

"Wow," I said. "I'm sorry." What do you say to someone about how they died? Do you say sorry?

She shook her head, still angry at how it sounded however many years later. "Now the phase just feels natural-like. It's like I've always been this way. I guess that's what happens when you're forever sixteen." She shrugged. "You'll see what I mean. You start to forget."

" 'Forever sixteen,' " I said. "Sounds like a movie."

"A *horror* movie," Ronnie said, laughing. "So how did you bite it? Car crash? We get a shitload of car crashes."

"Got shot by my own gun," I admitted.

She nodded. "Happens all the time. Like half the kitchen staff is 'shot by my own gun.'"

The idea that there was a kitchen staff blew my mind.

"What is this place?"

"It's kind of a fabulous speakeasy," said Ronnie. "It was built a long time ago, when a bunch of Prohibition-era folks crossed over. I guess some of these guys didn't find death quite as bad as they expected." She laughed and started to finish my drink. "Earth at that time may have had a lot of stuff this place didn't, you know, like babies, sunshine, breathable air. But mama, it did *not* have booze."

I knew that Prohibition was this time in American history when the government said you couldn't drink, if you can believe that. So I guess it made sense that a few folks probably thought being drunk and dead was better than being alive and sober. I sort of understood. Of course, I'd never heard of people getting so psyched to drink they'd be willing to die for it. Back where I came from, we just called those guys "alcoholics."

"So what is this I'm drinking?" I asked.

Ronnie grinned. She had a gap in her front teeth. It was cute. "Just a little recipe passed down from generation to generation," she said. "Making it is an art form, and *I* am the artist. I put a little bit of sol in every bottle."

"So it's moonshine?"

"No," she said, picking at her tooth gap with a finger-nail, just like I would have done if I'd had one. "I call it 'sunshine,' due to the lack of it."

"So when you get drunk . . ."

"You get burnt," she said with a laugh, eyebrows dancing. "You're catching on."

Ronnie was cool. That was a no-brainer. So I thought I'd ask her a question that had been nagging me ever since I'd talked to that mohawked punk hanging around front. I leaned across the table so we could talk without having to scream our heads off. "Is everyone really here to see Max's band?" I asked. "I mean, no disrespect or nothing, but isn't there more important stuff to do in the Afterlife?"

"You'll see," she said. She had the look of someone keeping a real juicy secret.

"And how are they going to play?" I asked. I thought back to Kevin nosing through the junk in the basement, digging for tools to fix his generator, which from what I'd seen could barely run a few sputtering lightbulbs. "Is this the Fiendish Lot *Unplugged* or something?"

Ronnie's eyes widened. "I said you'll see," she said.

Her leg had starting bopping around under the table, and she seemed distracted.

I felt it first, then I heard it—almost like when I'd been shot—the chiming of that giant clock high up on the front of the building.

The bells' heavy toll thumped through the floor, rattling up my backbone like a lightning rod. I grabbed the sides of my little table tightly as the floor moved under us. Ronnie snorted through her nose, trying not to crack up. Around us, the footlights on the stage started dimming and then puffed out completely, leaving the whole room dark as a black hole, except for the sols. That was when Ronnie started laughing. I guess she felt comfortable doing it in my face when she couldn't actually see it.

The bells tolled twelve times.

As they finished, a new sound rose up to take their place—a long, piercing note. It could have been a scream, or a howl, or some kind of electrical feedback, but whatever it was, it crowded out every other sound. It made the ceiling buzz above my head. Bits of white paint fell softly like fairy dust over the soft light of the crowd and the tables.

From all across the club, people began crowding the stage. There were more of them than I remembered, and a steady stream flowed in from the now-open doors. Hundreds of bodies packed together, shoulder to shoulder, a wave of creepy old dudes in trench coats and big black chicks in do-rags, shirtless guys with nipple rings, and just about every other freak you might find if you shined a flashlight into a dark corner. There were even some of those real faded-looking people. They shuffled with the help of other folks, who half carried them to the dance floor. Everybody trickled down and collected at the foot of the stage, staring up in a blank daze. Pretty soon, Ronnie and I had the main level all to ourselves.

Ronnie watched the crowd. "Like dogs to a whistle," she said.

Then, out from the shadows and the curtains, a figure appeared in the middle of the stage. If you blinked, you would have missed it. Like a magician showing up in a cloud of smoke, this guy just appeared out of thin air, only without the smoke, and barefoot. It was the little guy I'd met in Baltimore. Penny[20]. You couldn't

---

[20] James "Penny" Cruz, 1985–2001: slipped while cleaning his grandmother's gutters, impaled on garden shears.

mistake him for anyone else—that weird smallness, that baby face. If I hadn't seen him play a show before, I might have felt sorry for the guy, standing up there on that empty stage alone. He was so itty you could reach out and just crush him in two fingers like a gnat.

That horribly beautiful scream was coming from the guitar around his neck. Only there were no amplifiers and hardly a wire to speak of. All I saw was a single black cable. At the very end of the cable was a metal adapter that had been plugged right into Penny's silvery wrist. The note got real quiet but kept on screaming.

"Thanks for coming," said Penny, and since no one was talking—hell, no one was breathing—you could hear it perfectly, even without a microphone. "As you know, this is the first show of the new tour, so we'll be playing songs off our new album." There was a burst of shouts and applause, and Penny, head down, waited for it to wash over him before going on. "But first, I'd like to start things off right-like, with something we all know. I thought we'd play a few tunes by the Goobs for you guys, kick the tour off with some style." Whistles split the calm, and laughter. "That's right," joked Penny.

"This is called 'I Saw a White Light.'" The audience roared and the walls shook.

Raising a hand up high to strike, Penny gazed out over the crowd. Our eyes met in the smoky-orange smog lit by sols, and when they did, that little nut smiled.

A second later, a crazy chord tore the quiet a new asshole.

As it did, the audience flashed with light. So did I. Inside, I felt a satisfying tug from down deep in a place I didn't know I had. It was like taking a swig of bad whiskey or a wonderful case of heartburn. And that's when I figured out something. When Penny played, he was able to reach out from that stage, across that room, and somehow—I didn't know how—that little fruitcake was able to stroke my sol and make it purr.

The Fiendish Lot was the best damn band I'd ever heard, dead or otherwise. I know that folks often say the Rolling Stones are so old they should be dead, or that Paul McCartney got killed in a car crash and the Beatles replaced him with some look-alike, but man, the Fiendish Lot actually *were* deceased, and they kicked the hell out of any band that ever lived. Nobody who's ever seen them play will say different.

After that show at the Tick-Tock Club, I was pretty wiped out. Practically holding me up, Ronnie led me through a pair of swinging "staff only" doors that banged against the walls as we passed. Bent and rusted lighting grids and ladders hung from the walls, and the big black curtain stood like a midnight wall separating us from the stage, a few thick rubber cords slipping underneath. We passed backstage and then climbed a flight of stairs to a door with a big white star painted on it. Below were written the words "The Talent" and below that, scribbled in a drunken slash, "So Called."

The dressing room reeked with that unmistakable smell of stale beer and pot. I guess rock and roll has the same smell no matter where you are.

The room was circular with a sunken center that looked a lot like a giant carpeted hot tub. Steps led down into the pit, where there was a jumble of ratty couches and a coffee table without a tabletop, just four legs and the suggestion of a surface. Mirrors lined the curving wall, ending in another bar. The dressing room had probably been nice once, before the gaps in the sofa cushions had been stuffed to overflowing with cigarette butts and before the bar mirror had been smashed by a stool that still lay on the rug beside a pile of broken glass.

"Hey!" shouted a hoarse voice. "It's him! That guy!"

The voice belonged to Wes[21], the chunky bassist with that incredible shelf of hair. He lounged at the bottom of the sunken floor, on a pile of soft pillows that I quickly realized were women. "It's Jo-Jo!"

"Hey," I said shyly.

Not missing a beat, Wes jumped up, scattering groupies left and right, and climbed over people to shake my hand.

"I *knew* he'd show!" shouted a second voice, this one from behind me. Hand still locked with Wes's, I turned to see Edgar[22] sitting on an overturned bass drum in the corner. He and a couple of other dudes were playing poker in a huddle, gathered real close over a bong shaped like the Empire State Building. "Hey, little bunny," he called, and when he waved at me, I could

---

[21] Wesley Gilbert Borrow, 1975–1993: beaten to death on a military base in Okinawa.

[22] Edgar Fellows Borrow, 1975–1993: died suddenly and from unexplained causes in his bedroom in Bloomington, ID, on the same day as his twin brother.

clearly see the cards stashed up his sleeve.

Switching his attention back to his twin, Ed rubbed his fingers together, the universal sign for money. "Pay up, brother!" he said. "He did *so* die in that ambulance! And *you*, my friend, owe me a little something."

I watched as Wes, head down, walked across the room and handed over his payout: five cigarettes, the price of my life. Of course, Jesus was sold out for only thirty pieces of silver, so I guess I shouldn't have been too offended.

Ed chuckled as he snatched the smokes out of Wes's huge palm. He handed one to me. "You earned it, bunny. A hell of a way to expire."

Returning to his throne of fat, stained pillows and busty babes, Wes kicked back, legs up, his blue shoes giving off a deep watery glow.

He saw me staring and made eye contact, a crinkle of a grin at the corner of his mouth. "They're Elvis's," he mouthed, whispering so I could hear, "blue suede, and freaking chick magnets."

"It's true-like," added Ed. "Wes's most prized posessions did in fact belong to Mr. Presley. One of the many things the two men share, including a love of pastry."

Glancing around real impatiently, Wes picked up a stray combat boot from under the coffee table and hurled it across the room. The boot smashed against a door in the far corner of the room and left a perfect gray footprint on the paint. "Hey, back there, we got guests!" he shouted. Then he returned to Frenching with a busty girl[23] in a black-and-white leopard-print bikini top.

The door in the back of the room flew open and banged against the wall, and out walked Max and Penny, first one and then the other. As they came, Max ran her fingers through her hair, fixing its overblown tangle.

Now, women had always been a mystery to me, but every guy knows that hair-play is a telltale sign that a girl's either been making out or crying like crazy. Only the most intense feelings seem able to make them mess with their appearance like that. One hair out of place is one hair too many.

Penny looked fine. No lipstick prints. No sunken, weepy eyes. He bobbed his head to a song that wasn't

---

[23] Melanie Simms, 1939–1986: passed away from heart disease in an empty room in an empty house, with nothing but a stack of books beside her.

playing—at least not anywhere the rest of us could hear it.

The second Max saw me, she let out a loud groan. It wasn't exactly the best welcome I'd ever got. "Fantastic," she said, and not using the word in the good way, either. She'd ditched the suit coat and was wearing just the white dress shirt and black pants, sleeves bunched up, tie loosened around her neck. The tie swung back and forth as she leaned against the bars, ticked, frowning from her chin to her forehead.

"Hi, Penny," I said. If Max had gone traitor on me, then I'd need to find another person to get my back.

"Hi, yourself," said Penny, nodding at me, a slight smile on his lips. "Like the show?"

"Loved it," I said. "It was genius." I wasn't just buttering him up neither. The concert was the single most incredible thing I'd ever witnessed in my whole life— either of my lives, actually.

Penny waved his thumb in my direction. "Genius," he said to Max. "He said I was a genius."

"I wouldn't exactly be hanging my career on what Jo-Jo bunny tells you," said Ed. "Mama's got his pants on backwards."

He was right. I did.

Everybody busted out laughing, and I looked at Max for her to defend me, but the corners of her mouth didn't curl up or down. "Truth hurts," she said, shrugging, and at that moment, I felt totally alone. Any warmth I had inside seemed to fizzle, like a hot candlewick getting pinched between two fingers. Embarrassed, I put my prize cigarette into my mouth, not remembering that I didn't have a way to light it.

Penny dug around in his pocket; he pulled out a jet-black Zippo lighter and flipped the lid. "No harm done," he said in a kind voice. "Max is just messing around." He pressed a button and a yellow baby of a flame sprang up. "She likes to mess around." He turned on her with a look so angry I shrank back an inch. "Don't you, Max?"

They fought with only their faces, and then she must have surrendered, because she sighed. "Yeah, I love to mess around," she said. "That's me, the funny one."

"Can I be the witty one?" called Ed. "Or, wait, make it the poignant one!"

"I've got dibs on the oversexed one!" called Wes.

"Come on, take a seat," said Penny, directing me

toward the landfill of furniture tumbled into the bottom of the pit. "You're *my* guest."

"You can be the outsider," Ed called to me. "The one everybody comes to love."

Ronnie and me climbed down into the pit and got comfortable on the crappy furniture. Before she sat, Max went to the bar, kicked open a cabinet, and brought out a black metallic container about the size of a shoe box. She hoisted it high over her head like she'd won the Goddamned Stanley Cup. Taking off the lid, she pulled out a huge bottle of red wine. It lit the room with a warm red aura, like radiation from some atomic bomb. I could actually feel the heat coming off it in waves.

"Drinks are on my cousin Kevin and his bosses at the Department of Employment and Deployment," said Max. "One of these days that little bastard is going to learn not to mess with me."

"To the little bastard," we toasted.

I didn't have friends back home. Bart was about it. Sometimes I talked to other kids in the lunchroom at school, but the only thing I had in common with those guys was that, like me, they didn't want to pound anyone's face into the asphalt—but that's not really enough to build a friendship on. I'd always secretly day-dreamed that those mutant teenagers the X-Men might show up one day to tell me that I had a superpower, and then they would take me back with them to that pimped-out mansion they had outside New York City. I knew it was a dumb fantasy, but I also knew that a wish for superhero friends and a wish for regular friends had a pretty equal chance of actually coming true.

I enjoyed my time in that smoky dressing room. It was the first fun I'd had in a while, since Violet died. I knew the band would help me figure things out, even if Max wasn't glad to see me in the slightest. They had to help. I had nobody.

After Ed finished his tenth dirty story and the giggling died down, I spoke up. "So you went to Earth to test your songs," I said. "How'd it work out?"

"Who told you that?" Penny asked, squinting at me.

"Max," I said, worrying that I'd just given away some secret.

"Well, that's only part of it," said Penny.

"Call it a dress rehearsal," said Ed, in the middle of counting his poker winnings—cuff links, a few pennies, a paper clip, and one glass eye—all of it in full, blinding color. "Except Wes is the only one who wears dresses," he added.

Penny lay back, tapping a foot. "We're hitting the road for a few months," he said, yawning. "If you're going to tour, you've got to make sure the songs are strong enough to stand on."

"Tour," said Wes, gleeful, like a kid who just stumbled on a half-eaten doughnut on the sidewalk. "We're playing the whole Afterlife, mama, from the cliffs of Tophet to the Beaches of Acheron. We're even booked at the Edges, and from the stories I've heard, the lost sols there could really use a little of the Lot."

I didn't know what most of this meant, but I was starting to get the picture. "Wait. You're going away?" I asked, starting to panic.

"That's why it's called a tour," explained Ed. "Moving is kind of required-like."

I felt trapped. I didn't know what to do, to say. "You can't go."

They looked at me funny. "What do you mean, we can't go?" asked Ed. "This is not a democracy, and if it was, you wouldn't have a vote."

"He's right-like," said Wes. "You can look it up."

"I don't know anyone here," I said, stuttering in my excitement. "You guys need to help me figure out what to do. I did it for you, now you have to do it for me."

"But we're going on tour," Wes said, stating what I already knew. He leaned his head back into the lap of that girl with boobs so big that more of them seemed to be pouring out of her stretchy top than get held in by it. "Around here you got to *be* the album, mama. People hear it once, and that's it. Finis! There aren't recording studios around here. No repeat function."

"Ninety days, fifty shows, seven cities," said Penny. "That's the only chance most people will ever get to hear it."

"Ninety days," I said. "How can you even tell what a day is? There's no sunrise or sunset. Hell, there's no sun. It always looks the same."

"People go by twenty-four hours," said Ed, shrugging. "Why mess with success."

"I can't sleep," said Penny. He grinned wildly. "Once I found out I didn't have to, I stopped altogether."

"And he's been awake ever since," said Ed.

Penny slid forward in his chair, hands clasped in

front of him like a shrink. "So what's your problem?"

"I got to find my girlfriend, Violet," I said, glancing across the circle of faces at Max as I said the name out loud. Not once did she look at me, or anyone else for that matter. She just stared down into her cup of wine, face bathed in its pinkish glow. "She died a little while ago and should be here, but she didn't come for me at the station."

I waited as Penny rubbed his smooth, babyish chin and considered my problem. The others watched, drowsy or stoned, hammering on the wine, which was growing cold faster than we could drink it. My four cups sloshed around in my stomach and coated my insides with a wall of warmth that slowly cooled.

"It's easy-like," said Penny, snapping his fingers. "You come with us, mama."

No one moved. It was the quietest I'd ever heard the Tick Tock Club.

"You mean on tour?" asked Ed.

"It's perfect-like," said Wes, shaking his cup and making the wine fly all over the couch. "Our first shows are in Olam Haba, like three blocks from the MIA archives."

"Right," said Ed. "If he's going to find his wife, he's going to have to go there first."

"It's my *girlfriend*," I said, "and her name is Violet."

"Well, if you want to find Iris, you're going to need to go there," explained Ed.

"Ooh, yeah, and you can get us something from the gift shop," shouted Wes.

Before we could say one more word, Max jumped up off her cushion, a cigarette pinched in one hand and the near-empty wine bottle dangling in the other. "Fabulous," she barked. "So what you're saying is that this tour is going to be one big sausage party. Like the deck isn't already stacked-like against me."

"For the record," said Wes, raising one finger. "I have no problem with you recruiting more girls."

"Let it be added to the record that Edgar seconds the motion," said Ed. "He seconds it strongly."

"Oh, this is just great," said Max, growing more pissed. "This place is turning into a damned frat house."

"Like it wasn't already," said Penny, yawning and stretching.

Then I stood up too, pissed because I didn't know why she was acting so screwed up. After everything I'd done for her, this was the thanks I got—a big steaming pile of typical girl bitching. "What the hell is your problem?" I shouted.

"My problem is I don't like having you around," said Max, voice lower, colder.

I pointed right in her round face. "What did I ever do to you?" The others just stared, enjoying the show. "What's the big deal?"

"You want to know what the big deal is, Jo-Jo?" said Max, throwing her cigarette down into the ashtray and exhaling a long stream of smoke. "The big deal is that you think that because you helped us, that requires us to help you. I've seen people like you before. You have a look. You've got needs no one can satisfy. You're a hanger-on."

Knocking Ed's legs off the coffee table, she grabbed her bag and started up the steps out of the pit. "The big difference between you and us is that you helped us out for, like, twenty-four hours, and I got a feeling we're going to be helping you out forever." She threw back the last swish of wine, which was now a weak, watery rust color.

She slammed the dressing-room door behind her.

The rest of us sat in silence for a minute. Then Wes ripped a big fart. No one laughed.

"What look do I have?" I asked, not getting an answer. "Where has she seen people like me before?"

Ed looked up, thumbing the edge of one of his playing cards. He wasn't being a funny dick anymore. "In the mirror," he said. "That's where."

A few too many bottles of sunshine later and a smooch on the neck from Ronnie the bartender, and I called it quits. I stumbled up out of the pit and sat cross-legged on a pile of lumpy white beanbags that looked like giant blobs of lard. My dead body still buzzed with near-drunken heat. I fell backward, skull to carpet. Face toward the ceiling, I saw a skylight. There was nothing behind it—no moon, no stars, no real sky. Just mist. Just gray. Just a life after death that didn't mean much of anything.

"Hey, man," murmured Penny. He stood over me. Then he fell to one ass cheek, sliding down the highest peak of the beanbag mountain. Our heads nearly touched as we stared up through the window together. I didn't know what he was checking out, considering the night was a sea of nothing.

He began to sing quietly.

> *Yeah, it isn't all they say.*
> *I was in over my head.*
> *Yeah, it isn't all they say.*
> *Life looks better dead.*

He even did the guitar part with his mouth.

"What band is that?" I asked.

"Porcelain God," he answered.

We stared up through the skylight.

"You know, sometimes you can see stuff in the clouds," he said. "It's a game that kids around here play. Sometimes it actually works, even if it is all in your mind-like."

"I don't see anything," I said.

The fact that he didn't breathe sort of made me nervous. "You know, back when I met Max, she hardly knew how to keep a steady beat," he said, speech all slurred.

"Really?"

"Hell, yeah," he said. "You could see she had the

rhythm in her, she was just all over the place inside. Couldn't keep it together, and if your rhythm section doesn't have her shit together, it just makes everyone else fall apart." His hands rested on his chest. "I let her join anyway, because I knew she'd be a hell of a drummer when she just dropped her baggage and left it. We were called the Innocents back then." Out of the corner of my eye I could see the fool grinning. "Just for a month. That was a rough-like time."

"What was wrong with her?" I asked.

"Max had been in a bad place for a while," said Penny. "She'd gotten lost."

"Lost?"

"Her first couple years in the Afterlife, Max spent all her time searching for her little brother. He died when they were kids, and she spent a long time turning this place upside down trying to make it right-like. Or make it something."

Penny paused, his eyes wandering all over the black void. "I never gave much thought to dying," he said. "I just sort of accepted it and looked for what was next, you know? When they close one ride, you just go get in line for another."

I didn't know, not really. I was starting to miss my old ride.

I stared up through that round window like it was a periscope poking up into outer space. After a while, I began to see things in the mist, just like Penny said. Only I didn't know if I was making myself see them or if they were really there.

I saw me and Violet, together on a blanket in the park, which was the way it had always been and was supposed to be. I knew that. Everybody wants to try to hold on to the things that make them who they are, and that make them happy. No one wants to give up their baggage. Not when it's all they got.

6

I'm not a city guy. I hate the city. It smells like trash and pee, and most times it seems like there are more homeless folks than folks with homes, stumbling around with mismatched shoes and drinking from someone else's thrown-away Diet Pepsi. I'd never been to New York City, but I'm pretty sure I'd hate it.

So I was pretty disappointed when I showed up where the band told me to meet them, only to find a big grungy room full of straggly people. A couple of barefoot geezers slumped beside an empty newspaper machine. One woman had made a tent out of a trench coat and claimed a spot by the exit doors. Every few minutes an alarm rang and a surge of people suddenly grabbed their bags and rushed toward the end of the room, where a full tramcar thumped against the platform, wasted faces pressed against the streaky windows. The place was called Marrakech Tower, and it was a sort of bus station that stood on six huge cement legs over a section of the city.

The smell hit you first. It stunk like a bar john that hadn't been cleaned for a hundred St. Patrick's Days in a row. You couldn't escape the constant chatter of conversation, not loud enough to really understand but just low enough to drive you nuts. The place was so busy, there wasn't an open space to stand in. There were rows of chairs, each one of them filled. And like anything in a bad part of town, every piece of furniture was bolted down tight.

According to the big map on the front wall, the only way to get from point to point in the Afterlife was to take a tram, which explained the high mess of cables I'd seen strung up through the rooftops of downtown. The Afterlife was circular, with cities plopped here and there like chips in a cookie. A clean white border ringed the outside of the map, and next to it a skull grinned on a black warning label that read: "The Edges." Past that boundary, there was nothing but empty map. Talk about creepsville.

I hovered by the brochure shelf, watching an old

man[24] with no fingers on his left hand shift in his seat. When he got up to use the restroom, I pounced on the vacancy. I felt kind of bad for the old coot, since he was probably already having a tough time using the toilet with a stump, and now on top of it he was going to come back to his place to find my ass dozing.

Someone[25] in a chicken suit slouched in the chair next to me.

It was tough to tell if the person was awake or asleep. The feathery body just slumped there like a bag of trash. One of those signs hung around the chicken's neck, announcing: "When I Distract Others from Their Dreams, We All Lose."

After a while the chicken turned to me and spoke through a mesh hole inside its beak. "Didn't anyone ever tell you it's impolite to stare?"

"Sorry," I said, and moved my eyes toward the floor. No one had ever told me that.

I sat in my seat and tried to nap, holding a tote bag that said: "McGovern for President in '72," which I'd

---

[24] Lawrence "Apple" Fels, 1888–1953: complications from early onset Alzheimer's disease.

[25] Mitchell T. Amberson, 1971–2002: struck by meteor.

swiped from Max's house. Its insides were stuffed with a couple pairs of Kevin's extra clothes, which I'd also borrowed from the Inscos' basement. Every so often a tram car floated up the wires, scraped along the platform, and spit out an assortment of travelers, every one of them as pitiful as the ones who waited in the station. It was like Avernus was holding some sort of hobo convention, only it was never-ending and everyone was participating.

I stared around at all the folks crashed in Marrakech Tower. They didn't look like people waiting for their friends and family. They looked like people waiting to hear bad news, like people lying around just waiting to die. And I was one of them. For the first time, I knew that whatever I ended up learning about Violet wasn't going to be anything I wanted to hear.

To keep away the fear, I watched the front door and began to silently count.

10-9-8-7-6-5-4-3-2-1 . . . nothing.

I tried again. *10-9-8-7-6-5-4-3-2-1.*

At the beat of one, Max walked into the station, wearing a bright-white beehive wig and looking completely turned-around lost.

I was glad to see her.

She wore an old army jacket that had once been olive green and jeans with holes torn in them. Raising the dark sunglasses that sat far down on the tip of her nose, she checked out the place, catching sight of me right when I wasn't sure if she ever would. Out of reflex, she raised one hand to say, "Hi," but then caught herself, lowering it quickly. I guess she still hated my guts.

She came over, stood at my feet. "Hey," she said.

I looked up. "Hey."

"Trying to cry?" she asked.

"Since I got here," I said.

"Good luck," she said. She rocked on her heels, hands in her pockets. "Another day, another station. We've got to stop meeting like this."

"Funny," I said, not smiling. I didn't know what to expect from her anymore. "What's in the bag?" I pointed at the huge duffel bag she wore straps over shoulders like a backpack.

"Just baggage," she said. "That's why I'm late-like. Well, Ben also gave me a hard time, but that's to be expected."

"You guys like to go at it, huh?" I asked.

"It's the only way he ever actually looks at me," she said, not giving a yes or a no. "Fighting." Leaning over, she grabbed the handle of my stolen tote bag and pulled me to my feet. It was like we were holding hands without having to. "Come on, we need to get ready."

At a booth near the arrival gates a mass of people had started forming. On our left, passengers slept against the walls on piles of luggage, passing the time before their rides showed up.

"Where are the guys?" I asked.

"They went on ahead," said Max.

"Really?"

"Yeah," she said, craning her neck around the wall to see if the tram was coming. "I volunteered to stay behind and wait for you." Then she walked off into the crowd. I wiggled through the moving bodies and tried to keep an eye on the bulk of her bag ahead of me.

"*You* stayed behind for me?" I asked, catching up.

"Yeah," she said, eyes not meeting mine.

"I don't get it," I said.

Max stopped outside the doors to the platform, blocking my way. Now her hands were up in the pockets of her army jacket. Riders swarmed the platform, clawing their way into the sliding doors of the dangling metal box, which to me looked more like a floating Dumpster than something you'd want to ride around in. "I wanted to get you alone so I could apologize," she said.

"Oh," I said, getting quiet.

We stood together near the edge, where the concrete slab fell away to the city below. "Listen," she said. "I've got a problem-like." Taking a deep breath she didn't need, Max flapped her jacket's wings. "And no matter how messed up I am over my own stuff, it's not *your* problem."

"I'm sorry about your brother, Max," I said.

She didn't respond at first.

Then, moving a single hair out of her face, she whispered, "Me too."

We stepped on board just in the nick of time.

The trip out of the city took exactly long enough for the car to clear after a few stops and for Max to fall asleep on my shoulder with her hand in my lap. After that, taking a snooze was downright impossible. If anything, I spent the passing time thinking about how I should block out the feeling of her fingertips on my inner thigh—of course, doing, and thinking about doing, are two very different things.

Big, craggy peaks slid by outside the square windows, and we slipped in and out of clouds as we traveled across the empty countryside. Whenever you started to forget you were dangling fifty floors up from a saggy cable, the whole car would slide over one of the support towers and let out a screech, bouncing and sending wobbly shock waves through the floor.

Folks either slept with their heads thrown back against the wall, tongues hanging out, or they read books, like I imagined most normal people did on the subway. One big chick[26] with a head full of cornrows held on to a pole for support as she scratched out the boxes of a word jumble, like she was just crossing town for a coffee date. Most people did whatever it took to the pass the time.

Most people, that is, except for a small huddle sitting together at one end of the car. They didn't seem interested in going anywhere at all, really. They just sat bent over, faces fixed on the seat backs in front of them.

---

[26] Laverne Brown, 1958–2003: starved to death when feeding tube was removed, with her family's consent.

I wouldn't have noticed them if not for the fact that no one else in the car sat anywhere near them. A good two rows of empty seats separated them and the rest of us. I'd seen that kind of thing happen all the time back home, like when a dude who's down on his luck would come into a gas station to buy a coffee with the handful of pennies and nickels he'd snatched out of a storm drain, and everyone in the place would back up a few feet, like the smell alone would knock them dead.

Then there was the fact that they were see-through.

The folks at the end of the car were colorless, like everyone else, but to look at them was to try and catch sight of something that was constantly coming in and out of focus. They were missing something big, some important part of themselves. That light, that perfect, wonderful, pure-as-a-sunbeam-washed-in-reddish-glow— they didn't have it, or it was nearly gone. From the glum looks on their faces, I guessed that these people knew they weren't all there.

Max groaned and shifted in her seat. Then her eyes snapped open and she turned to look at me, surprised. Blinking, she sat up off my shoulder and worked her butt into the seat real good, trying to find a new, more-comfortable position, one that didn't include our bodies getting cozy.

"Max," I whispered, "what's wrong with them?"

"Who?"

"Them." I let my eyes do the talking.

"They're lost sols," she whispered, yawning.

"Lost sols? What does that mean?"

"It means they're fading away." She kept trying to find a good position but couldn't seem to. "It happens to everyone. It's happening to us right now."

"What?" I hissed. How could *it* be happening to me when I couldn't even feel it, when I didn't even know what *it* was?

Her eyes were wide open again, a dazed stare. "The sol is all that matters here. It doesn't last. Sure, it holds onto its old life energy for a while, but this place, this horrible, awful, no-good shit of a place, just kind of sucks you dry after a while." She tried to smile, and the tone of her voice got real low and gravelly, like one of those breathy phone-call killers from a horror movie. "No matter what you do, you will never escape."

"So life just fades away?" I whispered. "People do?"

"They call it 'residue,' that leftover energy from life," she whispered. "The colors, the heat, the fertility, all of it sticks to you when you pass over, but it isn't meant to be here. They've found some ways to hold it in. There's this metal you can make into boxes or bags, but it's hard to come by. Expensive-like. And it doesn't last."

"Like the frames on the walls in your house," I whispered. "They keep the pictures the right color, don't they?"

"Yeah," she said. "Like those." She laughed, like a hiccup. "You wouldn't believe the shit that Ben's squirreled away down in our basement. He used to have a job at the MIA, as a curator in the Endowed Objects Department. He went with them on all sorts of secret missions back to Earth to snatch stuff, but they laid his ass off when they found him taking his work home with him, if you know what I mean."

The ghostly figures sitting all alone together at the end of the car hadn't blinked since we'd starting talking. "It starts off slowly." I watched her eyes focus on the group of blank, almost-invisible faces. She stared at them longingly, in the same way people stand over an open casket and take it all in. "You lose your color pretty fast," she said, her voice flat, "and then you start to cool, like a baked potato out of the oven, eventually getting stone-cold-like. By the end, nobody will even want to touch you. All you want is to wander out to the Edges and roll away in the fog, like a candle going out." She blew on her flat bleached white palm. "Poof."

"If it could," she said, "this world would stick a straw into you and start sucking."

"What's there for it to suck?" I asked. "We're dead."

Inching over, she took my hand. Hers was cold, but so was mine. "You see the light, don't you, Jo-Jo?"

"Yeah, I see it," I said. "I can see everyone's."

Max rested her white cheek on my shoulder. "That's your sol. It's who you are, your purpose. I know it sounds all rainbows and angels and shit, but it's not. Feeding your sol is about not wasting your time or After-living weak-like. If you can figure out what you're meant to do, then you can feed your sol, take care of it." She sighed out a chest full of hollow air. "And let me tell you, nothing feels as good as sharing it."

"Then how come some people got sol more than others?" I asked. "How come some people look like they're on fire?"

She patted my knuckles, and the real slow, dumbed-down way she talked reminded me of the time when my sister tried to explain sex to me by describing a man as having a baseball bat and a woman as having a catcher's mitt. "There are a lot of reasons," she said, "but all I can tell you for sure is that you have to figure out what you overlooked when you were alive, what you missed out on the first time."

"I didn't miss out," I said. "Violet was all I needed." This was always the first thing that came to mind.

Max went on as if she hadn't heard me. "If you change your ways, your sol will burn so bright it'll be hard to look at. That's the way to go, in a flash of light, knowing you tore through this world like a meteor. But if you don't find a way to feed it, then this dead world is going to feed *off* it until you're history. You'll know it's happening, too. Trust me."

"Is that why it feels like I'm giving some big dude a piggyback?" I asked.

"You feel tired-like, drained. Your senses start to go. Vision gets blurry. Hearing and smell get real weak-like." She paused. "Then you start to forget. Your memories, they just start to sort of evaporate."

"And you fade away," I said, like I'd known all along.

"Like you were never here," she said, closing her eyes again, asleep.

When we glided into Olam Haba, it felt like deepest midnight, even though the world outside still looked the same—cheap and gloomy, like some haunted house that went crazy with the fog machine. Folks in our tram-car got up, swayed around on their feet waiting for the doors to open, and then lurched out onto the platform, an army of zombies.

Max and I went into the station and found the rest of the Fiendish Lot camped out in the corner of the room, talking so loud everyone could hear them. They'd taken over a few rows of bolted-down chairs and had built a little fort around themselves, like old-time pioneers circling their wagons. Bags, drums, and guitar cases sat in the middle of their little powwow.

Rush hour must have been over, because once the passengers from our car disappeared down the winding station steps and into the city below, the big open room sat practically empty. A lonely janitor[27] pushed a wide broom over by the ticket booth, sweeping what looked like dryer lint into a lopsided pile.

"Gentlemen," said Max, sitting down in one of the spare seats.

"Lady," said Ed. The rest of them tilted up their heads to say hi, and then quickly went back to what they were doing, which was watching Wes try to smoke a cigarette while holding it in his toes. It wasn't going real well.

I sat down on the floor beside them and yawned, rubbing my eyes. Next to me on an end table were a few open bottles of sunshine. I figured that taking a drink of that brutal stuff would be like gargling demon mouthwash. It'd probably sear the taste of tram stations off my tongue for good.

I took one of the bottles and started to tip it back.

"Hold up," said Ed, raising one hand. "Exercise caution, my friend."

I stopped.

"The ride from Avernus is a very long one," he said, "and not everyone is as civilized as you or I. When it

------

[27] Alceste Castelnuovo, 1932–1982: died of congestive heart failure during his fiftieth birthday party, face in his carrot cake.

comes to the urges of nature, my brother is, how you say, a savage."

Getting him, I put the bottle back on the table. I was careful not to spill a drop.

"Nasty," I said.

"*That* is why a dead man should not drink," he said.

"He could have at least marked the bottle," I said.

Penny unzipped one of the larger duffel bags, one that had patches sewn all over its black hide—from Rome, Paris, Kuala Lumpur, Shanghai, Tophet, and other places I'd never heard of—and started tugging out these big gray bundles of fabric. He handed one to each of us.

Unfolding mine, I saw that it was a weird poncho made from some kind of canvas. From the looks of it, the outfits had seen their share of action. Black, oily stains spread across the chests and arms like bubbles in a lava lamp. My poncho had a gaping hole in the middle of the belly, as though whoever had been wearing it last had gotten shot in the guts with a cannonball. When pulled up, the hood formed sharp, stiff triangles over my head.

"Now I know what I'm wearing to the prom," I said.

"I *loved* prom!" said Wes.

"Bastard stole my date," said Ed.

"Sad but true," said Wes.

Penny pulled his costume down over his head and then started picking up the equipment, a couple guitars slung across his back, a drum tripod in each hand. "Maybe we should get moving now that the happy bunny couple has arrived-like," he said. "We've got one show today, one tomorrow, and two over the weekend. If I'm going to be sitting on my ass, I'd at least like to be doing it on a couch instead of in a shitty tram station." There were murmurs of agreement. So we gathered up the rest of the instruments and, dressed like a team of space monks ready to rock, headed down the steps and outside.

We were met with a wall of rain. It came down in glittering sheets. I couldn't see ten feet in front of my face. I pulled up my hood and followed, secretly excited about feeling the pitter-patter of rain on my face again, even if it was in a storm.

We left the station, walking along a raised walkway. At first glance, Olam Haba was rain and not much else. A huge, flat cliff face rose up into the watery gloom to our left. As we got deeper into the city, whole buildings seemed to come together out of patches of wetness, shining like tall mirrors in the dark. All of them were perched on stilts, entire neighborhoods hugging the side of that lonely mountain. The streets were all those raised walkways, a network of bridges hanging over a deep nothingness.

We reached what was probably the main drag and got sucked into sloshing foot traffic. In that place we looked like clones of everybody else, in our thick robes and pointy, trickling hoods. The wide walkway was a busy market with stalls on each side. Salesmen hocked trinkets and pierced people's parts. Buyers pushed and shoved and kissed each other on the cheeks. It was your typical messed-up downtown nightmare.

As soon as we hit that Afterlife 5th Avenue, the twins tried to bolt into the sea of activity, holding their guitar cases over their heads to keep out the downpour.

"Hey!" shouted Max, and she reached through a tangle of strangers to catch Ed by one of his ears.

"Damn!" he shrieked. "What you do that for, mama?"

"Don't go running off-like," said Max. "We got a show in eight hours."

"Well, that's eight hours to do something else," said Ed, pulling free.

"Come on, Max," said Wes, whining. "I don't want to sit around the dressing room of the Flamingo. The springs in the sofa poke my butt."

The three of them stopped arguing and turned to Penny, who had nothing much to offer but a shrug. "I don't see why they can't go raise some hell," he said. "I can go get things ready at the Flamingo. The sooner these guys get there, the sooner they'll get bored-like. And we don't want the Borrow twins bored-like, especially with an afternoon to kill."

Foiled, Max hugged a snare drum to her chest and glared at the boys. "At least let us know where you're going," she said. "In case we need to search for your bodies."

"Wouldn't you like to know?" Ed said with a hint of playful evil in his coal black eyes. The second he said it, he shook his brother, who had already opened his mouth to speak. "And don't *you* go and tell them."

"We've got a show," said Max. "Don't forget. *Again!*"

They were already off. Ed pushed his brother's blobby body ahead of him like a snowplow, ramming folks out of the way as he headed off to sow seeds of trouble. The busy, jabbering, pointy-tipped crowd swallowed them up in the blink of an eye, sucking them into its core.

"Well, I'm going to the Flamingo," said Penny, shouldering his guitar and trying to keep the mike stands tucked under his arm from spilling out all over the wet pavement. "As usual, I've got to be the one who makes sure things happen as planned-like."

"You're such a martyr," said Max, sniping at him.

"See you there?" he asked.

"If you're lucky. I'm going to take Jo-Jo over to the MIA archives to look for something on his girlfriend."

"Sounds like a plan," said Penny. "Don't be late."

Max raised one finger and held it an inch from his nose. "You know, I should punch you in the throat," she said. "Give a damn once in a while, will you?"

They stared at each other, talking without saying words. It looked to me like a conversation they'd probably had a thousand times, I just didn't know what about. Then, with a shake of his head, Penny walked off in the direction we'd been going, humping off across one of the many bridges that connected the city's dots. At that distance, he could have been anybody.

Max didn't seem to know what to do. She looked at me and growled real mean. Then she looked at the ground. "Great," she said, throwing the snare drum down onto the pile of equipment that the twins had dumped in the middle of the walkway before bolting.

"Last I checked, I didn't have-like ten arms," she said.

Crouching, I took a drum in my hands. "Let me help," I said, "for once."

I didn't have one of those real brainy minds, but that being said, I wasn't no dummy. I could tell that the Afterlife was not all it was cracked up to be. It didn't take much to figure that out, genius or not. People scurried around, busy as ants, trying to make the whole world livable, hoping to feed their sols and make the most of second chances, even if on the surface it all seemed pretty pointless.

Take the archives of the Ministry of Immigration and Acquisition, for one. You'd been there before, even if it wasn't called the same thing. It could have been mistaken for a DMV on steroids if you weren't paying too much attention. And just like on Earth, it was a place that sucked the life right out of you.

Its great big round waiting room throbbed with a bright-white fluorescent light that constantly dimmed and brightened, like a lazy strobe, practically daring your brain to fire up a killer headache. All the seats faced one direction, toward a wall of small windows with numbers hanging over them on hooks. Over the hooks were signs that said: "Now serving" and then the number.

The workers sitting behind the windows could have been inmates lining up to chat with visitors through one of those walls of bulletproof glass. They looked homicidal. One glance at those steamy glares, and you wanted to turn around, forget whatever business you had there, and go the hell home. Maybe that was their master plan.

"I hate waiting," said Max. She adjusted her hairdo. The tall wig was starting to droop over all wacky, like the Leaning Tower of Pisa.

"It's funny," I said, sagging against the wall as people came in through the doors behind us.

"What's funny?" asked Max.

"For people trying to make the most of life, everyone sure does a lot of waiting around in this world."

Max grunted, and folding her arms she joined me against the wall. "Amen, brother."

That's what didn't make sense. For all the efforts to make the Afterlife seem special, hopeful, it pretty much seemed to have become a black-and-white version of regular life that was just rougher around the edges. I guess it made sense. Best intentions hardly ever turn into something real. More often than not folks just end up settling for what is, rather than for what they wanted. People are people, wherever they are. They screw up in the same old ways.

I ripped a number off a long paper roll by the door. It said: "13,093." As I wondered what my little prize meant, there was a sharp *ding!* and a pair of small, really jumpy little guys rushed out of a side room and dashed along the front of the counters, replacing the numbers on the hooks above the windows. At that moment, the line was somewhere in the vicinity of 12,704.

I rubbed my palms against my eyes. "Jesus," I said. "For a place with weak electricity, they really know how to make light that fries your eyes."

"Yeah," she said. "At least when you're at home, you can crank your own and sort of gauge how bright-like you want it. I think the government purposefully makes waiting-room bulbs to melt your brain."

I watched sad dudes shuffle up to the counters and then get yelled at by the tellers. "Who has a job here, anyway?" I said. "I mean, why would you work? *This* makes our sol all warm and fuzzy?"

"It's the penal system," said Max, raising a finger. "You do the crime, you do the time. For the most part, government employees are convicts. You do something naughty and you get sentenced to a job. You end up wasting a big chunk of your afterlife working, and not finding fulfillment. It's punishment."

"That blows," I said.

"That's the way it is," she said. "Some people got it real bad-like."

So we waited. For some reason, the time seemed to pass slower than it ever had. Max went through half a pack of cigarettes. She had a bad addiction, but one that was perfect for standing around looking pissed. That place brought out the worst in people. Every *ding!* made them bristle in their boots.

I watched one clerk[28] in particular. She sat behind

---

[28] Elvira Custer, 1966–1996: murdered by distant relatives after winning the lottery.

her little pane of glass doing her makeup—made up of nothing but blacks and whites and grays—and not helping anyone, not looking out at the room of worn faces waiting for the next available window, and not worried at all that she might get bum-rushed by a mob of angry chumps. The room trembled with that kind of crazy tension.

"I can't handle this much longer," I said, showing Max the number again. "Should we take a seat?"

"And stare at each other? No." She shook her head, which made her wig tilt back again to expose her dark curls. "I've done enough of that today, thank you very much."

But we sat anyway, because what else was there to do in a waiting room but wait?

We'd been sitting for what felt like an eternity when my number was finally called and hung up on those little metal hooks with a *ding!* As bad luck would have it, the window was occupied by the very same really bitchy-looking lady I'd noticed before. It took a lot for a person's frown to stick out in a whole room full of unhappy faces.

Max at my side, I eased my way up to the window real nice—or as Max might have said, real "nice-like."

"Hi," I said to the lady.

No reply. She blew on her drying fingernails.

"So I'm looking for this—"

"Hold on," said the lady, raising her palm to my face.

She examined the dull gleam of her nails in that queasy light, and then, at last, looked up, already irritated. "I need your request," she said.

"What request?"

"Sir, you need to fill out a request for assistance before I can help you."

"How was I supposed to know that?" I asked. "It doesn't say that anywhere."

"There are request forms over by the door," she said, flicking her pencil toward the waiting area. Then she started to turn around.

"I'll do it," I said frantically. "But I've been waiting for hours. Can you just help me? I'll fill out the form as we talk." As if she heard a starter's pistol, Max took off running across the room to fetch me one of those sheets.

"Fine," said the lady. She raised one eyebrow, giving some hint at attitude. "But you better talk real fast, mister." That annoying bell rang with a *ding!*

"I'm looking for someone who died," I said. Just then, Max showed up with the request form.

"I need to see your Afterlife Papers," she said.

I pulled them out of my pocket, unfolded them, and handed them over. Looking over the fine print and the signature, she gave them back. "You want records of the recently deceased?" she asked at last.

"Yeah, I guess," I said.

"We don't keep those records on-site," she said.

"Where can I see them?"

"You have to apply to have them unsealed."

"What do you mean apply?"

"Your request must be approved before it can be processed."

"How do I apply?" I asked, starting to stress out. I could hear all those fools in the seats behind me getting antsy. I was going to be one of *those* guys, the kind who took too long.

"First I'll need to see proof of relations, signed and notarized by your caseworker."

"A what?" I turned and looked at Max, who, for the first time in all the days I'd known her, didn't seem to have any expression whatsoever. "I'm not related to this person," I explained to the lady. "She's a friend."

"We don't do 'friends,'" she said, going as far as to make those air quotes with her freshly drying fingers.

"There is no way to find someone who isn't in your family?" I asked. I was starting to get just as pushy as she was.

"You can get on a waiting list to have your case reviewed by a ministry tribunal," she said. "You'll have to prove your relationship in order to be claimed as a non-relative family member."

"And how long does that take?"

She cocked her head and did a little shake of the shoulders, as if to tell me she was done. "It depends," she said. "It's a waiting list. You have to wait."

"So it's impossible to find my friend?" I said as the nightmare of what was happening became clear to me. The bell rang again. *Ding!*

"That's not what I said, sir," said the lady. "We just need to make sure we know who is retrieving the information, and for what purpose it is being retrieved."

I didn't know what to say next. I'd just imagined they had a couple of giant file cabinets chock-full of names, like an overstuffed drawer leaking mismatched socks.

"You need to fill out the appropriate paperwork and have it processed," she said, sighing. "Even then, we can't guarantee that the files you seek are ever going to be made available to the public."

"I don't know what that means."

"It means you need to go through the proper channels, sir," she said. "Just like everyone else."

I felt a hand on my back—Max. She supported me. "That's bull," I said, my voice getting real high. My chest ached and my head pounded from the lights. "All you have to do is go into one of those doors back there and check for me. Take one minute, and just look. Please."

"That's not the procedure, sir. We don't do favors."

"But you have to!" I shouted. I turned to the morons scattered in the rows behind me, all of them facing us, all of them watching like they were at the movies. They had to see that this whole place was all a big load of bull. Someone had to see that besides just me. "You don't even know Violet. You can't hide her away like some kind of top-secret project. It's just Violet."

Ding!

"Sir, you're getting excited. You might want to leave before"—and her expression got all "angry inmate" again, like she was about to shiv me in the shower—"before you do something you will regret."

"I'm not leaving." I'd never stood up like that for anything. Never.

The lady's voice got so frosty I could almost feel the chill. "We can make you leave, sir," she said. "But we would like to avoid that."

"Nope," I said.

Ding!

The security apes[29, 30] ditched us on the curb outside the archives, giving me two sharp kicks in the ribs for good measure. If I'd been able to bleed, I might have had a nice gash going above my right eye, but I couldn't, so I just felt the pain, but even that wasn't harsh enough for me to enjoy it. As the two muscle dudes walked back toward the front doors, Max jumped up, took off

---

[29] Saleh bin Tariq bin Imad Al-Filistini, 1915–1946: suffered stroke during a fight with his estranged wife.

[30] Peter Miller, 1987–2005: acquired immunodeficiency syndrome.

her wig, and hurled it at them. That beehive spiraled through the air like a missile, but when it hit the bigger of the two dudes between the shoulder blades, he didn't even seem to feel it. The jumble of wet hair made a squishing sound as it plopped to the pavement. We were flies swatting at people.

"You should have gone to hell!" she yelled at them.

When I didn't get up from the gutter, she sat back down next to me, legs splayed out in front of her in the cigarette butts and litter of paradise.

"Hey," she said.

I didn't look. I endlessly wadded my slip of paper in my fingers, my waiting-room number that had been good for absolutely nothing.

"Hey," she said again.

I didn't look. All I could think about was Violet wandering the streets, fading away like a ghost who'd missed her boat. With all my strength, I squeezed my eyes together, trying to force the tears. Nothing. How many times could I let down the girl I loved?

"Look at me, damn it," said Max, and she grabbed my chin and forced it toward her so our eyes met.

"I know what it feels like," she said, jaw set with a

fierce determination. "You feel powerless. You feel pointless. Like, if you can't do something to stop it, what good are you."

"Like why are you even here?" I added.

"Yeah," she said. "It's the worst thing in the world, losing someone you love."

I tossed my little paper number into the gutter at my feet. It blended right in with the rest of the waste. "Especially when you lose them twice," I said.

"Yeah," she said, looping her arm in mine. "Especially when you lose them twice."

7

You stand in line, like you're waiting to see one of those movies people buy tickets for way in advance. Only this is one show you don't ever want to see. You wait.

You stand, looking down at your scuffed brown shoes, which you would have gone ahead and polished if you'd ever had a ma to insist you did those sorts of things—like comb your hair, iron your shirt, wash behind your ears. All that crap usually falls into the "ma" department. Nobody just does that stuff on their own.

And you wait.

The line moves forward an inch or so. Bodies touch. Suit sleeves brush against each other with a scrape of static. The funeral director has got the music playing low, the favorite tune of the deceased—a little Lady Day, singing "Please Don't Talk About Me When I'm Gone." But it's real cold comfort in all that slow shuffling, that march of the dead. You move past the purple velvet curtains. They're the color of a heart, the real kind, not one of those paper valentines. By now you're sick of waiting.

Some folks have come to remember. Others cry a little. No matter why they're there, everybody who shows up on that rainy February night takes a good hard look. To see the horrible things people do to each other. To see what's lost when people make mistakes that can't be made right. To make them think about how they're living, and if they could be living better. Everybody who comes sees something different. I guess that's why they call it a "viewing."

As you get near the front of the line, you start wishing you didn't have to reach it. You remember that day in the park, when you first met her.

First, you saw her jellies on the grass. Then you spotted the deep brown feet that fit into them—shiny diamond decals pressed in all over the toenail polish. You couldn't help but stare. It was a look that glided up that body to those bright eyes, which flashed a smile you'd never, ever get over. At the time, you didn't think much of it.

Now you stand at her bedside in a suit you borrowed

from your pa. It smells like Camels. There's dried salsa on one of the cuff buttons. You look down at her body, and she looks back up at you, eyes *closed* this time. The clock on the wall ticks loudly—pounding—as you take your turn.

After all that waiting, you suddenly wish it would never end.

We stood around for like half an hour before the line moved, and Max and I stepped up to the velvet rope.

A few feet in front of us, past one of those propped-up signs that said, "Caution: Wet Floor," was this crazy book—the one that showed everybody who'd ever lived, and how and when they were going to croak. It was the book of the dead, and it sat there a foot away from me, under a spotlight that had burned out and was hanging from a frayed black wire.

The Last Minutes was about two feet tall and two feet across and fat with pages. It was like the King Kong of moldy attic Bibles. The edges were breaking off in crumbly bits, and I bet if you tried to pick it up, the whole thing would have turned to a smear on your fingers. Sitting in front of it was a little stool on wheels, as if someone was going to sit their ass down and read through all that tragedy.

The book rested on a metal pedestal. Off to the side next to it, an old guy[31] filled a folding chair. I couldn't tell if he was awake or not. He wore one of those uniforms and hats, the kind every discount security guard wears. From the looks of it, he was way too old to guard anything, and he had a belly like a bowl of jelly. Guy couldn't have chased a crook if he'd wanted to.

At first glance, *The Last Minutes* looked pretty stupid, ordinary. But I guess that's how you know when something is really important—when it looks just like stuff you've seen a million times, except there's a line of tourists curving around the block to see it. That's how we'd gotten the idea to see the book in the first place, when we were forced to squeeze through that wall of people blocking the sidewalk.

After getting booted from the MIA archives, Max and I had squatted on the curb for a minute squishing close together to get warm, with no success. Another

---

[31] Hoover Jones, 1920–1998: suffered a heart attack during the "Regional Output in the Coming Quarter" seminar.

storm had come in off the mountains in the distance, making the gray sky grayer and the dark rain darker. The rain fell, making our pointy burlap hoods all saggy. We didn't give a crap.

"I want to go back in an hour or so," I'd told her. I hadn't had my fill of the jerks at the MIA. Not yet. That conversation with that snooty lady in the window had only been round one, and I wasn't going down without a KO.

Max shook her head. "I can't stay," she said. The big, saggy duffel bag sat between her knees. She hugged it, protecting it from the rain. "I spent-like two years bugging those people. I won't do it again."

"I'm not asking you to," I said, sliding in closer so she could see my face through the downpour. I was trying to look as serious as I could.

"I recognized a few of their faces," she said, looking off into the dripping rooftops, thinking about the past, probably. "I remember them from last time I was here. That's a bad-like sign, mama."

"Then we won't bother," I said.

She smiled at me. "What happened to 'I want to go back,' huh?"

"I'll go tomorrow, on my own," I said. "You've wasted enough of your time waiting around for nothing."

"You have no idea," she told me.

If I hadn't been such a chicken, I'd have reached over and taken Max's hand. Because sometimes, even when it doesn't seem acceptable, or is even expected, you just want to touch another person. To hold someone's hand, even if it's cold and gray as a trout. There isn't a better way to remember that you're still a person.

So we'd gotten up and stretched, the gray water running down our ponchos to the street. We didn't get too far. After circling the MIA's big brick complex, we ran smack-dab into a line of folks snaking its way down the sidewalk. They stood in the rain, waiting to climb a set of steps that led into a different building. Neither of us was ready to hurry up and wait again. Not until we saw the saggy white banner tied across the doorway.

The MIA presents *The Last Minutes*,
the legendary book of the dead!
Traveling exhibition extended!

We thought it was a joke at first.

But when Max saw it wasn't, she grabbed us two spots in line.

We stood in the downpour until it became a dark and muddy drizzle. Then we hung out in the front hall-way of the MIA exhibition hall, which looked like every other big, sad room in the Afterlife—stained plaster and exposed wires, like they'd never finished building it and never would. The line moved fast. We passed the time playing Stud with a couple of studs[32, 33] in leather chaps, fans of the Fiendish Lot who about choked on their tongue jewelry when they met Max.

And just like before, we waited our turn. But this time we were rewarded for it.

The velvet rope was there for a good reason. People crowded to the front of the group without even knowing they were doing it. They bent their necks all out of shape to see it. Not because it was ancient, or because it gave off a barely there hum that made your teeth vibrate. No. They wanted to get up close to see the names.

They appeared from out of nowhere, filling the book's empty pages by the hundreds. Ink turned the

---

[32] Ferris Zogby, 1952–1989: hunted down by an abandoned daughter and shot in the back.

[33] Antero Koskinen, 1973–2003: fell asleep at his desk during an office fire—everyone else got out alive but hadn't known he was there.

white paper an oily black—left to right, top to bottom—and each page filled up real fast. When it did, the corner would lift up real gentle, as if caught in some breeze. Then the page would turn with a quiet creaky sound.

At one point, that old security guy dozing in the folding chair got his lazy ass up. Jowls wobbling, he waddled over to the pedestal and took this box-cutter tool from his belt. Then he sliced a big old hunk of pages right out of the book, dropping it into a chute in the wall like it was trash or something. Picking up a stack of fresh pages off the floor, he pasted them into the back. That way the book stayed nice and fat, for future generations of tourists and the heartbroken.

The names, they never stopped coming.

Max and I stood at the velvet rope, not saying much. There wasn't much to talk about. We knew we were looking at something bigger than our piddly selves. Then we stepped out of the way and gave the people behind us our place at the head of the line.

Back on the sidewalk afterward, Max handed me a warped cardboard coaster. It had a picture of a flamingo on it and an address. Then that girl was off like a shot.

She could really move when she wanted to get the hell away from something or somebody.

My guess is that after seeing *The Last Minutes*, everybody likes to have some alone time.

I trudged along the bone-cold walkways in the rain, not caring where I was going, not seeing the cracked sidewalk under me, but imagining my name filling a fresh and empty page: "Jonathan Joseph Dyas: shot with sock-drawer gun." Lame!

Olam Haba sucked. A wall of fog always floated a few feet in front of your face, and it seemed to pull away when you got too near, like it had a brain calling the shots.

Reaching the end of the next walkway, I stopped and looked up into the falling rain. As I did, there was a crackling pop, and the lights all over town went out.

A few blocks ahead floated a warm pocket of white, a diamond glittering deep in a coal mine. Above the door a glowing sign read: "River Styx Records." Wiping the rain from my eyes, I sprinted through the gloom toward the light. I don't know how it was even possible, but in those few seconds the rain had gotten even worse.

A bell tinkled as I opened the door. Standing on a

soaked black welcome mat, I shook like a dog.

Right away I noticed the music. It blasted from speakers mounted up in all four corners of the room. The quality was crap, like it'd been recorded in a closet by someone wearing one of those underwater scuba-diving face masks. But it was music I kind of recognized—the Who, I think—and that one detail made a whole world of difference.

The store was just a room, and a crazy cramped one at that. Wobbly card tables filled the floor, and resting on top were big cardboard boxes stuffed to busting with all sorts of junk, mostly records, but a bunch of other stuff too.

Like the music, I recognized a lot of it from my life, from—well, just *life*. There were these real sweet muscleman action figures I remembered playing with as a kid. I used to glue firecrackers to their backs and blow them up. A jumble of VHS tapes filled a couple boxes, and a stack of old raggedy comics leaned up against a pinball machine that would never ring another high score.

The walls were hidden behind a patchwork quilt of oversized music-store posters—Dead Kennedys, Circle Jerks, the Germs, NOFX, and even a newer one for

Sublime. A few still blazed in full color, locked bright and safe under black metal frames. The rest were the usual dull black-and-white you never got away from in the Afterlife, and I didn't know the names at all—the Goobs; Painted Ladies; Glowfinger; and Okey Dokey, Dr. Jones. But no Fiendish Lot anywhere, not that I could see.

To me, that shop—with its broken toys, old computer disks, and fuzzy dice—was a little slice of heaven. But to somebody else, it probably just looked like a collection of junk waiting to be lugged out to the curb. Just like Violet's Grandma Rafferty had always said, one person's trash was another person's treasure.

I hadn't seen him before, but in one corner of the room a real slick old dude[34] relaxed on a stool, slowly turning a crank on one of those electricity-generator boxes. Every turn made a click and then a low, grinding whir. Old dude looked to me like some kind of lazy outlaw, with them sharp-toed leather boots and cowboy hat drooped low over his face. His skin was wrinkly like fake car upholstery. In one hand burned a hand-rolled

---

[34] Barry Golding, 1870–1925: vaporized in a stampede of terrified cattle.

cigarette, even though he could have been dead, or stuffed, or both.

It was this guy who kept the music playing and the lights burning with the turning of his magic crank. Sure, the sound was tinny and hollow, like the shell of music without the insides, but it was a tune I knew, damn it, and I felt almost lucky for the first time in a long time.

When the song ended, another one started. I walked around the shop, row after row, and I browsed. It was something real normal that I would have done back home, which made it even more special in the Afterlife. Of course, in the old days, after checking the place out for a few minutes, I would have gone on to slide something down the front of my pants and mosey on out of there. I'd had real sticky fingers—but like a lot of old habits, I didn't have much interest in doing that anymore. What use did a dead creep have for a box of thrown-out action figures and old copies of *People*?

As if reading my mind, a low growl of a voice said, "You'd better not be planning on stealing something." I nearly jumped out of my skin.

There was a guy[35] behind the counter, which was funny because I hadn't known there was anyone else in the store besides me and the outlaw Jose Wales, who seemed content to stay in the corner pumping his handle.

Counter guy was chunky and wore thick Coke-bottle specs. The front of his T-shirt said, "Stop Looking at My T-shirt," but you couldn't help it. The tight fabric rose up just enough to show off his hairy belly button. That wasn't all. His soft yellowish-tan sol glowed above the droopy sag of his gut.

"I'm not going to steal anything," I said, playing the innocent.

"You look like Darth Vader on safari," said the guy, pointing to my pointy canvas poncho. He ducked behind the counter, where he was doodling with some pens and paper, distracted.

"Keeps out the rain," I said.

"Is it raining?" said the guy sarcastically. "I hadn't noticed." He chuckled to himself and kept working.

"You've seen *Star Wars*?" I asked. That mention of

_____

[35] Dwight "Ike" Lutz, 1935–1977: suffered heart attack on the toilet while reading pornography with his pants around his ankles.

Darth Vader got me thinking about the everyday life stuff about being alive, and I missed it.

"Who hasn't?" Then he looked at me close. "You still got a bit of a hue, mama. How ND are you?"

"I don't know," I said. "Maybe two weeks, maybe more. What about you?"

"Well I'm sure as hell not ND," he said, grunting. "I'm a Seventy-seven."

"What's a Seventy-seven?"

"Died in Nineteen Seventy-seven," said the shop guy, annoyed. "There's a bunch of us hanging around Haba. It's like one big class reunion all the time."

"And that's fun?" I asked him. The only thing that kept me from dropping out of school had been Violet. Just setting foot into the same building as my classmates was like taking some kind of test I was bound to keep failing.

"Seventy-seven was the peak of human civilization," said the shop guy.

Now, I'd never heard a single person say that about the seventies, *any* year of the seventies. All I knew about it was what I found out the time I cleaned our attic crawl space: old disco clothes. Damn if they weren't the fruitiest things you'd ever lay eyes on. Maybe Seventy-seven was the peak of civilization, but it must have been on some other planet where people were color-blind.

The shop guy leaned over the counter and got in my face. If he'd been on Earth, his breath probably would have smelled like chili dogs. "So you're into *Star Wars*, huh? Who's your favorite-like character?"

There was only one answer. "No contest," I said. "Jango Fett. He's badass."

"Jango *what*?"

"You know, the bounty hunter guy from the prequels," I said. "The hard dude who they turn into an army of clones."

A second passed as he sucked in a big breath, mostly to be dramatic. "They made a *prequel* to *Star Wars*?" he said.

"They made like three of them," I told him.

Sighing, he sat back on a stool and dug around in his ear with a finger. "Yeah, well," he said, glaring. "You see any movie theaters around here, smart guy?"

I shrugged. "I guess you've missed out on some stuff, huh?" I said.

"You could say that," he said. Then, thinking, he

began to explain. "You know, someone was telling me about this doctor who did a study, some dead anthropologist or something. He wanted to find out how quickly Earth culture trickled down to us here on the other side-like. Well, supposedly the Afterlife trails by like twenty, maybe twenty-five years." He finished scratching his itch and looked at his fingertip. "We're never on the cutting edge."

"That kind of sucks," I told him. "You get the leftovers of everything."

"You have to pick your interests in order to collect-like," he said, raising the very same finger that he'd used to go drilling around in his ear canal. "Me, I focus on pop culture and music, mostly. Just now I'm starting to get a nice-like flow of new stuff from the mid-eighties, some new wave, and even some gnarly heavy metal."

I smiled, feeling bad for the guy. "Then I guess you're not missing much," I lied.

"We survive," he said. "Still, sometimes it's like you're living in East Germany and you know everyone else out there is having-like a ball."

"There is no East Germany anymore," I pointed out.

"There's just Germany."

He sighed. "I guess I should have seen that one coming."

I watched the guy work. He was sketching cartoons, like the kind you might see in a daily paper, and dude had some talent. There was something special about it, though. Instead of a cheap ballpoint sucker, he used this real antique-looking fountain pen that he dipped into a black bottle that sat on a greasy cloth behind the counter. He didn't pay me no mind, and I watched as he pricked his fingertip with a needle and then inserted the whole damn digit into that makeshift inkwell. A soft amber light beam grew up from the inside of the bottle. When he dipped the pen back in and kept on with his sketches, I saw the difference, how suddenly them comics were jumping right up off the page, like the stick figures had got themselves a heartbeat. It might have just been my imagination, but I could swear that guy had worked a spell on his funny papers. Maybe drawing them was what he was meant to do.

I couldn't help but think back to Baltimore, when Harlan Hogg had used that crazy ink to give me a violet tattoo that seemed as alive as the real thing. Staring down at my hand, I could see that the flower had long since turned ashy and gone still as stone.

It was easy to tell that this guy was a no-nonsense type, a straight shooter, somebody who'd have no qualms chewing you out for not knowing who Jabba the Hutt was—even though he'd never actually *seen* Jabba the Hutt since, technically, the guy died like a decade before *Return of the Jedi*.

I leaned over the counter. "Can I ask you a question?" I said.

"You're not going away, are you?" he asked.

"So," I said, trying to sort things out in my head, "do you believe all of this stuff about sols?" I made eye contact, trying not to sound too serious or too joking. "To me it sounds like a load of bull."

The guy chuckled, his shirt inching up a bit more over his belly. He dropped one ass cheek back on the stool, where he kind of perched, like a big fat buzzard. "That's like asking me if the Earth is round-like," he said. "Or if David Bowie wears tight pants."

"So it's true?"

"You see them, don't you?" he said, holding up his pricked fingertip, which burned orange like E.T.'s.

"My friend says you lose your sol if you don't find your purpose," I said.

The guy made a face. "I've never heard it that way before," he said. "Sounds like a greeting card, or a song by Bread. Everyone thinks about it how they want to."

Resting his elbows on the counter, which was frosty glass set over a mess of old, rusty bottle caps, he snatched up a stack of beer coasters and began shuffling them like they were cards. They were the same coasters as the one Max had handed me—a flamingo on the front, an address on the back.

He seemed grumpier than he had a minute ago. "The time for Q and A is up-like, and as you can see, I'm busy, and the store doesn't exactly run itself." The place was totally empty, and the cowboy at the crank had most definitely fallen asleep for real this time. That, or died again. "So, a last question?" asked the guy.

"Yeah, one," I said. "You got-like any Fiendish Lot music in here anywhere?"

In the middle of his smart-ass smirk, the guy froze up. His T-shirt—which I couldn't help but look at, even though it told me not to—flashed. It wasn't the shirt that flashed, though. It was the sol underneath. It shined the color of honey.

There was a back room. There always was in joints like that. Secret stashes usually hid something you wanted to keep secret, or, in the case of the guy at River Styx Records, it held something you wanted to keep all to yourself.

"You like?" he asked as he closed the employees-only door behind us. The excitement was in his voice.

I *did* like. I liked so much I just nodded.

Behind the utility pipes and a big coiled metal boiler thing plastered with warning labels was the closest thing to a Fiendish Lot museum you'd ever see. Banners hovered from the ceiling on thin flossy wires. Below them, a silky black cloth covered a round table. Metal buttons lay on the soft, untouched black fabric, having been arranged with what could only be called love.

One button read: "The Fiendish Lot: the Second Coming." Another had a picture of a winged skeleton holding a guitar on it, and read: "Ladies and Gentlemen, Put Your Hands Together for . . . the Fiendish Lot." Pins scattered here and there showed pictures of fists grabbing lightning bolts. All the little doodads were merchandise from the band's other tours, junk that made sense in a store full of memories. A seamstress's dummy stood off to one side. It wore a black sport coat that looked like it had been set on fire by someone who'd changed their mind at the very last second.

The shop guy walked up behind me. "Penny wore that jacket when they played Tophet three years ago," he said. "That show saved my life." He stopped short. "I mean my afterlife." He grunted, like he was getting all choked up just thinking about it.

"I go to every show I can," he said. "For me, it's like going to church."

"Yeah," I said. We were strangers, but I knew what he was talking about.

"You want to know why no one will ever top the Lot?" he asked.

I turned around and looked at him. "Why?"

Pointing to his freckled wrist, he stared me down creepily. "They plug their instruments right into themselves," he said. When I didn't say anything, he shook his meaty hand at me and got real excited. "To touch people, to do anything worthwhile, you have to give a piece of your sol. So many people are afraid to do it. But if you do, it comes back to you twofold. We carry each other, mama."

I knew that's what I'd felt every time the Fiendish Lot had played—my sol and theirs crashing into one another in the air above the crowd. Everyone's in the room, sharing, mixing . . . and growing, getting bigger than you ever thought possible.

"Even Insco, the drummer," the guy went on. "She jacks right into these big amps that make the sound crazy loud. And what comes out"—and he tried to get a grip—"what's in the music, it's just an extension of them." He clutched at where his heart had been and threw his hands out in front of him, like he was letting loose a wild bird. "What's inside comes out."

"I know," I heard myself saying. I remembered—that sensation, better than any drug, like holding hands with a person without even being near them.

"Yes!" the guy said dreamily. "They explode with light, and you just bask in it."

Then I remembered what Max had told me. "Don't you have to be careful with your sol?" I asked. "Can't it get sucked dry or something?"

The guy was fingering the sleeve of the sport coat now, giving it bedroom eyes, like he was about to ask the mannequin to slow dance. "That's why they're hard-core," he said dreamily. "Every time the Lot plays, they give you everything."

I hadn't realized. "That's crazy," I whispered, thinking of all those lost sols on the train.

The shop guy smiled, buttoning up the front of the coat. He would have straightened the necktie if there'd been one. "That's rock and roll," he said simply.

The next time I saw Max, she didn't see me. It was probably an hour or so after I'd ditched River Styx Records. The rain had let up for the first time since I'd set foot in Olam Haba. It would have been a beautiful day, if not for the rolling tumbleweeds of damp fog, the dying sols stumbling around, and the occasional sap slumped in the gutter with an animal mask strapped across his ugly face. Other than all that, things were just peachy.

I was probably fifty feet from the Olam Haba tram station when I spotted her. Head down, hunched, that big duffel bag rising up over her shoulders, she zipped along the walkways, like the white rabbit trying to make some last-second appointment in Wonderland.

I thought about raising my hand and shouting. Hell, I was in the middle of doing it when my foot hit a pothole overflowing with gray rain, and down I went.

Max missed me. By the time I got back on my feet, she was a speck again.

I watched her go, knowing she'd never slow down. I wondered what kept driving her like that.

So I got up and followed.

I hurried to keep up as she motored through the city's web of twisty bridge-things, lugging that damn duffel. We walked for a long time, so long that I was starting to wonder if Max had gotten lost. There weren't as many houses on the outskirts. In a lot of places the walkways had collapsed, their stilts broken. Still, her pace never lagged, not even when she headed for a lonely little hut that sat tucked into the side of those massive gray cliffs.

I hung back, trying to disappear into the haze. But there wasn't a whole lot to hide in. And I was probably glowing like a half-man, half-lightning bug, so sneaking around was pretty pointless in the first place. I wasn't really the spy type.

Lucky for me, Max never looked back. She stopped at the warped door of that little hut and kind of collected herself. Then she knocked. I waited, standing like a moron in a puff of fog.

With no sound at all, the door inched open a crack. A face appeared and floated in the black gap like the moon. Take a skeleton and shrink-wrap it, and you had the old lady[36] who answered. She was barely there. Even from a good fifty feet away she gave me the willies.

She stared with dead eyes as Max spoke.

When the old woman moved to close her door, Max raised a hand and blocked it. She threw her lumpy duffel bag on the stoop at her feet, then unbuttoned the top flaps and loosened the strings.

A rush of light broke from the mouth of the bag, slicing through that haze like a sparkler popping. Max reached into the opening.

After all that dazzle I expected her to pull out something pretty freaking sweet, but when she took out her arm all she held pinched in her grip was this droopy

---

[36] Penabi Magboo, 1928–2002: bitten by poisonous spider after outdoor lovemaking session.

envelope. The paper seemed to glow like a flint in Max's fingertips.

A queer look settled on the old lady's cracked and ghostly face. I'd seen the same hungry stare in the eyes of a dog tracking a bone.

Hands trembling, she reached out. Max didn't pull away. They made contact, and something flashed— white and glittery—and I watched, breathless, as a bolt of pencil-thin lightning passed between them.

Crying out, the old lady hugged that dirty envelope against her chest. She practically crushed that thing into pulp, and as she did, a patch of blood-red color flooded her gray cheeks. Then so did a smile. The light of that piece of mail dimmed as the light in her eyes got brighter.

That old lady would have cried if she could have. She would have sobbed her eyes out. I didn't know what Max had brought her, but whatever it was, she'd been missing it.

8

"How you all doing tonight?"

It was one of those questions you weren't really supposed to answer. Still, the crowd screamed back at him.

"Last time we were in Olam Haba, we got arrested for inciting a riot." There were laughs, and then this chick[37] in the front row threw her panties onstage. Penny laughed and shook his head. "Keep this up," he said, pointing down at her beaming face, "and we're going to have to take you with us when we're done."

They went bonkers. They loved it. They loved *him*.

Penny didn't need a spotlight. His golden guitar—a Les Paul, I think—shined in the dark of the stage, the power cable connecting it to him with a glowing hot, branding-iron red. Raising his tiny hand, Penny hit a chord that made the floor seem to drop out from under people's feet.

---

[37] Cecil Mackenzie, 1985–2005: train collision en route to visit estranged lover, despite restraining order.

The dead air thundered once and went still.

I sat on the edge of the Flamingo's bar, my legs propped on a stool. Every time Penny played a note, the chord blew the hair back out of my face like I was standing on the edge of a tall building and the wind was rushing at me. It was warm, it was fast. I was sunbathing in the sound, in the sol.

The Flamingo was nothing like the Tick-Tock Club. I'd been to plenty of holes in the wall, but that joint was like the hole in the wall of a hole in the wall. With all its missing tiles, the white ceiling looked like a crossword puzzle.

Stepping back so that only his golden guitar stood out from the shadows, Penny spoke, his voice drifting up over the heads like smoke. "Max, would you do me the pleasure?"

Then Penny lit into a guitar riff that actually knocked a couple of bald dudes[38, 39] in front onto their asses. The rest of the crowd closed in around them, catching them

---

[38] Tim Carlson, 1921–1975: died in prison while doing time for fraud, evasion, and conspiracy.

[39] Tim Carlson Jr., 1960–2001: electrocuted for first-degree murder.

as they toppled like a pair of bowling pins. Grinning like a fool, Wes jumped up and down in his blue-suede shoes and became a blue-suede blur.

I strained, trying to make out Max in the dark clutter at the far back of the stage. She was barely there, lit mostly by her sol, like she'd swallowed a charcoal briquette and it'd gotten stuck on the way down. Back flagpole straight, she sat up on her padded stool, arms and legs dancing around all by themselves marionette-style as the rest of her stayed totally frozen. She screamed at the top of her lungs, a black necktie thrown over one shoulder. She looked happy.

Penny kept playing until he glowed so bright it was like staring into the sun. I felt the burning deep in my guts, but it was different. It was *my* pain. The music was dragging all of it to the surface.

Then he started smoking. A curl of flame shot up one shoulder and wrapped around his neck. He gritted his teeth, rocking like a maniac. Penny didn't need no pyrotechnics. Dude *was* pyrotechnics.

Violet. Violet. Violet.

I stumbled through the exit door to the alley, and

then fell hard on my knees in a puddle. It didn't hurt. Nothing about my body ever hurt anymore.

Head back, I inhaled deeply. I'd never gobbled so much air. Breathing didn't matter, not in that place, but still I felt like I was suffocating.

Violet. Violet. Violet.

I tried to breathe.

I don't know what Penny had done to me, exactly, but somehow he'd stirred up all the most painful parts about losing that girl—the stuff I'd gotten over, or worked through, or moved past—and rekindled it. My sol burned so hot in my ribs it was like choking on a stick of dynamite.

I slumped down against a garbage can and lay there for a second, worn out. The Fiendish Lot kept on going. As if an answer to a prayer I'd never make, the lights in the alley went out.

Alone on my ass, I glowed.

But I wasn't as alone as I'd first thought. Because when the song inside the Flamingo ended, it left a big quiet behind it. And that's when I heard the noise.

Shuffling—I heard the shoes before I saw the folks who wore them.

Turning real slow, I saw them standing in the alley nearby like a herd of cattle waiting around for the slaughter. Ghostly folks, about twenty of them, totally quiet, not moving, huddled near the door I'd just come bursting out of. They didn't look at me. No. To them, I was the invisible one.

The next song started, and the doorknob to the emergency exit made a pinging sound as it shook once in its socket and fell to the ground, rolling into a pile of dirty wigs.

Hearing the music, the phantom army shuffled closer to the wall, not really walking, but not floating above the ground either.

The closer they got, the colder everything felt. Their sols barely glimmered, like the coals of a campfire. "Do you want to go inside?" I asked the nearest one. It was a man[40], I'm pretty sure. His facial features were real faint, more like suggestions, some lines you'd doodle on a foggy car window. "You can go on in the door, if you want to."

I got to my feet and took a few steps, reaching out. He didn't flinch or nothing. My fingers went into his

---

[40] Tamba Karamoko, 1968–1999: drowned in the village well.

shoulder, drops of wetness forming at their tips.

Then I understood what I was doing. My stomach dropped out of me. One hand was almost completely inside the guy and he didn't feel a thing. His stare said it all. They were as good as gone, and before long, it would be like they'd never been there at all. "Do you need help?" I asked.

Violet. Violet. Violet.

"Please, let me help you," I said to the guy at the front, but I kind of said it to all of them.

Then somebody behind me cleared his throat. It wasn't one of the ghouls. No, it was a real person, like me. Without thinking, I yanked my arm back and took a step away from the man, holding my hand close to my chest. It was wet and clammy.

"He can't hear you," said a gravelly voice.

Max's grandfather stepped out of the alley shadows, and as he did, the brick walls went from a dull gray to a hot lava color. It was a miracle he'd snuck up on me at all considering he shined like a bright-red bike reflector. He'd fancied up nice in a gray tweed suit, complete with bow tie and all the trimmings, hair shellacked to one side. I hadn't seen anyone dressed up like that in a long time. And to tell the truth, the old man was the last person I ever expected to see at a punk-rock show in the red-light district.

Grumbling and stooped, he moved quickly toward me with the same cane action I'd seen him use before. He barely went up to my shoulders.

"What are *you* doing here?" I asked.

"I never miss a show," he said.

"*You* never miss a show?" I asked, shooting him the crazy eye. "What, are you some kind of super-fan?" I laughed. I couldn't help it.

"The biggest," he said. "I never miss them play. Not if I can manage." He added, "Max has no idea, and it's going to stay that way."

As the old man waddled past, the group of phantoms didn't move an inch, and he brushed up against them—and sometimes through them—but kept going, not freaked in the slightest. They tracked him, trained on his fiery sol like dogs on a scent.

"Can they hurt me?" I asked, not needing to explain who I was talking about.

The old man was heading to where the alley opened into the street, but he stopped long enough to turn back and smile. He reminded me of some kind of evil wal-rus. If I'd had his funky old-man teeth, I never would have opened my mouth. "They're harmless," he said. "Most of these poor sols were probably just heading out to the Edges and were drawn to the music. They always are."

"The Edges?" I asked, watching those murky gray humanlike shapes mob the half-open door, trying to squeeze through the gap.

"Those who've lost all hope, all reason to go on, make for the Edges," he said. He dumped his old pipe tobacco onto the ground. "You have to see for yourself. Walk in any direction and you'll get to the end of the world." He grunted. "Once lost sols reach the Edges, they simply quit trying to hold themselves together, and they break apart in the fog. It's beautiful to watch, actually."

It didn't sound like there was anything beautiful about it.

He chuckled and played with his cane, swirling the tip in a puddle. "You wouldn't understand."

"Where are you going?" I asked the old man. "I thought you watched every show."

"I do," he said. "But this time I have to leave a little, well, early."

"Do you know about the stuff Max has been swiping from your collection?" I blurted, meaning the objects in Max's duffel bag. I don't know why I ratted on her. "I followed her today," I said, spilling more of my guts. I knew he wouldn't say anything to Max. We had a lock on each other's secrets now. That was kind of like trust, I guess. "She went to a lady's house, and then gave her something."

"Did she?" asked the old man, flashing his unfortunate grin. "She's been doing that for years." He shook his head. "She doesn't think I know, but I do. When things you care about start disappearing, you notice."

"What are they?" I asked.

He tapped the tip of his cane against my boot, lively eyes hiding behind a wad of wrinkles. "We call them endowed objects. They once belonged to people, in their old lives. Now they're just pieces, memories. The government usually takes them when you arrive here and destroys them. But me, I save them if I can."

"So what was Max doing?" I asked, confused.

"Returning possessions to their rightful owners, I suppose," he said.

"Sounds like a lot of work," I said.

"Oh, it's more work than you realize, and terribly painful. Most people can handle the pieces of their old lives, can keep the past behind them where it belongs. Others, however, become too attached." He watched my reaction closely, and then kept talking. "Max tries to help them all. She is always trying to make up for what she sees as her mistakes. She tortures herself for the happiness of others."

"What do you mean?" I said.

"Some things sit on a shelf and you look at them from time to time," he said. "Other things grab you deep inside and don't let you go. They affect how you live your days, and for how long. You never know how you'll react until you face the possibility of losing what you've already lost again."

I thought about what he said, and then pictured Max high on her stool. "She doesn't look tortured when she's drumming," I said.

"That's because it's what she was born to do," he

said. "Just because people get second chances doesn't mean they take the hint." Then, without any warning whatsoever, he drove that cane right down into my big toe.

I leaped back, knee up and howling. The old coot gave me the eye and said, real cool, "Do you get me, son?"

I did, or so I thought.

In front of all those transparent spooks, the old man looked like the Human Torch. When he spoke, the tiniest rays of light trailed from his wrinkled lips. You had to get right up in his face to see it.

"Hey, man, you look pretty shiny," I told him. "You feeling okay?"

He laughed, an empty sound, like he was talking into a hollow coffee can. "Not everyone fades away," he said. "Better to burn out brilliantly than to never burn at all."

Shrugging, the old man shook his head at me and hobbled off toward the open road, passing a fresh crew of phantoms as they joined the mob near the Flamingo's back door. I watched him go.

Problem was, I didn't know why I'd been given a

second chance. There were a million things I wanted to redo, but none of them would change who I was or what I'd done in my crappy life. Hell, what I *hadn't* done.

"Do you think my girlfriend is going to the Edges?" I shouted after him. It was loud enough that, if we were anywhere else, people would have looked up to see what the ruckus was about. But not in the Afterlife.

"Why, is your girlfriend dead?" he called back.

"Yeah," I said.

"Then I would recommend you leave her that way," he said.

When he reached the alley mouth, all the darkened lampposts came alive again with a clunk and a fizzle, electricity punching back through the wires. The night burst open with twinkling white, like we were caught in a giant camera flash. It blinded me for a second, and when the spots cleared I couldn't see the old man anymore. He was gone.

A heavy bass line started up inside the Flamingo. Its thump made the manhole next to me jump out of its slot and then roll around in the metal opening like a quarter before settling back down with a thud. The Fiendish Lot had started their second set of the night.

It was going to be their last in Olam Haba. Then they'd be moving on again, another stop along the countryside and another step nearer to the end of the world.

And I'd be going with them.

TRACK 3:
WITH BANGS AND WHIMPERS

9

MISSING

Violet Rafferty
18, African American
About 5' 6" and 114 lbs
Dead for 6 weeks (give or take)
Please go to Radical Hernia with any information.

I began hammering, missing the head of the nail, squashing a thumb—damn. Barely felt it. By that point, the numbness had gotten so bad I could hardly move my fingers. The stubby electrical pole was already plastered with a collage of flyers, so mine barely stuck out at all, like a single curse word on a great big bathroom wall covered in scribbles.

When I finished hanging my sign, I sat down on the curb, basking in the warmth of the house behind me. It was on fire. It cast just enough real light for me to see by, and it hardly made any noise—or maybe I just couldn't hear it. Figures moved around me on the sidewalk—ghouls—groups of those slow-dying shadow people. These days, they seemed like my only company.

One whole month had passed since my night in the alley outside the Flamingo, but there I was, still surrounded by ghosts.

Sparks bobbed and looped overhead like a swarm of lightning bugs heading south for the winter. The house fire started to die out, but it didn't matter since something in Gehenna was always burning. It wasn't a big deal. You got used to it. If you could stand the charred, Cajun-blackened skies and the ungodly roasting smell, then you might even call the place cozy. If you didn't have a soft spot for arson, then you might like the huge piles of landfill trash building up along either side of the street like snowdrifts. Honeymoon spot, that city sure wasn't.

Across the street, the Fiendish Lot was playing a gig at this three-story Spanish-language joint called Radical Hernia. You could feel their rumble under your feet. You felt it through the soles of your boots as they stuck to the hot, gooey black asphalt. If you didn't know better, you'd think an earthquake was coming, or that an army was marching home from war.

The shaking got so bad that about halfway through the band's first set, a bunch of these worried construction guys were called in to reinforce the supports that kept the second and third floors of the building from crashing down on the first. Of course, I think the possibility of being flattened got the die-hard fans even more wound up. They stood outside cheering as the construction guys scurried around like Santa's elves.

I hoped those dudes had figured out the problem, because when the band started up again, that whole damn building was still rocking nonstop.

Not everybody went back inside after the excitement. The streets and sidewalks outside the band's concerts were always packed with fans, the crazies who followed them from town to town. You found them sitting in little circles on the curbs smoking and jabbering, passing around the sunshine, or just lying there like bums, listening to songs they'd heard a hundred times but never got tired of. They loitered like it was their job.

Then, of course, there were the spooks, the lost

sols. They were guaranteed to show up every time the Fiendish Lot plugged in and played, no matter where, no matter when.

They always seemed to arrive from out of nowhere, phantoms at the end of the street lit from behind by the fires. It would start as a trickle—one or two—but in just a few quick minutes it would become this steady flow. They came for Penny's crazy glow on the way to the Edges. Or that's as much as I could figure out from what I knew, which was squat. Always squat.

The ghouls were the reason I'd started hanging around out front of the band's shows instead of inside with the fans.

As I sat there with the hammer in my hands, weighing me down, I saw them. It was a scene I'd gotten real used to over the last few weeks: a faded wave of ghosts shuffling down the street toward me and a crowd of "normal" people stepping back to let them through and keeping a safe distance.

That was my cue to move. Standing up and jogging across the road, I hurried down the empty space between the two mobs—the buffer zone where neither of them had any interest in being.

Near the front of the pack of ghouls was a pretty normal guy[41] with little round squirrel eyes and a bald spot. He'd probably been in his forties when he died, but was now barely there at all, his skin as thin as an onion peel. Walking alongside, I took the old guy's frosty, trembling arm the best I could manage. He was freezing through and through, like he'd been hibernating in a meat freezer.

"Hello," I called to him. "Can you help me?"

Every one of those cold, damp bodies pushed blindly past me, even as I tried to stop them, even as I searched their dazed faces for one that I'd find familiar. But my fingers passed through every sleeve and every shoulder, coming out soaked on the other side. They herded toward Radical Hernia and the warmth of the sol bleeding through its open windows from the stage, and I nearly got trampled under the cold dead feet.

"Shit!" I shouted. I clenched my fists and screamed it again. Getting angry was the only thing that made me

---

[41] Kichiro Ishikawa, 1912–1962: contracted syphilis from one night with a prostitute, died of dementia.

feel alive, like I wasn't about to lose my mind and vanish into the background.

I sat back down on the curb and punched myself
in the skull. Then I did it again. My head was already
ringing, so it didn't matter if I made it louder, clearer.
Crying with no tears, I buried my face in my palms. I'd
never felt so damn cold in all my life.

Unrolled "MISSING" posters lay around me on the
sidewalk, totally worthless. Words didn't mean anything. Ghosts couldn't read, could they? I wished I had
a picture. I could show it to folks so they could recog-
nize her. So I could. Because, well, I couldn't remember
Violet's face no more, even when I tried my hardest and
squeezed my eyes shut tight.

As I dry-cried, I couldn't help but notice a group of
Fiendish Lot fanboys hanging around by a lamppost on
the corner. They were sort of half watching the phantoms and half watching me.

"You know, there's easier ways to get laid-like," said
one guy[42], calling across the street. "You probably don't
need all the signs and shit." A tattoo of an eagle, its

_____

[42] Anthony Morris, 1959–1982: drug overdose from some really
bad junk given to him by a pimp named "Donkey Kong."

wings spread, hid his whole face. His buddies giggled, even though what he'd said wasn't all that funny.

"He must have very particular tastes," said one of his buddies[43], and they all laughed. They had fancy British accents, even when they laughed.

I turned around on my butt so I was facing the flames of the house fire. I'd dealt with bullies all my life, and I'd be damned if I was going to do it in the Afterlife, too.

Their leader went right on blabbing. "It's bad-like enough we have to deal with all the husks out front," he said. "Now we have to deal with a husk lover."

Shaking, I got up. I picked up one of my posters and set to work hanging it. It was something to do, to take my mind off them, off everything.

I finished slamming in the nail I'd been hammering into the alley wall. Hammering I could do. I could do that real good.

"You know, there's a place for people like you," said the first guy's hilarious buddy. They were walking up now, probably to kick my ass and leave me busted up

---

[43] Hollis Wallace, 1940–1962: sunk in a squall, picked apart by eels.

in the street. It wouldn't be the first time that had happened. "There's a reason your kind drift out to the Edges," he said, voice full of poison. "Nobody wants to look at you, mama. You remind-like everybody of what they lost. You bring us all down."

I wasn't sure, but maybe *their* purposes in life were to be huge assholes. Everyone, and I mean everyone, seemed to be trying to get in my way.

About an hour or so earlier, before the band's show, Max pulled me behind the backstage door to give me a talking-to about how I'd been acting lately. She'd been a dream in glowing orange and knee-high boots, hair in corkscrews around her shoulders, eyes touched with a crescent black moon of mascara. The Radical Hernia had never seen a girl like her before.

"Hey," Max had said, creeping close. I'd always liked how she did that. "Jo-Jo, *hey*."

"Hey," I answered, a wisp of fog coming from my lips.

"I," she said, wrapping her arms around her chest, hesitating. "You," she said, and tried to look into my eyes but couldn't do it. So she stared at the poster instead— my pathetic, pictureless excuse for a "MISSING" poster.

"You can't keep doing this," she said at last.

"I've got no choice," I told her.

"Listen to me," she said. "You know this is wrong-like. You *know* it."

I'd taken out another nail. "Maybe this is what I'm here for—did you ever think that? I've got to try something."

She grabbed me by my collar and jostled me good, not that I needed any help shaking. "This isn't trying," she said, trying to stay calm. "This is giving up-like."

And for that moment I didn't know what I was saying. "And is that so wrong?" I muttered, dropping the hammer with a crack.

I heard paper rustling, and then felt her push something into my hands. "This came for you when you were out posting stupid signs," she said.

I looked down at the snooty official letterhead, my name at the top:

> TO: Jo-Jo Dyas
> RE: Violet Rafferty
> Dear Mr. Jonathan Joseph Dyas,
> Due to the lack of records supporting

your claim and the judgment of the Recently Deceased Panel, your request to be considered as a non-related family member of the deceased Violet E. Rafferty has been denied by the Ministry of Immigration and Acquisition.

If you intend to pursue this matter further, please wait an additional six weeks before resubmitting your application. Additional administrative fees will be required. Please review the policies and procedures on the back of this sheet. Thank you very much for your patience and cooperation.

Albert Dudley,
Chief Justice
Recently Deceased Panel
Ministry of Immigration and Acquisition

I'd rolled up the paper slowly and then crumpled it in my hands.

"This isn't why you're here," Max had said, a comforting hand on my shoulder. "Nobody knows-like better than I do." She'd kissed me on the cheek. Not once, but twice. Then she had pulled open the backstage door and slipped inside, vanishing into the roar of the sound check. Even gone, I felt the weight of her touch. Her lips.

That was an hour ago. Now she was lost in her drumming, and I was lost in a sea of fucking flyers. Remembering that anger, that helplessness, I looked up from my handful of nails and into the faces of those three English punks making fun of me. They'd moved closer, crossing the street, circling for the kill.

"Why don't you just get lost?" said one of them. "It's too late for you, don't you know that?" There were only a few feet between us now.

Max thought I'd given up. She'd never been more wrong. I'd never give up, not even when everyone else had written off Violet. I'd fight until I couldn't fight no more.

"What's your move, ghost boy?" asked the leader, his boys at his side.

The last thing I remember before swinging my fist was Max's sweet voice saying, "This is wrong-like."

But it was too late. Words couldn't stop me. Max was inside with adoring fans at her feet, and I was out in the street getting my face punched in by an Englishman with a fist the size of a softball.

10

When I came to, I was lying in a puddle of something. I didn't want to know what. I'd been dumped into some sort of wooden cart. Wheels squeaked below the floor, and every bump in the road knocked my head against the planks. I couldn't quite open my eyes yet, so I just listened, nose full of a stench that made BO seem like one of God's greater blessings.

I'd woken up right in the middle of a heated conversation. Two dudes were arguing over who would win a smack down between Superman and Thor, which was a no-brainer for anyone who's actually read a comic book. The sides pretty much boiled down to:

1. Not only is Superman strong and fast and can fly, but he can also shoot heat vision and see through shit.

2. Not only is Thor strong and fast and can fly, but he also has this mystical fucking sledgehammer.

Hell, I'd forgotten a lot in the last weeks of my fade, sure, but I still knew a thing or two about superheroes. My brain had its priorities.

"Hey, he's stirring," said a voice. The cart stopped. Then the hands came.

To be honest, I was pretty sick of being grabbed, tossed, wrestled, and pounded on by folks in the Afterlife. When I finally worked my eyes open, I could see that I was being dragged down a long cinder-block hallway. Up near the ceiling, a row of wide, flat windows had been blacked out with patches of dark cloth. For the first few seconds I stayed sort of spacey, floating, feeling those faceless hands pulling me along the cold stone, staring at that blacked-out view.

A door clanged open somewhere nearby, and suddenly we were in a little jail cell, loneliest-looking little place you ever saw: rough stone blocks, a couple of benches on the walls facing each other, scratch marks crisscrossing the walls. In the corner, a tiny metal toilet stuck out of the stone wall. The seat might have fit, maybe, half of my ass. A small black sign with white lettering hung from the flusher handle. It said: "Out of Order."

None of this inspired much confidence.

Whoever had me dropped me to the floor and then slammed that door shut. I stared up at the white paint peeling off the concrete ceiling and shouted, "For the record, dude, Superman could never beat Thor!" as loud as I could muster. "Superman is an alien, but Thor is a GOD!" Then I crawled over to the closest bench. The cell's one small window was also blocked by one of those bolts of black cloth, not that any view in the Afterlife was worth seeing.

Resting my head against the wall, I looked myself over for damage. There was a ragged cut on my thigh— right through my damn trousers—and two of my teeth had been knocked clean out of my head. Not that any of it caused much pain. Even with all the bumps and bruises, I lay there out of it, in a cloud of numb.

I'd have cried if such a thing had been possible, but there was nothing doing. So I sat, quiet. After a few seconds I got hip to a strange sniffing sound. For the first time, I looked into the shadows at the other end of the cell, deep pits of black, and I saw him.

A guy[44] in a bear suit sat on the opposite bench,

---

[44] John Stearns, 1972–2004: died from unknown causes, alone on a sidewalk, surrounded by people who did nothing.

his paws on his knees. He silently stared at me with a pair of googly eyes. Hanging from his neck was a sign on a wire. It said: "You *Can* Teach an Old Bear New Tricks."

As I checked him out, he waved at me.

"Hey, Pooh," I said back, a little creeped out.

He waved again and then shrugged.

I decided to quit blubbering and check out my digs, which I guessed was the drunk tank and which I *knew* was the winner of the "most urine-smelling place I'd ever been" award.

I was stiff and it hurt when I walked, but I still dragged myself up off the seat and poked my achy head through the gap between the door's metal bars. At the end of the cell-block hallway sat a messy rectangular desk with five gray lockers lining the wall behind it. The guy[45] in the chair looked to be some kind of cop, and he snoozed with his legs up on a file cabinet that was dented to hell and dusty. He snored with a fake motorboat sound, like he was doing it on purpose. Even in a world where people didn't need to sleep, the

---

[45] Henri Claude Lautrec, 1960–1997: smothered by a jilted lover who mistook him for his rival.

fuzz still found ways to be lazy.

Everything about the place looked pretty normal, except that on the wall above the desk was this shelf, kind of like a coatrack, but instead of coats the five metal hooks held a line of giant animal heads. From left to right there was a dog with a long red tongue, a panda bear, a chicken with that piece of rubbery skin that hangs from their necks, a gorilla, and—the weirdest of all—a big old elephant noggin with serious tusk action poking every which way.

On a separate prong below the rest hung a tangled jumble of signs fastened to loops of twisted wire. I'd seen those little things all over the Afterlife—from Avernus to Tophet to Gehenna. The topmost sign dangling from the pile said, in big fat letters: "Human Beings Are Meant to Evolve. *I* Didn't." I wasn't totally sure what all of it was about, really, but to bare my soul and be completely honest, I couldn't think of a better way to scare folks straight than locking them up inside sweaty animal heads with signs chained around their necks.

I gave the bear across the cell a look. "What kind of nutty stuff you guys into around here?" I asked.

Yogi just shook his head real sad and mumbled

something behind that fuzzy face. I couldn't hear a damn thing he said. For all I knew, he could have said, "Don't ask me," or, "Do re mi."

I must have fallen asleep, probably out of boredom, because I was woken up real good when the big metal door clanged open.

A big gorilla of a guard[46] stood in the cell doorway. He wasn't dressed in an animal suit. He was just huge and puffed up with muscles, the kind of body you get from a lifetime diet of steroids. "Are you Dyas?" he asked.

"Don't you even know, mama?"

"Quit bitching and come on," he said in a thick accent, maybe New York-ese or New Jersey-ese, the hell if I knew.

The guard slid the door open and grabbed my arm. As he did, my roommate backed away toward the far corner of the cage. I didn't think he could have put up much of a fight, anyway. He'd already had his claws yanked out.

---

[46] Jocko Sweet, 1961–1991: victim of an aneurysm after a minor traffic altercation.

The cop shoved me out into the hall, slamming the door shut again. "I'm sick of hauling in you ghouls," he grumbled. "Get a clue, will you. The rest of us work hard to contribute, and all you do is leech." He forced me ahead of him down the hallway, which was now strangely quiet except for the scraping of boots and angry muttering. "Eventually people are going to quit taking care of you. You'll really be on your own. Then what?"

I didn't know what he was talking about. I'd done a lot of leeching off people in the past, when I was pimply and alive, but I hadn't done much of it since. If anything, I was now trying to stay the hell out of everybody's way.

He took me to a visiting room, a long wall broken up into a series of individual stalls. Each dividing wall had a number stenciled above it in white paint. I got directed to stall #4 and sat down on a small stool, only to find Penny's round baby face gazing back at me through six inches of safety glass.

"Penny," I said. "God, dude, I am so glad to see you."

He shook his head, pointing to one ear. In the middle

of the glass barrier in front of me was a round rusted speaker. It took me a few seconds to find the black switch on the wall, and I flipped it.

"Hey, Penny," I said again. "I'm glad to see you, man."

"Wow," he said, sidestepping any hellos. "You look bad. *Real* bad-like. I hadn't realized how bad you'd gotten. Your sol's like a little candle, man." Behind him on the other side of the glass was yet another damned Afterlife waiting room, filled with folding chairs and sad faces.

"Can you get me out of here?" I asked him.

"Well, we're working on it." Then he thought about it. "Well, *we're* not working on it so much-like. But your caseworker is, some guy named Uri. They called him down from Avernus."

I was kind of stunned by this news. It was the first time in my life that anyone was fighting for me instead of against me. "What was I arrested for, anyway?"

"Fighting," said Penny. "The cops nabbed you instead of those other guys because they hate lost sols." Then he leaned in close to the glass and whispered into the speaker, his voice breaking up. "And like I said, you look bad, mama."

"Really?" I knew I'd been headed down that road, but I couldn't be as far gone as all that. It had only been a couple of weeks, hadn't it? Maybe not knowing that you're fading away is how it gets you.

"I'm sorry, Jo-Jo," he said, exhaling and setting his forehead up against the glass with a squeak. "I kind of missed it."

"Missed what?"

"Missed *you*," he said. "I lost track of you. I should have been paying closer attention. I always figured you were in the crowd somewhere."

First of all, it wasn't the guy's responsibility to follow me around like a guardian angel. God knows I'd never had one before. Second, I wasn't working the streets without being noticed. Plenty of folks saw me, one in particular.

"Max knew what was happening," I said.

From the look on Penny's face, I couldn't tell if this was news to him or not. He just nodded, chewing on his bottom lip. "Yeah," he muttered. "That makes sense."

I looked around at the guards napping on their feet near every entrance. "What do the cops care if I'm fading away?" I asked.

Sighing, Penny said, "The government likes everything around here to be in order-like," he said. "The spooks sort of do their own thing, but they give off a pretty depressing vibe. So the cops try to grab them, teach them lessons so there aren't so many stumbling around like zombies."

"Teach them, huh?" I said, thinking of my bunkmate, the world's saddest circus bear.

"I think it scares the cops to see lost sols as human, like them," Penny said. "So they make them into monsters."

That made sense to me. I was afraid of clowns for just such a reason. I thought of the long red shoes and the oversize hula-hoop pants, and shivered.

Then something Penny had said earlier struck me, and I moved in closer to the glass, noticing the face prints squished across its gray surface. "Wait, so if my agent guy is getting me out of the clink, what are you doing here?" I asked him. Penny was probably the biggest celebrity in the Afterlife. He always had boobs to autograph, afterlives to change.

"I have some bad news," he said. "It's Max."

A familiar blast of fear zapped my brain. I'd had so many nightmares of getting a phone call just like this. I guess once you've gotten it—the voice of a broken grandmother on the other end of the line—you live in fear of the next time it happens. Some days, you can't hear anything but those five words: "I have some bad news."

"What about her?" I asked.

"It's not Max exactly," he said. "It's her grandfather, the old man."

The fear eased but still seemed to eat away at my insides. "What about him?"

"He's burning up. He's dying."

That didn't sit right with me. "Isn't he already dead?"

"You know what I mean-like," said Penny. "He's passing on-like. He's not long for this world."

"Oh." I remembered how he'd looked last I'd seen him, like a glow stick that had wandered away from a rave—the exact opposite of how I was probably starting to look.

"Max left the tour to go home."

"And you're going too?" I asked.

Penny swallowed. "No," he said, staring hard at me

guiltily. I wasn't sure why. I'd never questioned his choices, and I sure didn't feel like starting. I had enough on my plate, thank you very much. "I've decided not to," he went on. "I learned a long time ago that we all make-like choices, we all give up things. It's what you have to do to survive, to grow." His strange beady eyes stuck on me. It was like looking into two empty windows with nothing and nobody behind them.

"What did *you* give up?" I asked.

He was impossible to read, a total freak show. "Max," he said. "I gave up Max."

Had I missed something? "What do you mean, Max?"

Penny flipped the switch to his speaker and the crackle died. He was thinking, maybe wondering if he should keep talking. Obviously he'd started a ball rolling and now was a little nervous about where it was headed, or if it was going to roll over him on the path to wherever it would end up. Sitting back up, he turned on our microphones and cleared his throat. "I loved her," he said. "I still do, as a matter of fact."

I didn't see what all the fuss was about. "Good for you," I said, feeling annoyed, maybe even a bit jealous.

"So why don't you go out with her?"

"Because loving Max is all about me," he said, jabbing a finger in his chest to make the point. "Me, me, me. She'll never return-like the feelings, but I feel them anyway. I can't help it. I always will."

"That's how it works," I told him. I knew all about that from Violet. I could see that he felt that way about Max. She was special too, to him . . . and to me.

"Maybe," he said. "But should I spend my entire afterlife pining away for someone because it makes me happy-like, even if it has nothing to do with her happiness?"

"If you care about her," I said.

This answer almost made him crack up, and he shook his head, a smarty-pants smirk on his pretty face. "Jo-Jo," he said, getting close to the speaker, so I could hear the pop of his lips through the wires. "As far as we know, a person may only have one extra chance to do something great-like after screwing up the first time. So instead of moping around after the girl I love, I'm doing something that actually makes a difference. Life is a series of forks in the road, mama. There is what you want, and there is what matters."

His voice crackled in and out, so the words sounded sliced up into bits and jumpy. "My afterlife isn't about me. It's about what I can do for other people. It's all about giving them a few more moments of living." He thought. "Like the Artifacts said:

> *All I want is all I want*
> *And what I want is you.*
> *All you want is what I'm not*
> *So now I need to choose."*

Again, I had trouble believing what I was hearing. "So you're not going back to be with Max?" I asked.

"No," he said sadly. "The band's going to hang around in Gehenna for a couple days. Bob Sumo is going to take over for Max on the drums." Penny thumbed over his shoulder at a guy[47] with a ponytail who was sitting under a big black poster that said, "Maintenance of the Sol Is a Virtue."

Finally, after all that time together, I saw the normal guy underneath all the trappings. No more famous rock

---

[47] Robert Drake Sumo, 1988–2004: cracked skull during miscalculated stage dive.

star. No more super-musical genius. Penny was just a wimp kid prone to the same selfish weakness as the rest of us. Oh, and he was acting like a total tool. "If you were Max's friend, you'd get your ass to her front door, pronto. That goes double if you love her. She needs her friends."

For a guy who could turn into a ball of fire, Penny was a wet blanket. Looking at me with big weepy eyes, he nodded, because he knew I was right. Still, as always, he was putting on a show, but this time just for me. "I never said I was strong," he whispered. His voice sounded hopeless, the same way I'd felt gazing up at the jail-cell window to find it all covered up. "And I never said I was right. All I said was that I'd made my choice."

"Right," I agreed. "And I've made mine."

I went back to the jail cell again. Head ringing, I sat up on the metal seat and pressed my knees to my chest to convince myself I was warm. My bear friend still sat on the bench across from me wearing that public-service announcement of a sign around his neck.

We didn't say much, just sat on those two benches staring at each other. A lot of the time I wasn't sure if he was awake, but every so often he'd scratch the back of his head with a clawless paw, or go over to drop those furry legs and sit on the can. I couldn't really tell if he was using it or not, but he'd sit there for a good five or ten minutes and sort of hang out.

Eventually, the big cop who'd taken me away the first time came back. Grumbling, he cracked our door and kicked the bear awake. Then he dragged him out by the ratty collar of his bear suit. And even though I wasn't the one getting set loose, I felt kind of glad that they were letting Smokey go. Bears belong in the wild—even fake ones that wear Velcro tennis shoes with zipper pockets.

Before walking down that long hallway, the bear man flashed me a big-eyed look through the bars of our cell. I couldn't see his lips moving underneath that giant head, but a muffled voice came out of the mouth hole. "Thanks, man," he said. "I couldn't have gotten through the night without you." And off he waddled.

I didn't know what I'd done, but I was glad to have done it. Helping others had never really been my thing.

After I'd been a guest for a grand total of twenty-two hours, they booted my ass out of the Gehenna drunk tank.

As soon as I hit the streets, I headed for the tramway station. Around me, the fires were still burning, tongues of smoke standing perfectly straight in the windless night, like rusty nails sticking up through a rotting floorboard. Hurrying through the reddish haze, which smelled suspiciously like the taco place a few blocks from my old house, I thought about Max, the old man, and Penny. It was less thinking than worrying. I saw their faces on every stranger and every faceless specter I passed in the barbecued streets of that hell of a city.

At the tram station, I grabbed the next car across the desert to Avernus. The trip was a lot longer than I remembered, and bumpier, too. At one point we skirted along the borders, and, head to the window, I gazed out over the cliffs to where you couldn't see what was what anymore, where the fog of the Edges waited past the cables and the rickety electrical towers. All that emptiness was kind of inviting, really. Better than the sadness that was waiting for me at the other end of the tramline.

When we swayed into the capital city, a wall of blackness filled the windows. An announcement crackled through the overhead speaker letting us know that the whole place was trapped in a temporary electrical blackout, and as the car hit the station, it came to a stop a few feet shy of the loading dock. The black outside was so solid you wondered if you'd smack up against it like a bug on a windshield. Everyone watched their step as they hopped from the open door to the waiting platform.

I followed the people in front of me through the station and down the steps. Their sols gave off just enough light to get around, but once they reached the street they went their separate ways, and I started to freak out. The buildings ahead had all been smothered in the inkiness of that blackout, and there was no way I was ever going to reach Max if I had to feel around in the dark like Ray Charles looking to cop a feel.

Luckily, I didn't have to. My fading sol was still burning strong enough to light my way. It was a miracle.

It took me two hours to cross the city alone in the dark, and by the time I reached Little Anglo, I was sprinting. I don't know why. Something inside told me that I needed to get to Max as fast as I could. I kept picturing Violet—in that covered casket, stretched out on her grandmother's floor, in trouble and me not anywhere nearby to help her when she needed it. That was the last time I'd moved that fast, to reach the girl I loved too late. So I tore down the block, jumping up on the broken sidewalk and nearly tripping over a folding table that had been left along the curbside, and then up the steps toward the only front door in the whole world that I recognized.

The front door of the apartment flew open before I had a chance to knock. And there she was: Max.

She stood in the doorway, lit from behind by a weak white lantern.

She'd been trying to cry. I knew without seeing a single tear on that moon face.

I wanted to say something, but all that came out was sputtering. Before I could finish, she grabbed me, hard, and hugged me like she was trying to kill me.

"Where have you been?" she said, voice shaky.

"I got tossed in jail," I said.

"Like I care," she whined, crushing me tighter. Suddenly, she lost all strength and her knees gave out. Together we made a pile on the floor of the entryway.

"Ben," she whispered.

"Is he dead?"

Max choked out a laugh. "Don't I wish," she said. Then she started sobbing with eyes as dry as Death Valley.

Just that once I wanted her to shed some real tears. So I could reach up and wipe them away. And for the first time since I'd died, I forgot about Violet. For just one second. I was too busy thinking about Max, who lay right there on top of me.

11

"How'd you get the news?"

"Messenger," she said, hands playing in her lap. They looked for something to do to keep all those restless fingers busy. "Here comes this delivery dork, almost wetting his pants-like when they let him into the dressing room. And before we can even say, 'Hey, welcome, pull up a chair, douche bag,' he lays it on me that my grandfather is on the brink-like of death. Talk about surreal." She picked up her drumsticks. The wood was chipped away from years of use, like a couple of chewed-up pencils.

The lights were on now, and the living room of the house hummed with electricity, bulbs sputtering. I sat next to Max on the love seat, tucked into the angles of the bay window that looked out over the street. No one was out. The lights of a house several blocks away blinked on and off, as if the whole building were hoping to send messages with Morse code.

All through our conversation, Max and I watched her cousin Kevin, who gently rocked back and forth in his chair at the living-room table. He was acting like one of those kids with a mental glitch, the kind who can memorize an entire phone book but who still needs to wear a helmet in case he throws some kind of spaz. His face was stretched tight and pale with sad.

"How long has he been sitting like that?" I asked.

"Two hours," said Max.

"Where is the old man now?" I asked.

"There," said Kevin in a robotic voice. He lifted one arm and pointed down the long hall that led to the bedrooms.

"I can hear you talking about me!" shouted a raspy voice. "Remember, you punks, this is supposed to be a *good* thing."

I shot Max a confused stare, but she shrugged. "He sounds much better than he is," she explained.

"I'll say," I said. Inching forward, I peeked around the corner and saw a pool of light spilling from one of the doorways onto the floor.

Snarling, Kevin stood up and kicked his chair across

the floor of the living room. It banged against the wall, making one of the old man's prized picture frames hop from its nail and slide down to crash against the floor— a photo of a nuclear explosion. The glass smashed into a billion pieces.

Kevin stomped into the kitchen and sat down in a different chair, but kept right on brooding like he'd been doing before.

"What was that?" yelled the old man from down the hallway. "What broke? How many times do I have to tell you to keep your hands off my stuff?"

Max jumped up and followed Kevin into the kitchen, twirling a drumstick in each hand. She stood over him, and the two glared at each other like the first one who blinked would turn to stone.

Kevin never had a chance. Max is the single most bullheaded chick you'll ever meet. He looked away, trying the silent treatment since the staring contest wasn't getting him anywhere.

"What's with the extra drama, mama?" demanded Max.

"Oh, shut up," he said.

"I said, what's your problem?"

"What's *my* problem?" asked Kevin, almost laughing. "What's *your* problem? Just leave me alone, will you?" He actually reached down, grabbed the seat of his chair, and then with a bunch of squeaks turned the whole thing around so she wasn't in his face. "For once don't stick your nose where it doesn't belong. Just go be with your friends." His voice was hoarse from all that tearless crying. "We've never needed you around before. We don't now."

Then Max pointed at him, like she was about to go all, "Make my day," on his pip-squeak butt, but she didn't say that. She said, "Well, I'm not going," and then turned around and headed over to join me on the love seat.

Once her back was turned, Kevin stood straight up off his chair. For a second I thought he was going to send the chair flying again. Instead, he clenched his fists and every other muscle on his tiny, ropy body and flexed all of them together, transforming into a crazy shaking little ball of rage. If that squirt had been able to explode into flames like Penny did, he would have for sure. We would have been toast.

"Why do you pretend to be so upset now?" he

shouted at Max. "He was never worth sticking around for, so why do you act so sad that he's moving on? How can you be such a liar?"

Max flinched, like she'd been stabbed in the back. She spun on him and hissed, "Say that again."

"No problem!" he said, still tough but starting to get scared. He was back in her sights, and that freaked him out. "All you ever do is fight with him," he said. "What do you care what happens?"

But then I realized that Max wasn't mad, not really. Her body was buckling with feelings, but not the angry kind. Stepping forward, she took Kevin's trembling fists in her hands.

"It's what we do," she told him softly. "That's how he and I love each other. We fight. It's weird, but it works. You know it works. You know *us*."

Kevin tried to stay pissed. I understood that. It made him feel like he had a way out of all that sadness, and that he wouldn't be trapped inside it forever. But he wasn't a fighter. And he was a sucker for Max—just like the rest of us.

Turning his wobbly hands over, he wrapped them around Max's and squeezed. "I actually think the arguing is kind of cute," he said quietly, calmly. "Sometimes I'd pick a fight with him just because I got jealous."

"Don't quit your day job," said Max, smiling, "as the peacemaker, I mean."

"Don't worry," he said. "Nobody does 'bitch' like you do."

I sat in the bay window, still waiting for the first punch, but it never came.

From down the hall, a weak voice called out, "Keep it down, you brats! Old guys are trying to die around here. Ever hear of a moment of silence?"

I volunteered to sit by the old man's bedside so they wouldn't have to, so they could hash out what they would do once they were on their own.

Perched on a stool by the old man's bed, I stared out his window at a patch of asphalt littered with gutted pillows and a flipped shopping cart. Leftovers of the old man's experimental flower garden bent dying between the black cracks. The strangled green stalks were turning a sickly gray. In a day or two those itty-bitty seedlings would be like everything else in the Afterlife, just like something you remembered from life on Earth, but

323

sucked dry of whatever had made them matter once.

As I teetered on the back legs of my stool, the old man suddenly opened his eyes and looked at me.

Now, everybody knows that "look." At the end of the horror movie, the slashing killer is dead, but some dumb, stacked chick has to walk over and make sure he is, only to have those devilish eyes flash open and scare the living shit out of you. Well, that's what happened. When the old man's milky-white eyes rolled back, I just about had a stroke. The legs of my stool went sliding out from under me as I got folded in half between the chair and the wall, hitting the floor with my ass.

I struggled to get up and not look like a total jerk, but it was too late for that. Righting the stool, I sat back down and waited for the insult I knew was coming, but he just lay there watching me.

Even though he'd been tucked under heavy blankets, they couldn't hide how much he'd brightened. The truth was clear right there on the sheets. A crispy, burnt layer of fabric rested under his glowing shoulders, and when he turned his head, you could see the curled-up flaking chunks of mattress that'd been all cooked.

"You can't fluff a pillow worth a damn," he said at last.

The insult didn't bother me. What had I expected?

"Yeah, well, it beats me smothering you with it," I said.

"Please," he groaned. "It would be doing me a favor."

He coughed, mostly to clear his throat. "Does it hurt?" I asked.

"Not a bit," he said. "It feels like floating in water while you're falling asleep."

"Sounds like a bad idea," I said. "You could drown."

"Too late," he said. "Already did that once, in my toilet in Albany."

That made me laugh.

As we sat in silence, his shrunken eyes swept over me, lingering for too long. He had something on his mind, and I didn't like the feeling that he was getting ready to lay it on me. I wanted to fill the quiet with sound, even if it was just chitchat.

"Why aren't you heading out to the edge of the world or whatever?" I asked.

"Eh," he said. "I'm not searching for anything. Besides, I always found walking the world to be too tiring. I learned to embrace my afterlife and settle down.

Burned real bright, thank you very much."

"So now you're all done . . . embracing?" I asked. His outline was so hard on my eyes that I had trouble paying attention.

"Looks like it," he said, managing a shrug of those fiery shoulders. "I gave up on regret a long time ago."

That had a real nice ring to it. I looked out at the old man's garden again. His plants may have shriveled up and died, but he had clearly grown, changed, since his time dead. Seeing those strangled weeds made me think back to the last time I'd watched over a person's bedside. Only that time the bedside had been a casket.

It was the night before we buried Violet, when the guys from the funeral home prepared to shut her up for the final time. I'd waited by the open lid and talked to her dead body, going on for so long that the funeral-home guys brought me a chair to sit in so I could get comfortable. I was pretty sure they didn't do that for just everybody, either. I kept thinking somebody would throw me out, or make me go home, but no one ever did. I sat and talked to Violet like I'd done so many times before, as she fell asleep in bed or slowly woke up in the morning to find me there, always there.

At last, the funeral-home guys came to close the casket, and I stepped aside and let them take her away. The home had closed hours before, but they'd let me stay on through the cleanup, the vacuuming, and the darkening of every lightbulb in the building. It was funny. Seconds after they rolled Violet's body out of that big room, I totally blanked on what I'd told her. Maybe all that matters is that I'd had a chance to say it. No regrets, just like the old man said.

Sitting beside his bed, I felt weirdly calm. The jittery glow of the turn-crank lamps made everything around us seem like it might disappear at any second, as if we'd never been there in the first place.

"I think things will be better when you leave here," I told him. "I don't know you too well or anything, but it sounds like you were good to your grandkids, and that's more than a lot of folks can say." I paused. "Most folks are assholes."

His eyes closed, the old man smiled. "Agreed," he said.

I kept talking, seeing as how he wasn't interrupting or telling me to shut up. "I don't even know if real death exists," I said. "But I like Max's idea. How the universe is just one big Disneyland, and we're all just moving our way from part of it to another. If that's the case, then we'll eventually have to wind up in one of the nicer places, with the clear skies and those green bushes carved in the shape of animals." I pictured heaven, or something like it. "I'm not sure if the best place would be Fantasyland or Adventureland, but both sound pretty good to me. Although Fantasyland might have the haunted house in it, and that might be kind of scary."

One eye—like a sun—cracked open. "Sounds great," said the old man, "but don't ever bullshit a bullshitter."

Instead of backing down under his wrinkly frown, I held my ground.

"I believe it too," he said at last. He took a deep, empty breath, watched me. There were still traces of a smile on what I could see of his face. If I'd ever met my grandpa, I'd have wanted him to look at me that way, with approval. "I hope things do get better," he said, "for your sake and mine."

"What do you mean?"

"You're as dim as a dying candle," he said.

I looked down at my fingers with their nearly transparent tips. He was right. Coughing, he tried to inch forward but had some trouble. "Come here," he whispered. So I leaned in closer.

"You're an okay kid," he whispered. "You may smell bad and look like a hillbilly, but Max thinks you're okay. She always has. That's not enough for some people. But it's enough for me."

"I'll take care of her," I said, trying to sound noble.

He chuckled right in my face. "*She'll* take care of *you*," he said. Then he couldn't stop giggling.

Nothing stings like having an old fart spend his last moments laughing in your face. "I could still smother you, you know."

"Kid," he said, "haven't you learned anything? We don't need to breathe." He paused. "Well, except maybe to laugh." And then he did just that. And what do you know? I did too.

On the morning of my third day back, the old man began to glow the most dazzling orange from the inside out. I wasn't sitting with him when it started, but I felt the heat from all the way down the hall and around the corner.

By afternoon, he was burning so bright you couldn't

329

even go into his bedroom anymore. I tried, but was blinded, and saw spots for half an hour afterward. So we waited, watching as the glow crept down the hallway, like sunlight inching its way across the asphalt on an early morning.

That was when folks started arriving—a lot of people, forming a line across the porch and down the steps, long enough to reach the sidewalk. Ancient old guys shook my hand and smiled crooked smiles. Young girls with pigtails and tattoos hugged me and tried to weep with joy, like I actually had something to do with what was going on.

For every saggy-faced geezer I helped out of his coat, or old biddy that hugged me for way too long to be comfortable, I wondered: Had this many people come to my funeral? Of course, it was one of *those* questions. The kind you know the answer to almost even before asking the question. My answer: a big fat *no*, to be sure.

I'd never made much of an effort to become part of anyone's life back on Earth, so few people would have missed me when I was gone. I hadn't left many empty Jo-Jo–shaped spaces.

But, from the looks of the mob filing through the

doorway, Ben had made a lot of friends. Whatever he'd done, it was pretty clear he'd had himself a big old afterlife.

The old man's sunny orange glow grew brighter, and warmer, and after a while his cranky shouts from the second bedroom stopped altogether.

"It's time," said Max.

The visitors moved outward to the walls of the living room and stood in a circle, their backs pressed to the plaster, facing the middle. Max and I rolled the old man's bed into the living room by propping the metal legs up on little wheeled dollies that somebody had brought with them—probably for just such a reason. Once the bed came to a stop, the people closed in.

The whole time, Kevin sat apart in a corner of the kitchen. He slumped on that same chair, eyes to the floor like he was napping.

No joke, the old man shined. His sol had gotten too big for that little space, and it lit the room with soft and beautiful warmth, like he was a star about to explode. It was impossible to look at, but I still couldn't look away. I didn't want to.

Max sat on the bedside and held Ben's hand. "We've

come together this evening to show the man Benjamin Insco that he has lived a meaningful afterlife," she said, as if she was reciting from scripture. I'd never heard her voice so clear, so adult. There weren't any slang or cuss words. She might as well have been praying. "We celebrate him," she said. "And we shall continue to celebrate him long after his light burns out."

I watched the old man. Everyone did. The light coming off him had gotten so crazy intense it hurt your brain. But no one turned from the sight, not one person. I think it was because we knew this was the last time we'd see him. It was his "viewing."

In the middle of all that weirdness, Max got up, and, setting Ben's hand carefully on the pillow, she walked into the crowd, which parted to let her through. She stepped into the kitchen next to Kevin.

People waited. The old man got brighter and hotter, whitewashing the walls.

Max crouched by Kevin's chair and put an arm around his shoulders. He shook real bad. Pulling him close, she whispered in his ear for a long time. Then, after a few minutes, they got up and headed back to the living room—together.

They sat on either side of the bed and took the old man's hands and clasped them in their own.

"Thanks, Ben," said Max, quiet.

"Thank you, Grandpa," said Kevin, his voice all over the place with feeling.

Ben didn't say or do much. His body turned a piercing orange and then red and then the color of pink lemonade. He seemed pretty content to just gaze up at Max, and then at Kevin, and then at Max again—back and forth until his eyelids began to sag and the glow grew so wicked the rest of us had no choice but to look away.

Then his sol broke over the room in a wave, and for a few seconds I was blinded by his blaze of glory.

And I actually felt it—his body becoming his sol, and his sol becoming the light, and the light breaking apart into nothing, like steam off a hot car hood. I don't know how I could tell, but I could. I'd lived a lifetime of ignorance, but that, I knew.

Then the light weakened and died. Only spots were left crackling in the corners of my vision. Ben was gone. All that was left was his burnt shape on his sheets, a wisp of smoke.

But damn, man, what a way to go.

Still on the bed, Max leaned over and rested her forehead against Kevin's arm. He kissed her on the top of her head. They didn't have anything left to say to each other.

Then Max turned to me. I was sort of reeling from the whole ordeal myself and feeling a deep, cold spot of grief forming in the pit of my stomach. The last thing I expected was to feel happy.

But for a girl whose grandfather had turned into a one-man meltdown thirty seconds ago, Max looked awesome. She looked *hot*. She was still crying, but with a great wide grin, cheeks burned brown, hair blown every which way like she'd just spent a day at the beach and didn't care how she looked because she felt fantastic.

I think I loved her.

12

The day after the old man's big exit, there was nothing to stop the three of us from sitting in the crawl space under the front porch, drinking from one of his old bottles of port wine marked "1878." On any other day I might have felt like some high roller drinking that fancy shit, but not that morning. That booze kicked like a mule going down, and it had the taste of sour grapes.

"Death is so stupid," said Max. She sat with her arms around her knees, head pressed up against a rafter. Rain beat on the porch above, silver trickles coming down through the cracks.

"I wish death would die," added Kevin, who had not stopped tossing pebbles since we got there.

I took the dusty bottle from Kevin's fingers. "Did he really even die?" I asked. "Maybe he just went to some Afterlife afterlife?"

They didn't have a response to that one.

Water dripped right onto Max's head with a tapping sound, but she didn't move. I'd never seen her so out of it. She hadn't said much, not since her grandpa went supernova and burned a permanent shadow onto the dining-room wallpaper. What are you supposed to say after something like that happens? For the last twelve hours she'd kept her lips good and plugged, looking off into space.

I knew that look. I knew it real well.

Sometimes there's just nothing you can do to shake the sad. It clings to you like static on your clothes. Every time you forget it's there, you touch a doorknob and get jolted back into remembering. The longer you walk around avoiding it, the worse it builds up, to the point where other people don't want to come near you because you might zap them and make them sad too.

Kevin burped, and then thumped his head back against the cinder blocks. "So what are we going to do with all this stuff?" he asked. He pointed off to where the crawl space opened up, a pit of gravel where a thick black tarp covered a mountain of square lumps. A corner of the tarp had been thrown back, leaving a dark opening. The three of us stared into it.

When Max had told me that the old man liked to collect junk that people carried over when they died, I figured she meant he had a shoe box in his closet. I was way off. When I saw his "secret" stash, I realized it wouldn't have stayed secret for long, not at the rate it was building up.

Stacked on the gravel were crates, maybe a hundred of them, maybe more. Inside of each were black sacks, some the size of coin purses, others as big as body bags. They were made of the slick, metallic fabric that Max had told me about, which worked sort of like leg warmers to trap the energy inside the objects and keep it from breaking out and vanishing into thin air. Each and every one had a small paper label with writing on it.

Even with the stuff tucked away safe in those satiny sacks, you could still feel their magical crackle. Crawl spaces are usually pretty gloomy, but ours was lit with a toasty light that colored all the grayness of the stones a solid gold. It was like we were having a happy hour in the belly of Fort Knox.

"I say we give it to the MIA," said Kevin. "In case you haven't noticed, this town can use all the power it can get."

"I'm not-like going to let them burn it," said Max, real cold.

"Why not?" asked Kevin. "Who needs it?"

"Nobody needs it," said Max, "but it's not ours to burn."

"Hey, nothing lasts forever," said Kevin. "What would be the point?"

"Duh, to last forever," said Max, shoving him.

"Think about it," said Kevin. "Peaks and valleys, right? You have to take the bad with the good. Otherwise we wouldn't feel anything."

"I could do without the bad," I said. "I'd still manage."

"I'm with you," said Max.

"I don't know," said Kevin, shrugging. "When you know something is coming to an end, you tend to make the most of it."

Max sucked on this for a second. Then she nodded toward the heap of bags and boxes underneath that black tarp. "I think we should return everything to its owners," she said.

"Yeah, someone should really do something about that," I added, knowing her little secret. "Have anybody in mind?"

457: Kelly, Reginald, of Savannah, Georgia, 48. Heart attack, 1978. Daguerreotype of old woman.

1,091: Chiang, Jules, of Boston, Massachusetts, 94. Pneumonia, 1990. Stick of incense.

2: Thatcher, Bernard, of Hampshire, U.K., 7. Influenza, 1918. Crucifix of wood, most likely given as gift based on inscription.

1,412: Escobar, Richard (Ric), of Mexico City, Mexico, 22. Decapitated, 2003. Small diamond earrings in the shape of pistols.

Every one of them had touched someone's cold body in the last minutes: a Bible tucked under an arm, a favorite suit brought out of storage, or a guitar that some fool never got around to playing. It felt wrong, picking through the leftovers of other people's lives. Each name was some dead person. Maybe they'd died scared, or alone, or fighting with all they had left inside them.

Now the very last link some folks had to that important moment sat on a shelf in some guy's musty basement. I understood why the old man had done it. He'd wanted to keep them safe, protected. But they weren't doing anyone any good under those dripping porch boards.

They were just fading away, sitting on the gravel losing their luster.

Since the old man didn't really have any possessions of his own, we went through his collection to sort of tidy up our heads a little, and to show some respect for what he'd spent most of his afterlife doing—snatching other people's heirlooms from the incinerator fires. Standing knee deep in black bags, it was hard to know if he was the world's biggest pack rat or just an old fool with his heart in the right place.

"There is some weird stuff in here, man," I said picking through a few of the smaller bags and peeking inside. That old saying, "I wouldn't want to get caught dead *fill in the blank,*" really made sense to me now.

"Don't even get me started on this pile over here," said Kevin. "I want to wash my hands after this."

"I wonder how many of these people died happy?" I said.

"It's funny-like," said Max, emptying a box of little black bags. "It doesn't matter who they are, every single person I've ever met-like in the Afterlife admits to having some regret. They could have had the best life ever, but they still think there was something they should have done differently. It's kind of cool-like." One side of her mouth curled into a smile.

"I don't know if I feel that way," I said, peeking into a big bag about the size of a sleeping bag. Down at the bottom was a pair of bicycle tires.

Max sat back down again, a tarp draped over her head like a hood. "What," she said, "you think your life was fine and dandy-like? Listen, no offense, but I saw some of your situation, and you could have used a little help."

"I wouldn't do anything differently," I insisted. "Well, maybe a few things—like, I'd probably be nicer to people." I closed the bag and thought hard. "But I wouldn't want to mess too much with how things happened, because in a way they all led me to Violet, which was when things finally got good."

"Here we go again," moaned Max.

"She's right," chimed in Kevin. "I barely know you, and even I'm sick of hearing about this person."

I raised my arms in a giant shrug. "Why is everyone always on my case about this?" I asked. It was about time I got a damn answer.

"Seen a mirror recently?" said Max coldly. "You'll

understand." She was talking about my fade, how I was getting weaker, like those ghouls out ghouling up the streets.

"I've got time," I said, trying to convince her. "This is my life now."

"Your life, huh?" said Max, hopping closer on her butt. "I'll tell you why I'm always on your case about this." She held up one of the tags that went with a magical black bag. "Remind me, how old were you when you died-like?"

"Seventeen," I said. "Give or take a few months." I honestly was having trouble getting the timing exactly right. Remembering details was tough.

"And how long did you know Violet?" she asked.

"Almost two years," I said. I wasn't sure where she was going with things.

Max shook the slip of paper in my face, her eyes harsh. "You were seventeen, mama!" Corkscrews of dark hair jiggled in her face as she railed. "You lived for seventeen years, but you talk like you only lived for two! I'm not a mathematician, but those numbers seem pretty messed up-like."

"Quality not quantity," I said quietly, picking up

another sack. Untying its string, I eased open the top and released a funnel of light. Inside, a couple of gold teeth rolled around in the midnight folds of fabric.

"Get your face out of that bag and look at me," said Max. I knew that tone in her voice. She wasn't asking. She was giving me a direct order.

"What?" I said, turning. Max Insco wasn't the only one who could get bitchy.

"What I'm saying is that you talk like your life didn't even start-like until you met your stupid girl-friend," she said. Her powerful voice grew and filled that musty crawl space. "I'm sure Violet was incred-ible, Jo-Jo." The way she said it, I knew she meant it. "I'm sure she was beautiful and exciting and sweet and smart-like, and everything, really. But there was a Jo-Jo before she came along. Life doesn't start when you fall in love."

I stared into her dead eyes, and there was so much feeling behind them. Max wanted me to move on. She wanted it more than I did.

"That's how it happened to me," I said real matter-of-fact. "I was nothing before Violet. If you knew me better, you'd know that."

There was no sound but for the streaming rain and drip.

"Okay," said Kevin, snapping his fingers together and looking pretty awkward. "Let's all get back to work, shall we?"

"No!" Max said sternly. She stood up perfectly straight under the tarp, water sliding down the sweeping plastic to the gravel. "I am sick of it."

"Sick of what?" asked Kevin.

"Sick of him and his lovesick," she said.

"So am I," he said, shrugging, "but what can we do about it?"

"Oh, I've got some ideas," said Max, and her pissed scowl downshifted into this sly smile. It was not a look a guy wanted to see pointed in his direction. No, sir.

"What?" I said. "It's not like you can change history. I'm dead."

"True," she said, "I can't rewrite the past. But I *can* show you the present."

"And how the hell are you going to do that?"

"I'm not. *He* is." She turned to her cousin. "Kevin reincarnates for his job."

I stopped, bottle at my lips.

The runt only shrugged. "Hey, it's a living."

Seeing as how I thought reading was for freaks, I'd never had much use for libraries. Folks were always saying that "reading takes you places," but from the look of all those dusty old books and cubicles, it wasn't anyplace too interesting.

The place Kevin worked looked like a library, like the place the rest of the world stashes its super-nerds so they could all keep their annoying questions to themselves. We walked in the front door, trying to stay quiet but doing a pathetic job of it, as Max knocked her shin on a file cabinet and yelped—but only for a second. Kevin flattened a hand over her face to keep the shriek from leaping out.

The lobby rose up real high through the whole center of the building, maybe ten or twelve floors all the way to the ceiling. Balconies on every level circled the walls and looked down on the floor below. Despite being roomy, the place had been jammed with so many metal shelving units that it felt like you'd accidentally wandered your way into a crowded closet. Way up at the very top, a skylight shaped like a star gave you a glimpse of those gloomy heavens overhead. In the Afterlife, skylights were kind of pointless, really, since the words "sky" and "light" didn't really have much to do with each other.

The three of us hurried across the floor to a hallway, single file because you couldn't fit around the hundreds of shelves any other way. As we shimmied past, I saw that the drawers were packed with little slips of paper, like those Dewey decimal cards they'd had in libraries before computers showed up. One time, when I'd left school and cut through the parking lot out back, I found all the old cards tossed into the Dumpster, thousands of slips of creamy cardboard.

"Come on," whispered Kevin, motioning us toward the corner of the lobby, where a single set of staircases wound up to the higher floors.

"Couldn't we have taken the elevator?" I asked, ready to pass out on step 216, four steps from the end of our climb.

We'd scaled three long flights of stairs before reaching Kevin's floor. It didn't matter that we didn't need to breathe—I still felt winded by the time we opened the door to the Office of Reincarnation and spilled onto the hard carpeted floor.

"Listen, I'm just an intern," said Kevin. "There's one elevator, and it's only for full-timers."

"He may be an intern," said Max, dropping down next to me. "But he's an intern with a key and full security access."

"Not if he keeps coming in after hours," said Kevin. "Now come on."

At one end of the fifth floor, behind a small horseshoe-shaped desk, sat a night watchman[48] with his nose stuck in a book called *For Whom the Bell Tolls*. The cover showed two folks getting it on, and both of them were losing their shirts.

Kevin gave the watchman a little wave and leaned one elbow on the edge of the desk, suave. It wasn't a good look for him. "Hey, Malcolm," he said.

"Hey, Mr. Insco," said the watchman, glancing up. His thick glasses made him look like he was about to go scuba diving.

---

[48] Malcolm Wittinger, 1924–1973: died in an airline flight of tourists bound for a swingers resort in Mexico.

"Busy tonight?"

"Nope. Dead." The watchman took a breath, eyes flickering up from his read to take a good long gander at me and Max. "Are you working tonight?"

"Yeah," said Kevin, nodding like he was buried under the workload, a monster deadline, the big faker. "It's a busy time."

"Okay, then," said the watchman. "Have a good one."

Tapping the desk once with his pointer finger, Kevin muttered, "Right." Then he took two steps toward the stairwell before rocking back on one heel. "So, can I bring you anything from the other side?" he asked the guard nicely.

Malcolm the night watchman closed his book and took off his glasses, setting them on the desk in front of him. He folded his hands together. The room was so damn still you could hear the guy's keys jangling in the pocket of his trousers.

"I've made a list," he said, like he was a kid talking to Santa Claus.

The waiting-room hallway was lined with inspirational posters, but instead of saying "Teamwork" and showing a bunch of guys rowing a boat, or "Courage" with some joker climbing a mountain with one of those spiky axes, they said things like "Shame" and had a photo of a blond freckly kid frying ants with a magnifying glass. At the end of the hall, Kevin unlatched a wall full of locks and then pressed a ten-digit code into an old grungy keypad and said his full name twice into a battered old intercom. The speaker buzzed. A red bulb blinked. The lock clicked. Kevin opened the door marked "Stacks" and brought us to his place of business.

I hadn't been expecting anything too exciting, but by far this was the least interesting place I'd ever been. Like all rooms where Kevin worked, the floors were crammed with shelves, drawers were pulled from their tracks and stacked on top of one another, and dust coated everything. A small conveyor belt, like the one for bags at the airport, ran along the wall, curving into a little hole in the wall that was covered with rubber flaps. On the far wall was a door. It looked pretty normal—gray, paneled, a knob that had been all deformed from years of hands grabbing it and turning it.

"Can I get a Coke?" I said, pointing to the big machine in the corner that I had just sort of figured was a soda dispenser because that's what it looked like.

"We do *work* here," said Kevin.

I walked around. The clunky old machine wasn't a cooler but this vintage punch-card computer. There was a slot for where you stuck a thin card, and there was a lever next to it that had been repaired with string and a bit of chewing gum. The manufacturer plate on the front said: "GROD INDUSTRIES," and the year had been scratched off with a sharp object.

Rectangular punch cards, which I now assumed went with the machine, littered the place. I tweezed one from the closest filing cabinet with my thumb and pointer finger. It had a mess of tiny squares missing from the surface, forming a sort of pattern, like somebody had gotten bored in that messy little dump and decided to invent paper Tetris. At one end of the card were the words "2—Dearborn, Michigan: 48126" printed in an old-fashioned computer type.

And there were hundreds more names and places where that one had come from—hell, maybe millions. The Office of Reincarnation was chock-full of them.

"What is all this?" I asked.

"These are the stacks," said Kevin. "They belong to the Department of Employment and Deployment, which is where you go to get jobs back on Earth."

"You can get jobs back on Earth?" I asked. Earth, I could barely picture it.

"Not any jobs you would actually want," said Kevin. "You've heard of reincarnation, right?"

"Is that when you come back as a camel or something?"

He smiled, thumbing through the box of cards. "Well, reincarnation says you can come back to life by being reborn into a new body. Some people like to think that you can come back as an animal, but we don't do that. It's against our policies." He looked like he was going to say more but then ended with, "There was an incident, with a tapir. That's all I'm going to say."

"So no animals," I said.

"No animals," Kevin confirmed. "Anyone going back has a job. Most of them are gathering material for basic survival"—and he counted with his fingers—"for construction, clothing, and infrastructure. The rest of the guys out there . . . well, their orders are classified. But there's always a trickle of people coming and going."

"So why the hell isn't everybody zipping back and forth?" I asked.

"You need an object to do it, to focus your path on a particular spot on Earth, and we only retain a certain number of items for that purpose. The rest are shipped down to the rendering plants at the bottom of the mountain so that we can have electricity."

"Got any open jobs?" I asked.

He smiled. "No. Only people willing to give up everything are sent back. It requires total seclusion, no contact with anyone. You're supposed to help people get the most out of life during their time there, to avoid ending up, well"—and he gestured to the Afterlife at large—"*here*."

"I want in," I said. I missed wind and birds and bacon cheeseburgers.

"No way," he said, laughing. "It's too stressful. You have no idea. Too many people have snapped under the pressure and lost it. They've blown their cover."

"Really, like who?"

"The guy who shot Kennedy, for one," said Kevin,

raising his eyebrows. He stopped on a card, read it, and then moved on, thumbing.

I walked up beside him, noticing Max peeking into the rubbery mouth of the conveyor belt hole. "No shit?"

"On my honor," he said, raising one hand like he was giving an oath.

At last, he whipped out a card and held it up, reading it silently as he stepped away from the drawer and up to the weird soda-machine computer. "This should work perfectly," he said, mostly to himself. "Industrial accident, three people dead."

"And that's a good thing?" I asked.

Shrugging, he pressed a button on the rickety old keyboard and the computer bleeped and blooped. "Hey, when you want to travel in a group, the occasional exploding fry cooker can really come in handy."

That didn't sound like any fortune cookie I'd ever read.

Kevin inserted the card into the slot and the machine suddenly rumbled to life, chugging with a rattle of nuts and bolts. Down came the lever and practically broke off in his hand. The conveyor belt jolted and started moving. It slid real slow, empty for a few seconds until a small black box appeared and brushed under the rubbery curtain. We followed its progress round the curve and to a jittery stop in front of us. I recognized the black material. It was the same as all those sacks in the cellar, the same as Max's magic duffel. With a last robot gasp, the computer shut down.

"Voilà," said Kevin. Grinning from ear to ear with a workman's pride, he snatched up the box and cracked the lid. He reached in and took out a handful of something and handed some of it to me, and some of it to Max.

In my palm, I held a fancy, yet totally bogus, gold watch. The glass face was shattered with a couple spidery lines down the center. The thing was busted but good. Yet even though it would never tick again, that watch was still slightly warm and alive in my grip, a hot potato.

In her palm, Max held a gross pink retainer, like from somebody's mouth. Kevin, he had a diamond wedding ring.

"Thanks for giving me the nasty one," whined Max.

I slid the watch onto my wrist. Kevin put on the ring. Max . . . well, Max *held* the retainer in two fingers, completely grossed out.

Kevin dropped the empty box back to the belt and herded us across the room toward that lonely, beat-up-looking door with the worn-down knob. "We'll have thirty-six hours," said Kevin, "give or take twelve."

"Give or take *twelve*?" I said.

"Hey, man, life-tripping isn't an exact science," said Kevin. "Don't be afraid. When it's time to come back, you'll feel the tug. Don't fight it. There's no fighting the Open Door."

"Is this the door?" I asked, checking out the squished metal knob.

"Do you see another door, bunny?" asked Max, antsy.

"Looks old," I said.

"It's one of the most ancient parts of the Afterlife," said Kevin. "It's been here as long as we have."

"What, fifty years?"

"No, 'we' as in 'people,' stupid," said Max. "You're hopeless."

Just then, the door rattled, as if something big was

fighting to get through from the other side. The closer we moved toward it with our little objects, the more the hinges pulled against their screws. I didn't like all the special effects, made me antsy.

"I think this is a bad idea," I said.

"No," said Max. "I'm going to show you what you've left behind, good or bad."

"It doesn't make a difference," I said. "What's done is done."

"Doesn't make a difference, huh?" she said. "Funny. I was thinking the same thing about your whole crummy life. Care to prove me wrong?" She winked pure evil.

Then I noticed the old beaten gym mats on the floor at my feet, and the one on the opposite wall. Looked like a landing pad, but for what?

"Just go into the light," said Kevin, cool, smooth, comforting.

"Hell no," I said.

"Relax, fool," said Max.

"*You* relax," I managed to get out before a rush of wind tore the Open Door wide and snatched my legs out from under me.

I screamed as Kevin banged into me. Together we cracked up against the door frame and went spinning this way and that into nothing. The whole time, Max was whooping it up. She was having a blast, as usual.

TRACK 4:
WAS IT A WONDERFUL LIFE?

BALTIMORE

I screamed as loud as I could until—

"Excuse me, sir?"

It was a voice.

It twittered in the back of my mind, singsongy. I thought it might be my conscience telling me something important, trying to get my attention. But I knew better than anybody that if I had a conscience that loud, I'd have turned out totally different.

"Sir?" said the voice again.

It was a girl, her accent full of signature Baltimore sass.

"Excuse me, *sir*, I've called the police. They should be here any minute."

That made me open my eyes, and it was the color that struck me first. Hard.

It came at me from everywhere at once, a million different colors. I had to shut my eyes it smarted so much, every ray a needle to the brain.

Then I smelled the leftover traces of cooking meat, and if I'd had a full stomach, I might have just emptied it right there in the orange-and-red plastic booth. Sure, I'd never been no food snob, but the smell of that beef was so strong, so ripe with grease, it about cured me once and for all of my carnivorous ways.

Sounds crashed over me—cars whooshing from the street outside, a conversation across the room about someone's surprise birthday party, and two stoner employees at the closed cash registers counting out their cash. After bowling me over good, all that noise settled into an easy background rumble, like engine noise.

"Sir?" asked the voice, and a finger tapped me, and very slowly I turned my head to look into the blank face of a girl holding a mop and a bucket.

"What?" I said, feeling the deep buzz of my voice shaking through my chest. I remembered it, and it felt damn good.

"Sir, you're naked . . . by the children's play area."

And so I was. And so we all were, naked as the days we were born.

Max, Kevin, and I sat cheeks to seat in a booth of a

burger joint on St. Paul Street in downtown Baltimore. Outside the front windows, streaks of yellowy lightning lit the wet walls of the skyscrapers. Rain streamed down the glass and made the full moon look like a melting ice cube in the dark sky. I grinned at the sight, plastic seat warm against my thighs, floor sticky against the soles of my bare feet.

I gasped for air, though I still didn't need to breathe.

Lucky for the three of us, the restaurant was closed. Otherwise we might have had a riot on our hands, or at least a charge of public indecency. It wasn't too lucky for the night manager, though. She gripped that mop handle like it was a baseball bat, and made this real unfortunate face that brought out her green braces, which made it look like she'd just munched a box of apple-flavored candy. Her name tag said, "LITTLE BIT."

"Where'd you come from?" she asked, suspicious.

"Never mind that," said Max through a hefty moan. "Tell me, girl, is the kitchen still open?"

For once, I didn't care. I didn't care that I walked out buck-naked into a trash-strewn alley at whatever o'clock on a whatever night in downtown wearing nothing but a knockoff Rolex, because I felt fantastic. And I never feel fantastic about nothing.

The three of us skedaddled out of that burger joint just as the police were getting close enough for us to hear their sirens. As we stumbled out shoeless onto the asphalt, a rat heard us coming and darted quick between two plastic trash bins. Beautiful. Everything was cold and wet, and the night sky had a deep plum color through the drizzle.

I could hardly keep under control. I felt like sprinting through the streets, which was weird, I guess, since the ground was littered with glass, and disintegrating hamburger buns bobbed in the pothole puddles. Still, I wanted to dash through the intersections shouting at the top of my lungs—no, *laughing* at the top of my lungs. I was alive! My sol felt like a Molotov cocktail.

"Settle down," barked Max. "You look like a couple of head cases."

Kevin acted about as hyped as I was, like he wanted to run a marathon in nothing but his hairdo.

One time, when I was just a little-shit kid, back when my ma had just passed on and our pa was off in mourning, which meant getting trashed with the guy who helped him snake sewer lines, my sister and I snuck into this motel down by the 295 expressway.

It was just some low-rent Super 8 or Motel 6 or one of those chains that's got a number in the name, but they were swank enough to have a hot tub for guests. We spent an hour in that hot tub talking about Ma and stuff we'd remember about her no matter what happened— come hell or high water, as they say. We laughed about the way she'd leave our clean laundry on our beds, all the pieces of clothing laid out in outfits to look like an invisible person was lying there. Or how she would sit on the TV remote and pretend to have magic powers, waving at the screen as she shifted positions, causing the channels to change. That trick had us going for a long time.

At the end, we climbed out of the hot tub and jumped into the cold of the pool, and it felt like dropping into a bucket of ice water. Every cell in my body cried out in pain at first, but then a feeling of calm washed over me. I felt alive. I felt glad to feel. I felt lucky.

That's what it felt like when you came back from the dead. It's not every day you stand there wanting to celebrate just standing there, just being alive. You wanted to thank somebody.

Max covered her naked body like an expert, arms thrown over her top and bottom. Still, in the places where she was too big for her arms to cover, the skin popped up around her fingers. I would have stood there gawking if I hadn't suddenly felt my own bits and pieces blowing in the wind. I moved to cup myself, and Kevin followed my lead.

"Right," said Max. "First course of action, clothes."

"Then what?" asked Kevin.

"Then we pay a visit to an old friend," she said.

Ten minutes later, we walked into Harlan Hogg's High Art tattoo parlor on Baltimore Street, dressed in trench coats we'd stolen from a Goodwill box at a Unitarian church that had left its doors unlocked. To strangers we probably looked like a team of strippers that had fallen on hard times, but to Harlan, we looked like the last people he wanted to see strolling in his front door. He sat behind the counter reading *Glamour*, boning up on "Sex Tips You Won't Find Anywhere Else." And he was relaxed.

At the door chime, he jerked in his chair. Then,

when he saw the three of us, we got a quick preview of what that old biker would look like in the Afterlife—his face went from piggy pink to pale in a split second, the poor bastard.

"You," he wheezed.

"Me," I said, though he could have been talking to any of us.

"Oh, keep your boxer shorts on," Max told him. "First order of business is beer. Take us to your liters."

After two Pabst Blue Ribbons and three hours of Grand Theft Auto, Kevin fell asleep on the beanbag sitting in the corner of Harlan's home theater, right under a black light poster of a skull with fire for hair. Kevin had never seen a video game before, and he took to it like a guy who'd just figured out that you could use your privates for something other than peeing.

Max and Harlan were down the hall in the tattoo parlor. I could hear the electric buzz of his ink gun. It sounded like they were shaving.

Camped out in a leather easy chair, I watched the sun start its rise through the bars of Harlan's window. Light crept over the rooftops and stretched yellow down the road. It was like a dam had busted and was flooding the city. You forget how nice sunrises look when you're stuck in a place that's got none. Even a hellhole like Baltimore Street looked sort of beautiful in the morning. All the neon shuts off. Cops ditch their beats and go home to see their kids. Even the sketchy folk who wander during the wee hours seem to disappear, replaced by business dudes hurrying to the office.

As I slumped there finally hitting that real sweet spot of snoozing, it dawned on me: It was a new day, another chance to screw up—like I always did—or to make up for all the times I should have done better but didn't. Maybe there was something to what Max was saying after all.

It was funny. I'd had a gun to my own head, and I'd died. But only now was I starting to see why being alive was so cool.

Harlan's tattoo parlor looked just like it had when we'd left it, meaning it was still a dump that smelled like disinfectant and clove cigarettes, only now the smells were about fifty times stronger and reminded you what real queasiness felt like. Crossing the parlor, I noticed a stench and then saw somebody's leftover lunch bag sitting on the counter, untouched—a burrito, I could tell by the day-old funk of it.

"I see you didn't take my advice and go home." Harlan Hogg was bellied up to his secret workbench wearing nothing but a pair of wrinkled flannel boxers and black cowboy boots. He had rubber gloves jammed up to his elbows and goggles snapped over his dark sunglasses. He looked like Chewbacca from *Star Wars*, if Chewbacca had been shaved and poured into a pair of jockey shorts.

I stared, but he was too busy to care, fiddling with a pair of big plastic tubs full of that magic ink. He swirled blues and greens with a glass stirrer, tasting the mix with a fingertip to the end of his tongue.

"Morning," he said.

"Morning," I said, walking in. "Listen," I told him. "Lose the cable bill and invest in some pants, mama."

He raised his eyebrows over the top of those plastic goggles and then grunted. "Hey, man, some people do their best work in their skivvies. I'm a dynamo in nothing but my boots and my booty."

Then Harlan pushed the jugs of ink out of the way

and, snapping his goggles up onto his forehead, he took off his sunglasses and showed me his eyes. I didn't think it would be such a big deal, but it was like looking through a window that had just been wiped clean.

People are funny that way. One second they're a drain-clogging dust bunny, and then when you see a pair of milky-blue eyes peeking out, you're suddenly able to pick out the face underneath all the tangles. It's like the old-man beard he'd been sporting was just a disguise. Harlan Hogg didn't look all that much older than the rest of us, maybe thirty-five.

"What's it like, Jo-Jo?" he said. "Over there, I mean?" Searching me with those big blues, he mindlessly played with the skull ring on his middle finger. "Isn't like what I expect, is it?"

"I don't know," I said. "What'd you expect?"

"Something better than this," he said.

I had no comment, but I think my face gave me away.

His voice grew soft, real un-Harlan-like. "I lost my wife a ways back," he mumbled. "We got married young." He swiveled the skull ring in circles. "It feels like a million years ago now, but I still remember it pretty good." He tapped his chest with a closed fist. "She got cancer in her left breast." His voice cracked a bit.

When he looked up again, the dark sunglasses had found their way back over his gaze. With eyes covered, his beard seemed to rise up and swallow his face. "I always hoped she went someplace nice," he said, dry mouth smacking. "You know? So I could sleep at night."

"Yeah, I know," I said.

Jaw clenched, Harlan looked up at me. "Would you do me a favor, man?" he said, voice pretty wobbly for a biker dude. He dug around for his pocket. But he wasn't wearing pants, and it's tough to empty the pockets of your underwear when there aren't any. Holding up one long, hairy finger, he slid off his stool and left the room.

When he came back, he was walking slowly with his hands cupped together in front of him.

A small seashell earring rolled around in his palms. It was the kind you might drop five dollars for down at the harbor, as cheap as cheap gets.

But Harlan carried it like it was worth a fortune.

He shuffled close to me. "Her name is Carol Ann

Hogg, or Jensen. That was her maiden name." The earring looked like it had never been worn or just once, maybe. "Take this with you. Take this and give it to her."

"Don't you want it?" I asked, knowing that if I did take it, I'd never see Carol Ann Hogg, or Jensen, or whatever the hell her name was. It didn't work like that.

"She died wearing only one of them," he said. "She's probably been looking for the matching piece."

I didn't know how to tell him the truth without hurting him. "Trust me, man," I said. "It will do you more good if you keep it here. Over there, it won't matter much."

But he shoved those meaty hands right under my nose. "It hasn't done me any good," he said. "I got closets full of reminders. I got a head full of them." He took a deep breath. "To tell you the truth, the more of her stuff I give away, the better I feel."

I took the earring, and since I didn't have pockets either, I just closed it in my fist until I could locate a pair of pants.

Wiping his forehead, he sat back, took out a cigarette from where the pack was secured in the waistband of his underwear, lit it, and blew out a smoky stream. "I should have never learned to do this," he said.

"To do what?" I asked.

"To tattoo."

"Yeah, and why's that?"

With a shrug, he chuckled. "You should never get it into your fool head that anything in life is permanent."

Toting my fourth beer—its teeth sinking sharp into my head, like real alcohol should—I walked down the apartment hallway to the small second bedroom. Against the wall by the closet I made out the shape of a futon on a skinny wooden frame. A bright yellow beam of sunlight cut through the blinds and across the pillows and over Max's sleeping face.

I crawled onto the futon and collapsed with a groan. I couldn't sleep, even though I wanted to. Alive again, my body worked like a crazy powerful radio, picking up every signal that the world was sending out. The sheets were so clean and crisp it almost hurt to lie on them— I felt every single stupid stitch. Around me, the lights from the hall and the sunrise and the closet all burned with jagged edges, like shards of glass.

So I lay there for a while, one hand behind my head, sipping from my warm bottle and thinking Max was long-gone asleep, until she rolled over and looked at me.

Our noses touched. I don't think she meant that part to happen. Her breath was bitter, nothing but sour beer between us.

"Do you think Penny and I make a good couple?" she asked.

"Are you serious?" I asked.

"No. I'm kidding. That's why I asked."

In that shaft of alley light, her head looked sort of cut off, alone and bodiless. Maybe I was sick, but I thought she looked so kissable just then, and I hadn't found anyone kissable for . . . so long. Weeks ago, just that thought alone would have made me feel like a total A-hole. But for whatever reason, it didn't anymore. Just because someone looks kissable doesn't mean you're going to do anything about it.

"I don't know much about relationships," I confessed. "Do you like him?"

"I used to," she said. Then she snuck a hand under the sheets and took the bottle away from me. "Has he told you how much he's in love with me?"

"No," I said quickly.

"You're a liar."

"Yes," I added before she could attack.

She went to take a drink but then smelled the warm beer in the bottle and wrinkled her nose, handing it back. "Penny and I tried it once-like," she said, "when I was a big bunny. It was good then, when I needed him, when I needed someone to save me. But we're very different. Little things, like when you lived-like, can make a big difference. It's so stupid."

"What do you mean?" I asked, setting the bottle on the ground and pulling a blanket up from the foot of the bed.

"Like, I grew up in the seventies when punk was exploding. Every single day I wore this blue blazer with fake chevrons pinned to it, and for a while I had my hair in spikes. I ditched my sixteenth birthday party to see the Damned. Penny wasn't even *born* until 1985." She scratched her nose and shifted, trying to get comfortable. "See, that's messed up. But it's even more messed up that something so stupid and trivial means so much-like to me."

"It's not messed up," I said. "Where you come from is important." And then I remembered my little house on the corner. "But it's not everything."

"You're right," she said.

I lay there staring at a crack in the ceiling and thinking about Penny, the little guy who could go up in flames like a can of hair spray meeting a match. "I don't think *when* he lived is the thing," I said. "I think it's that Penny's a dork, or maybe he was when he was alive. Maybe he was real different than he is now, and when he died, he took that starting-over thing to heart." I threw the blanket over me, over us both. "I bet that underneath all the rock and roll, Penny's pretty vanilla."

This seemed to hit her someplace, a soft spot. Her face stayed real still like a statue. I was so used to her only breathing every once in a while that it was strange watching the sheets rise up and down above her boobs. She still didn't need the air, but maybe being home again made her wish she did. Made her wish she was really alive and not just playing house. "I guess you can't really know someone when you're dead-like," she said softly. "Who they used to be, I mean."

I liked the way Max looked. I always had. There was always something electric behind her smile, a crackle, like she was the one in the band who should have caught on fire, not Penny. "Isn't that why we go to the Afterlife," I asked, "to do a better job of being us?"

And at that she flashed a small smile. "That's the best way I've ever heard it put-like," she said. "I never liked the whole *'This one thing is your reason for being!'* thing. It scares me shitless."

"You always seemed pretty sure about it," I said.

"People make you feel like if you don't find the one thing you're meant for, it's over. It's done. What if I'm meant-like to do a lot of things? What if I can make a difference in more than one way? What if I want-like to play music, *and* see the world, *and* write books, *and* try to find my brother, *and* do whatever else I want to do?"

"I don't think it's about what you do," I said, being real picky with my words. "I think it's about *why* you do it."

Her mouth was the only thing that moved. "Yeah?" She paused. "Then tell me, mama, *why* are you looking for your girlfriend?"

"Because . . . I think she would maybe want me to?"

"You think she would maybe want you to spend your whole afterlife looking for her?" asked Max. "You think she'd maybe want you to be miserable-like, for years and years and years?" She waggled a finger in my face. "You think, but you don't *know*."

I didn't have a response to this, but luckily she kept talking. "But you aren't afraid to talk about the past, about how things about it still hurt. I think that's why you mean so much to me. Most guys don't do that, Jo-Jo. Most *people* don't. They just pretend it never happened." Her smooth fingers slid down my neck. They weren't cold, because I was dead now too, unlike the last time we'd spent together in that stinking city. We were the same now, me and Max.

I rolled over, and we lay there almost nose to nose. Our legs bumped together, our wrinkly puckered kneecaps kissing. The room was dark and silent and small, the walls boxing us in on all sides. "You remind me of my old life," said Max. "I'd forgotten a lot, but you've brought it gurgling back up-like. You remind me of living even though you're dead."

"Is that a good thing?" I asked, hopeful.

"It's agony," she said.

Up close, I could see Max real good for once. I'd never seen someone carry so much sorrow around on her face like that. I wanted to reach out and smooth the creases.

"Good night, Jo-Jo," she said. Then she moved in close and kissed me softly. It felt like a snowflake landing on my cheek. I could still feel it as I drifted off to real sleep for the first time in a long while.

BALTIMORE

Harlan let us borrow his minivan. For some reason, I'd just assumed that a dude with a ratty beard and an old black leather vest, named Harlan Hogg, would own a Harley-Davidson, or one of those choppers with the long front wheel, and a helmet with a spike on top. But he had a minivan, with a car seat strapped into the back. The moral of this story: Never judge a freakishly huge biker by the size of his 'stache.

When we left Harlan's place, we looked as normal as a trio of dead teenagers was ever going to look. Max wore some baggy, flowery number that had belonged to Harlan's dead wife and made her look like a forty-year-old housewife getting spruced up for a church potluck. As for me and Kevin, we had to borrow from the Hogg himself, meaning leather, and we ended up looking like a couple of junior members of that old disco band the Village People.

Even though we'd been under the needle and gotten some color, there wasn't any saving us from the stares of the passersby on the street. Walking along Gay Street, we got about five ogles and a couple of flat-out jaw drops.

My first and only time in Harlan's torture chair had left me looking pretty much exactly the same as I always had, except my skin was a sick shade of orange-brown. Harlan had admitted to messing up my mix, but only after I called him on it.

Kevin ended up with a pretty classy brownish tone, like a walking sweet potato. It made him look a little more handsome and less like a pasty-faced runt. His sunken eyes sparkled with flakes of gold.

Then there was Max. She'd kept her skin its regular ice-milk white, but her eyes gleamed with bright blue centers, like they were a couple of frozen spearmint Life Savers. Her curls moved in the morning city breezes, blowing everywhere and black, a big old dead head of hair.

We tore out of there with Cheap Trick on the stereo, windows down all the way and Harlan's rabbit's foot key chain swinging against the steering block like the ticking of a clock. It felt good to be on the road again, the wind making the hair on my arms stand up. Just like old times—*alive* times.

"Where are we heading?" I asked, heading south toward the busy harbor.

"We're going back to your old neighborhood," said Max, feet on the dashboard. A hula dancer wiggled between the fuzzy bedtime slippers she was wearing instead of real shoes.

I hit the brake and nearly bumped the shiny sports car ahead of me. "What?" Traffic was already backing up from Pratt Street, the spot where all the tourists went to spend their hard-earned bills on crab T-shirts and water taxis.

Max grinned goofy and turned to me. "Jo-Jo Dyas, *this* is your life."

I waited for the rest of what she was saying but then saw that she was done. "Is that a joke or something?" I asked, glancing over but keeping my eyes on the stoplight.

"Well, yeah," said Max, getting this deflated look on her face. "'This Is Your Life!' It was a TV show, bunny. They brought on people from the contestant's past and surprised them. They had to guess-like who the person was."

I shrugged. "I never heard of it."

"Just drive," she said, sinking low. "Or maybe I should get out and walk. Then you can do what you do best, and follow a girl around."

My sister had lost a lot of weight since I'd seen her last. This would have been a good thing if Carrie had done it for any other reason but grief.

I was looking down on her from the roof of the auto-supply shop behind my old house. From up there, the whole neighborhood looked as small as I'd always thought it was.

Carrie sat in a chair on the back patio, and asleep in his beat-up blue playpen was her baby, my nephew. I stared, speechless for a sec. I could hardly believe I was back there, secretly walking around town even as I was buried somewhere with maggots for brains.

"That's my house," I said, pointing it out. "And that's my sister, right there."

"Wow, really," said Max sarcastically. "What are the odds?"

"You're a bitch," I said.

"I know," she said, smiling.

Max leaned back against a big metal box, maybe a ventilation unit, and stretched out. Then she reached into the side pocket of her dress and took out a small plastic case as big around as a box of cigarettes. Unsnapping the lid, she slid out a small, folded pair of sports binoculars. The University of Maryland Terrapins logo was printed on the side but starting to flake off. "I come prepared," she said, passing them to me.

"Where'd you get this?" I asked.

"Harlan Hogg," she said, "from whom all blessings flow."

Sticking the eyepiece to my face, I scanned the blur of the street and then swooped down into the backyard, where bees zipped in and around the overgrown rosebushes Ma had planted back when I wasn't even a drunken burp in my pa's throat.

I zoomed in on the kid asleep in his little padded cage. A huge dragonfly lazily circled but zipped away when I turned the focus knob, like it knew I was watching.

The kid looked pretty good. Carrie had fattened him up, and he wore shoes, something he'd never had before.

He'd never needed shoes when I knew him, or at least I didn't think so. A couple months ago he could barely stay on his feet for more than three seconds. I tried to picture him walking, arms above his head, little hands tucked in someone's big hands. I guess that someone could have been me if I'd been around, to guide him around and to hold him up.

I went back to focusing on Carrie. Her face filled the whole eyepiece. I stared unblinking at that big white shape, like a scientist checking out the surface of an undiscovered planet.

I'd never really looked too hard at my older sister. Little brothers aren't supposed to. Sisters are gross and mean and like to torture you just because you're small and because you pee standing up, which they point out is pretty damn weird. Their floors are littered with twisted bras, and they got magazines about boys stashed just about everywhere.

If it weren't for our fights, which could get real nasty, Carrie and me never would have talked at all. We were two different species, sort of like natural enemies, and every day we'd fought our instincts and got along just well enough not to rip each other to bloody pieces.

But as I sat there cross-legged on the roof across the street and watched her, Carrie didn't look much like my sister. No. She looked more like our ma. She looked older, smaller, not so much bad as skinny and ready for a really long nap.

"You know what's funny?" I said to Max.

"What?" I broke her out of some brood she'd been in.

"It sounds messed up, but Carrie ain't that bad-looking," I said. "I always just thought she got pregnant because she put out. I never thought much about how other guys saw her, you know?"

"I'm sure it was a little bit of both," said Max, sitting up. She came over and took the binoculars from me and squinted through the lenses. "But you're right. She has a classic face. Like if Ingrid Bergman waited tables at Denny's."

I let Max watch for a few more seconds. "You think she misses me?" I asked.

"Probably," she said. Then she waited. "Did you ever give her any reason to?"

I looked over my shoulder and glared at her, angry words at the ready.

She was right, though. I hadn't given Carrie much

cause for hurting over me. My death might have been a relief, even. "Yeah, but who does?" I said after a long while.

"I did," said Max.

This burned me bad. "Well, not all of us can be awesome," I snapped at her. "Maybe if Carrie had been less of a bitch to me, I'd of liked her more."

"Don't get mad at me," said Max. "It isn't my fault that you feel like you could have done better."

"I did okay," I mumbled, snatching away the binoculars. "I did fine." Squinting at me with wicked eyes, she lay down again on the gravel, belly-up.

As I continued to spy on Carrie, the sun flashed off something. I blinked. A small gold cross hung from around her neck. My no-good, sleeping-around, cold-medicine-swigging sister had found religion.

"Huh," I said.

"What?"

"Carrie's got a cross on," I said.

"Doesn't take much," said Max.

"It would for Carrie," I said.

"I guess she misses you," said Max, picking gravel off the dimpled white soles of her bare feet. Stretching, she stepped into her slippers and got up. When she stood, the dress fell around her with a swish. "Are you coming?"

"Give me a few more minutes," I told her. Then I looked across the cracked street at the tiny figure sitting alone in her lawn chair, like a doll left behind in one butt-ugly hand-me-down dollhouse.

Max looked up. "What did you say?"

I thought about my life. It hurt to do it. "I said you're right," I told Max. "I should have done better."

I don't care who you are, some famous movie star with a two-million-dollar face and a ten-million-dollar pad or a guy sitting in his cardboard box under a bridge counting aluminum cans, at some point in your life you wonder who's going to come to your funeral—and you damn well hope there's going to be a good turnout.

My dream service went a little something like this: My pa would show—released from prison, most likely, or on the run for breaking parole, just sticking his neck out long enough to come to my casket side and apologize for everything he'd ever done *to* me, and not done *for* me. Then Carrie would come up to the altar and drop down on those wrinkly knees, which were usually caked with crud, and thank her lucky stars for such a wonderful brother. She'd weep into her paws and wish me back to life simply so she could show me what a mistake she'd made in treating me so bad, like that time she'd made me eat a half pound of dirt just because she'd lose five bucks to a friend if I didn't. There was a whole parade of people I expected to come and beg for my forgiveness, or to confess to how much they'd always loved me, and so it went, on and on until the imaginary cops were clearing traffic for my pimped-out purple hearse.

I used to like those daydreams. Funny thing was that every single person who'd walked down that aisle came to pay for their sins. Not a one of them showed up because they'd actually liked me.

I thought about that as I pulled under the trees of St. James's cemetery, finding a nice cradle of shade where we could sit and get our bearings. The sun was out and cooking us in the front seat. It made the sticky, spilled coffee on the plastic dashboard heat up and smell like a burnt-down Starbucks.

Kevin had woken up some, and sat in the back

eating leftover breath mints he'd found under the seat—the whole freaking box, like they was popcorn. He'd gobble one piece, get the rush of flavor, and then gobble another.

"We're here," said Max, reading the sign in front of the church. She flipped the switch that made her seat lean back and reclined, stopping when she was eye level with the van door.

"What are we doing here?" I asked, resting my head up against my window. I was pretty worn out after seeing Carrie and the kid. A second look back at my past and I'd get whiplash.

Max took out the binoculars and did some reconnaissance. "Well, while you and the world's mintiest man were beating on computer-game hookers over at Harlan's place, I was making phone calls."

"And what did you find out?" I asked, not really caring all that much. I was lost in my head, reliving this time Violet and I had gotten ice cream on 36th Street, not far from where we were sitting in a stuffy minivan staking out a cemetery. It'd been a day just like this one, where breezes made the maples brush the rooftops.

"See for yourself," said Max, handing me the specs.

"This better be good," I said, and, yawning, I put the lenses to my face again and half expected to see some long-lost relative sobbing over my unfair death, a sight that was probably supposed to make me all weepy inside.

I didn't see nothing like that. Instead, I saw the headstone. It was rectangular and gray—ordinary, a squat white cross. In the middle of the marble was the engraved name: "Jonathan Joseph Dyas." The rest of the lettering got so tiny it was like some vision test with a sick sense of humor. Adding insult to injury, a splatter of fresh bird poop messed the top.

I read the name again. "Is that my grave?" I screeched. I pushed against the lenses, as if that would somehow shoot me across the lawn and leave me graveside.

"No, it's the other Jo-Jo Dyas's," said Max.

"Holy shit," I squealed, leaning so far into her lap I nearly cold-cocked her.

"Something's written below your name," she said, grabbing back the binoculars.

"What is it?" I asked, panicking.

She twirled the dial and focused her view. "Wow," she said.

"Wow, *what?*" I cried out.

She rested the binoculars on her knees, jaw hanging open. "It says, 'A Loving Son and Caring Brother.'" Then she made a stunned *eek!* face. "Can you believe that?"

I couldn't. "That's crap," I insisted. "I was a lousy son and brother, and everybody knew it."

Max looked at me funny, and I stopped short. Saying that out loud sort of shocked me right out of my tantrum.

I *had* been a bad son and a letdown of a brother. Sure, my pa may have done his share to screw me up, and Carrie never would have won a medal for being a good sister, but it's not like I'd ever stepped up and carried the ball either. I was just another Dyas, I guess. Rotten and no good and now, to top it all off, worm food.

We sat there for a while and cooked in the sun, all of us thinking quietly to ourselves as kids passed by on their way home from school. Face-to-plastic, Max inspected the world without ever removing those binoculars, as though nothing she saw through their screwy mechanism was actually happening, and therefore it couldn't touch her.

Suddenly stiffening, Max craned her neck to look down the street behind us. "Don't move," she hissed. "Stay quiet-like."

Burrowed deep in our seats like grunts in a foxhole, we peered over the open passenger window at the walk leading to the gate of St. James's Cemetery. A young guy was hustling along the sidewalk, chain dangling from his baggy back pocket, backpack over one shoulder.

There was something all too familiar about that swagger, a bad something, and it left me cold even with all that electrified life pulsing through me. It made me wish I'd had more good memories of life to go with all the bad ones. Almost every time that I looked back or remembered, it was something I wanted to stay far as hell away from.

Max tracked that homeboy all the way down the walk to where he cut a sharp right into the cemetery, and then she sucked in a quick lungful of air. "No *way*," she muttered. I don't think she meant to say it so I could hear.

"What?" I asked, elbowing in.

"Nothing," she hissed.

"My ass it's nothing," I said, and wrestled with her for

the binoculars. We fought back and forth again until we broke into a fit of slapping, and then finally she surrendered and handed them over.

It was a good day for surprises. At the foot of my grave—which was still pretty fresh, mind you—stood White Knife Johnson, the prick who had killed my girlfriend and then helped in my own death on the blacktop of Charles Street.

I couldn't think of what to say. Moments like that demanded some seriously high-class reflection. What came out of my mouth would say a lot about how far I'd come since that horrible night in the darkness of downtown.

Who was I kidding? I wasn't some poet. "I ought to walk over there and pop that bitch right in the mouth," I said.

"You'll do nothing of the kind," said Max, grabbing my arm. Her grip was cold, a metal vise. "What good-like would it do?"

"Make me feel better," I said, going for the door lock. "Teach him a lesson."

"Listen up," said Max, snapping me around in my seat to face her, "the only one who needs a lesson around here is you, bunny."

With a grumble, I went back to squinting into the eyepiece. I was seeing it, but I didn't believe it. Legs apart, White Knife Johnson was standing in front of my headstone.

Max gestured out the window. "You see? He's visiting you, stupid. He's sorry for what he did."

I glared at her, raging inside. "And you know that for a fact?"

"Of course not, but why else would he be here?"

The cushions behind us squealed as Kevin crawled around getting comfortable. "Wow," he said from out of nowhere. Then he sat up. "That is just wrong."

I turned around and caught Kevin staring out the big backseat window. Then I turned to see what he was gawking at.

"Max!" I screamed.

Out there in the graveyard, glancing over his shoulder real careful in case anyone was watching, White Knife Johnson had folded down the front of his baggy jeans and was taking a nice long whiz on my grave.

We all sat there, unsure of what kind of response to have. Groggily, Max shook her head and then looked out the window again. That little gangster was still going at it, right out there in the light of day.

"He's pissing on me!" I whined.

"I can see that," said Max, reaching over into my seat to start the engine. "Wow. It seems that my lesson has taken a turn for the worst." She looked back. Yup, it was still coming. It's like he'd chugged a six-pack ahead of time. Actually, I bet that's exactly what he did.

"You'd think they'd have someone around to keep things like that from happening," said Kevin. Then he rubbed his eyes. "I guess not."

White Knife finished, shook, and then took off at a jog, snapping his top button as he vanished into the trees across the way, the very same maples that had once made such a pretty whisper.

For a few seconds, there wasn't much to say. Until I went off, that is.

"Well, God, thanks a lot, Max," I shouted. "I'm real happy we came just in time to see *that*. Now I can rest in peace."

"What?" she lashed out. "Did you expect him to hug the ground and cry?"

"No!" I said. "But I didn't think he'd pee *his* name on *my* headstone."

Kevin's face floated between ours. He was wide awake now, listening real close to the soap opera unfolding in that lime-green Plymouth Voyager.

"Yeah, well, what makes you so special?" said Max, getting mean.

I punched the dashboard, which made the glove-compartment door pop open. "I never said I was special," I said. "I'm the opposite of special. I'm as normal as they get."

"You say that like it's supposed to mean something," said Max. "You're always complaining that your life didn't mean-like anything, that it only had meaning when you met Violet."

"Well, you can't argue with the truth," I said. "You want proof? Why don't you go out there and check out my grave. Take a whiff."

Max threw her arms up into my face. "Save your self-pity. I'm sick of it. If your life doesn't have meaning, you have no one to blame but yourself."

As she raged on, Kevin slowly inched away from her wrath and into the cave of the backseat. Nobody wanted a piece of Max's action when the timer was ticking—because when it hit zero, she'd blow.

"The world doesn't owe you anything just because you're born-like," she barked at me. "You can't show up and expect to matter, not for doing what billions who came before you did. Being alive, you didn't earn it. You didn't meet-like any special requirements. You just showed up, bunny."

"And what did *you* do?" I asked coldly.

"My life was a mess too," she said. "But now I make a difference."

"Is that what you call it?" I asked. Max was always educating everyone else on what she saw fit. Well, it was time someone spoke truth to her for a change. I slammed the glove compartment closed and it made the whole van shake.

"You're only trying to screw with my head because I'm not giving up," I shouted, getting in her face. "You gave up on your brother, and the only way for you to feel okay with that is for everyone else to give up too."

"Shut your ugly face," said Max, not yelling anymore.

"It's true," I yelled. "You screwed up and left him, and now it's too late."

"I said shut up!"

"No!"

"This is about you, Jo-Jo!"

"That's what you keep saying, but you don't mean it!"

Then she nearly head-butted me in the process of shrieking, "I'm trying to save your life!"

That's how the conversation ended, with Max turning toward the open window and resting her head on the sill, forehead in the sunlight. I bet she would have started crying if she could have.

I felt awful. If anything, Max was proving her point too well. Without Violet, without something good to hold on to, I was nothing but a trash can full of bad memories. I was no good without the love of a good woman. Worse, I was becoming unlovable.

"Give me the keys," she said. Her voice was very unlike Max, without any feeling tucked in it whatsoever.

"Why?" I asked.

"Because it's my turn to drive," she said with her eyes on the traffic that passed slow and lazy for a weekday rush hour. The lights of the intersection blinked yellow.

We switched places, me in the passenger's seat and

Max behind the wheel. As I was climbing in, I adjusted the mirror so I could see what was going on behind us. A class of schoolkids filled a crosswalk holding hands. "What's the next lesson?" I asked. "Are you going to tell me that if life gives you lemons, make lemonade?"

Her face had a pale, cloudy quality to it, like she had a hangover or something. "No," she said flatly. "We don't have that saying in the Afterlife. We have one of our own."

"Yeah, what is it?"

Eyes worn out and glassy, she looked at me with a smile that wasn't happy in the slightest. "The saying is: When you're surrounded by darkness, you have to make your own sunshine."

The effect of the Open Door was supposed to last about thirty-six hours, but I could feel its hungry pull after only about twenty. Like that babe in that movie *Jaws*, I was floating there in the front seat of the minivan minding my own business when out of nowhere came this tug. At first, it was hardly noticeable—might have been a bump in the road. I didn't think much of it, really. Then, just as I was starting to drift off in a sunbeam, a fly buzzing around my head, the Open Door sent a warning shot.

For a second I thought Max had steered us right into a fender bender.

But in reality I hadn't moved an inch.

"Did you feel that?" asked Max. "Whatever we used to get through is losing its spunk-like."

"What does that mean?" I asked.

"It means we're not going to be here much longer," said Kevin, who had woken up from another nap and decided to join the land of the living, even if only for the last few hours of it. The fool had spent almost his entire vacation from being deceased passed out in a pile of old, soiled receiving blankets that looked like they'd seen one too many spit-ups.

"Should I be freaking out?" I asked.

"Nah," he said. "You'll start feeling a pull. Like you're a fish with a hook caught in you." He showed me, one finger curved up in his craw, a spasm of the wrist.

"We should find a place to sleep it off," said Max, pulling to the side of the road. "Know a place?" She actually looked at me, which she hadn't done for half an hour. Not since our fight.

"What kind of place?" I asked.

"Beats me," she said. "What about someplace pretty?"

I wasn't a tour guide, and what I knew about the city was limited to how much five dollars and a light-rail pass could get me, but if I knew anything, it was where a girl could go to drift off in the evening sun surrounded by flowers.

Sherwood Gardens looked better than I remembered it, with or without the freaky sol buzz I had going on and all that slow twitching of my insides.

As we coasted down a hill and slowed at a stop sign, I caught a smell of sweet landscaped greens outside our open windows. Waiting for the other cars to cross, Max leaned her head against the door and closed her eyes, feeling the day's dying sunlight brush her face.

It was a frown I'd never seen before, one I can only describe as gut-wrenching, heartbreaking, sol-crushing sadness. Just seeing it sitting there brought me down a notch too, because it was my sharp words that had made her feel so shitty.

Young folks walked around us, college kids, I guessed.

Only college chicks could afford to spend so much to look so trashy. As for their boyfriends, they looked a lot like Kevin did, as if they'd just pulled themselves out of a dark car after yakking in a seat-back pocket. Across the road in the garden, a group of them milled around with blankets and sleeping bags, all forming a circle around a big white sheet that'd been stretched and hung over a pair of poles to make an outdoor movie screen.

I'd been to a drive-in once, back when Bart and me were still buddy-buddy. We'd been huffing glue for a few hours beforehand, so I don't remember much, except that the place was crowded with sleazy old dudes and the movie had "XXX" in the title. This was way different. In the bushes lining Sherwood Gardens a cardboard sign poked up from the curb, taped to flimsy wire wickets. It said: "Johns Hopkins University Summer Outdoor Films. *The Seventh Seal*: 7:00." There wasn't an "XXX" to be seen for miles.

"Who wants to see a movie?" I asked.

Max raised her hand, and when Kevin took his sweet time, she grabbed his arm and yanked it up.

She parked the van on a side street lined with land-scaped lilies. We found an old flannel Washington

Redskins blanket in the payload of the van, and I stuffed it under my arm, waiting as Max helped Kevin to the sidewalk. He took it slowly, wobbling as she whispered, "Baby steps, baby steps." Hoofing it across the street to the park, we were met with cool, overgrown grass that slapped at our shins. It felt real nice.

Sherwood Gardens is this beautiful old patch of land in a swanky Baltimore neighborhood where I could never afford to live, but where I could show up any time I wanted and walk the grounds for free, even nap under a dogwood with my shoes off. Once upon a time, it had been some rich fogy's private garden, and his neighbors took it over when he died. From what I've heard, they raised millions every year to pay for all those flowers. You can see every penny in the petals.

I couldn't help but think of my Violet, and not just because that place was full of blossoms. We'd met in that field two years before, even though it felt more like one long lifetime, which I guess it kind of was. As I lost my shoes and went black-and-white barefoot through the grass, I wondered what Violet would have thought if she could have seen me.

When we reached the open clearing where the kids

were gathering, Max blew a strand of hair out of her face and then kept it afloat on a long blast of breath. "Wow," she said, inhaling the air, tasting it. It was perfume to her, nothing less. Flower beds sprang at every turn, and cool blue shadows darkened the evening trees. "I wish it went on like this forever. I just wish it went on and on, and we could keep walking and never reach the end. It's paradise-like."

It *was* paradise. Max had it right on the money.

We chose a hump of grass underneath a tree that I recognized, and I unfolded the blanket for the three of us to sit on. We lay back flat on the ground, dozing as the Open Door plucked our insides like we were a trio of fancy string instruments. It was a feeling like no other. The sun warmed our dead feet for those last few minutes before it set. And soon the murmur of the crowd got quieter and the hum of the crickets got louder, darkness with a bright-white screen and the munching of microwave popcorn.

I lay there kicking myself for going after Max so hard back at the cemetery. Sometimes when you're pushed so far to the edge, there ain't anything to do but push back.

That or you can step out of the way real fast and let the other person fly off the cliff. And that was something I never wanted to do to Max. She was the one person who'd stayed with me all this time, through every step of my stupidity.

I reached out and found her hand, glad when she didn't pull away. "So have you ever gone home?" I whispered. "Have you ever seen what life was like without you?"

She shook her head. Her hand felt cool, almost damp.

"Why didn't you?"

"I couldn't," she said. "It was too hard."

There was a giggling sound and then a whir. Out of nowhere, sprinklers came on behind the trees and the whole crowd exploded into drenched craziness. I jumped up and started to tug our blanket out of the spray, but Max just lay there like she was in a trance watching the drops of water twinkle in the beam of the video projector. While everyone else hightailed it for cover, she sat there until her straggly hair hung on her bare shoulders and the blanket had turned a darker shade of red.

I half expected the living ink to come melting out of her eye sockets and ears, to drain away like a painting left in the rain. But it didn't. The only thing that ran was the mascara she'd dabbed under her eyes—Harlan's dead wife's mascara. It made two perfect black streaks down her face, from cheekbones to collarbone.

Then the spraying stopped and the pranksters who'd brought the sprinklers got nabbed by some chaperones and dragged away. The swish of water was replaced by a lot of folks laughing. Coeds rushed around to clean up, to do damage control and get their little movie night back on track. The water had woken up Kevin, just enough for him to stroll a ways off and get a closer look at a blonde in a now-wet T-shirt. As for me, I just stood there looking foolish, a blanket in one hand with a girl on it. Max stayed motionless.

"He used to spray me with the hose," she said in a voice that gave nothing away.

I waited. Then asked, "Who did?" as I pulled as hard as I could, dragging her across the slick grass as if I were trying to do that crazy trick where you pull the tablecloth out from under the place settings without knocking all the dishes over. I dragged her about ten feet until we reached a dry spot under a different tree.

Settled again but soaked, I plopped down next to her and crossed my legs. She dried her eyes on the sleeves of her shirt and leaned down toward me, hesitated, and then put her whole head in my lap so she could stare upward into the mess of branches overhead. Birds moved quietly in the leaves like ghosts.

"Who used to spray you with the hose?" I asked again.

"Clark," she said, "my brother. He used the hose, squeezing down with his thumb to make-like the water into a stream."

"I used to do that to Carrie," I said, "back when she was little." I pictured my sister as I'd seen her from the roof, all grown-up-looking. Then I remembered her wet to the bone and shrieking like a cat in a bathtub. We'd had some good times, all right.

"I pretended it bothered me," said Max. "I don't know why."

"Because family is family," I said. "You're supposed to find them annoying."

"Is that right?" she said, trying to smile. "Since when do you dole out advice?"

I shrugged. "Think about it. Who else out there will take your shit and not give up on you? They're your practice. If they don't test you, they're not doing their jobs."

She laughed. "I guess you would know."

I laughed too, but I also sensed that we were getting back into good territory. Max's bursts of words came after a long stretch of silence. With her legs folded in front of her, she stared off into the evening, eyes on the totally empty white screen. To look at her hypnotized face, you'd think she was following a whole story line.

"What happened to your brother?" I asked.

"He got hit by a car," she said, monotone. "He was riding his bike. Some guy spilled coffee on his pants and looked down just long enough." She closed her eyes and hummed. It wasn't a sigh or a sniffle but a musical note, a way to sum up all that anger and sorrow into a single sound.

She gazed into the big white sheet stretched out across the grass as the fabric rustled gently in the breeze. "He was ten," she said. "He'd just gotten back from summer camp the day before. He was on his way to his friend's house, to tell him he was home. The stop sign was two blocks from my house. You can see it from the kitchen window."

I understood her pain. "How long did you look for him?" I asked.

"For about three years," she said. "I just kept thinking about him out there alone-like."

"I know the feeling."

She looked at me, eyes so artificial blue they reminded me of how fake our time on Earth was, and how we didn't belong there, no matter how much we wanted to. "I didn't want to tell you about him," she said.

"Why not?"

"Because after a while I started to forget him," she whispered, and as she said it, her face struggled to stay put together. "Years passed. You know? Now there are only these little pieces I remember-like. And, well, I don't like to think that it's what you have to look forward to."

"It's weird," I said, thinking out loud.

"Everything's weird." She sighed.

The college kids had got themselves all worked out on a collection of blankets around the movie screen, like a mess of life rafts circling a shipwreck. At long last, the movie started. There were cheers and a couple of burps. I couldn't have cared less.

After taking a breath and twiddling her fingers, Max made eye contact again. "Tell me what you mean-like by that. What's weird?"

I looked around at all the little things that are part of life, from the curving blades of grass to the kicked-off tennis shoes flung alongside the sidewalk. "That you forget," I said. "That all of the big stuff slips your mind, but small things, like getting soaked with a hose, those are the things that bang around in our heads forever."

"Looking back is tough," she said. "It makes it easier if there are good things to remember when you do."

I looked at her. She was so pale she was almost glow in the dark. Her sol had gotten a bit dimmer, but nothing to worry about. Not like mine. It reminded me of winter nights in the car with Violet, when her glassy black skin had gone as cold as ice. All I wanted to do was make her warm again. Make *them* warm again. "Max," I said, "I want to have good things *now*, too."

She raised one eyebrow. "You don't say?" she said. "Isn't that what I've been trying to tell you all along-like, you asshole?"

"Yes," I said, hanging my head.

"Moving on doesn't mean forgetting," she said.

"Not when I have help," I said.

"You've got me," she said. Then she sighed and rubbed her eyes. "That is if you quit being such a bunny, *bunny*."

I had trouble thinking of us in any other way except for sitting on that blanket, wet from the sprinklers, together. She looked up at me with a smile that told me everything was going to be fine and that even though I'd be afraid, I'd never be alone.

I stroked her hair, and then I said, "I think I'm falling in love with you."

As I said it, the crowd of college kids reacted to something happening on-screen, and the mixture of laughter and whistles didn't exactly jive with the seriousness of my sudden confession. That must have been why it took Max a second to register what I'd said—the three easiest words in the English language. When she did figure it out, she didn't look too happy. Not at all.

"You are a moron," she hissed. "You are the world's biggest moron."

I paid the response no mind and craned my neck

down to kiss her, trying to reach back and re-create the moment we'd shared so many nights ago down in the sweltering heat of the stream.

"Keep moving and I'll bite your lips off," she said, and she meant it.

I stopped a few inches from her face. "What's wrong?"

She stared up at me with mascara-streaked cheeks and slits for eyes. "Don't you dare try to make me your girlfriend," she said. "I know what happened to the last one."

I sat up again. The kids on the wet grass were laughing so hard.

In the dark and wet, Sherwood Gardens looked nothing like I remembered it. The memory was all wrong. There was no Frisbee, no dog, and no girl in jellies with a smile like a sharp white slice of pear.

I was still me, and Max was right, about everything. I couldn't even be by myself long enough to find myself, what I was meant to do. For me, the only way life was ever worth living was if someone else's love made it so. It was pathetic, *I* was pathetic, and only now did I see how pathetic.

I looked down at Max. She shook her head in disappointment and rolled over to try and catch a few winks, alone. Before closing her eyes, she yawned real big. "Besides, I'm not that into you," she said.

I wanted to cry or to smash myself in the skull with my fists, but I didn't. Instead, I turned away. I couldn't look at her anymore. I could hardly keep from jumping to my feet and running down the street, away from paradise and its flowers and all the little things I'd once loved about it.

"Why did you have to go and do that?" she whispered, furious. "Why?"

The old black-and-white movie played on the big stretched sheet. It didn't look like it made one lick of sense, some Euro flick with a bunch of those words at the bottom of the screen. At one point, the character of Death, the Grim Reaper, was playing chess against a knight. I got the gist of the story enough to know who the man in black was. He wore a big robe and was real creepy-looking, with white makeup and dark lips.

At about that time the numbness started, first in my head and then sliding down over my eyes. The sound of the Swedish or Swiss or whatever the language they were talking began to fade slowly, like the turn of a volume knob. At that point I felt so much like sleeping that I didn't put up a fight.

Everything felt tingly, but I kept right on watching that movie. And the more I stared at the Grim Reaper moving around on-screen like a bad guy, the less frightening he seemed. In fact, caked up in all that pale makeup, Death looked a lot like a clown.

She chose to park several blocks away so as not to attract attention, because in that swanky neighborhood, people know which rich-guy car belongs to which rich guy. Then, hand in hand, the two of you raced the rest of the way, dashing across intersections that were sure to turn busy in a matter of hours. Dogs bark, but the windows stay dark.

The air floats in a place between warm and cool. You barely feel it, like there is no air at all, like you are on one of those space walks, where the astronauts move in slow motion. Together, you hurry into the park, into a mysterious undiscovered planet, a place of quiet mansions sitting up on the hilltops, where tall fence gates stay good and locked, and where one walk-in closet is as big as your whole damn house. You are aliens there, explorers in uncharted territory.

Reaching the tree where you first met, the two of you

roll out the blanket. It unfurls like a flag and settles on the wet grass. Flat on your bellies and close together, you creep across the ground, rolling the fabric around you to make a big old love burrito.

Knees knock. Hot breath fills up that small space, and you wait. You expect somebody to have noticed by now, to have spotted the two unfamiliar shadows sprinting through the tulips. But no one does. You are invisible. You are more than aliens now. You are ghosts.

You want to get as close as two people can get, so you take off your clothes and pile them at the foot of the burrito. You take out the condom wrapper and tear it open on the dotted line, careful not to rip the center where the important part has been tucked away. With help, you wiggle into it, not liking the pinch—hating the pinch and the sound of the rubber snapping. You climb on top, and your weak, ugly, stringy little arms shake with the weight.

Before it starts, she whispers, "Be careful, I'm a virgin," using the V-word, which you've never heard outside of some bad joke your pa might tell to some of his stupid, toothless friends. You are a virgin too—a no-brainer. You can't believe she may have ever thought any different.

417

Everything you do seems wrong, from the rhythm to the angle to balance. Still, she keeps her hands on your neck, pulling you closer, so you know she's doing A-OK. You are too concerned about the pain on her face to enjoy much of it. In fact, it doesn't seem like enjoyment has anything to do with it, really. It's about getting closer than you ever thought you could. It's about sharing something you don't just share with anybody. It's about sharing you.

She makes this sound that she's never made before, and it's not at all easy on the ears. It's over, fast, and neither of you reaches any kind of ending. But that's okay. It's okay. You don't see that she's crying until you move out of the way and let the moon come through the leaves overhead to wash over her face.

The girl you love cries like crazy in the crook of your arm. And nothing matters but making those tears dry up fast. There is no other thing.

"Are you okay?" you ask.

"Yes," she says through the shaking.

"Did it hurt?"

"Yes." Then she slips in a breath. "It hurt, but in a good way."

TRACK 5:
LIVING ON THE EDGES

13

I don't remember nodding off during the movie, but I did. And when I woke up, the only part of my body I could feel was the big toe on my right foot, and I flexed it over and over, hoping the feeling would spread to the rest of my leg. No such luck. I was just this big toe floating through space, for all eternity.

The insides of my ears started to crinkle, like they were stuffed with tinfoil or had been tuned to some TV station that couldn't get reception. I opened my eyes and found nothing but blackness, an outer space without all the stars. Hell, I could have closed them shut again and not even known the difference.

After a few seconds of that, I heard the whooshing.

I felt all stretched, like some parts of my body were moving far ahead of others.

Then the wind stopped, and so did the sound, and that's when I felt myself flying through the air.

I had just enough time to say, "Whoa," before whacking a padded piece of wall with a loud, back-shattering crack and dropping hard to the floor. In front of me, the Open Door roared with a blast of wind, and then, creaking loudly, it slammed shut and locked. Silence.

The room was still and normal, except for the fact that my bare butt was pressed to a stained old gym mat on the floor.

I sat dazed for a few seconds. Then I smelled something real funny and looked down to see that expensive watch on my wrist smoking like a burnt toaster waffle. It wasn't gold anymore, but a cracked and ashen gray color—or colorless. It looked like it should have hurt, should have burned against my skin, but it didn't. When it stopped giving off little puffs of smoke, I went to touch that watch, and when I did, it fell apart into about a thousand pieces.

"Dang," I said. "I broke it."

That's when Kevin staggered past making the universal face for "I'm going to barf." It was a good sign when I heard him get sick in a hallway trash can. It meant my ears were working again.

We'd shown up back in the Office of Reincarnation.

"Ugh," said Kevin, wobbling back up to me. He slapped his face once. "Did I do anything stupid?" he asked.

"You wet your pants in the back of a minivan, but other than that, no," I said.

"Double ugh," he murmured. He walked buck-naked across the room and took our clothes off the hooks on the wall. The first hook was already empty.

"Hey," he said, glancing over his shoulder at me. "Have you seen my cousin?"

"Remind me who that is again?" I said, feeling a weird ringing in my ears. Not the good kind, the Fiendish Lot kind, but like I was about to get a bloody nose.

"Max," said Kevin. "Have you seen Max?"

We walked back to Little Anglo through the weakly lit streets of Avernus, with its tall towers and its frayed and saggy electric lines sparking in the pitch black. The wooziness made it so we didn't have to say much, not that we had much to chat about as we avoided the potholes and ignored the kooks in their oversized heads doing jigs for a bottle of sunshine. For once, the runt and I had our minds on the same thing: Max, who could have been anywhere. The one place we knew she wasn't was with us, which was where she belonged.

I felt sorry for Kevin. When we stomped in through the rain-splattered front door of their duplex, he actually broke into a run to check the bedrooms—but he came up empty-handed. The chick had split.

The Insco house was cold and dark and full of echo. The old man's bed still sat in the middle of the living room where we'd left it. We hadn't even changed the sheets after he'd burned to a crisp a couple days before. In fact, the place still smelled like fried old guy. It wasn't a very nice thing to say, but it was by far the best way to describe that certain stink.

I wandered into the hallway, walking to the very end, where Max's bedroom door hung open in front of a grandfather clock that had long ago ticked its last tock. I'd never seen Max's room. During my time in the house, all the action seemed to revolve around the old man's deathbed across the hall, or down in the cellar where I'd slept my first as a Newly Dead bunny, with my face pressed into the ass-smelling community futon.

Max's bedroom was almost completely empty. The small bed had been pushed into the far corner of the room, and beside it stood a desk, equally bare and just as plain. Big white squares marked the parts of the wall where she'd once hung posters or picture frames. Bent nails still stuck from tiny holes in the crumbly plaster.

I noticed something as I stood in her doorway. There wasn't a single knickknack. The bed was pure white, not decked out with any decoration or defining marks, not even a cute little throw pillow for kicks. No diaries. No stuffed animals with a loose button eye that was dangling by a single string. No security blanket. I found it kind of funny. For a girl with such a hard-on for souvenirs, Max didn't really seem to have any of her own. It was like that room was some black hole of memories, sucking up any kind of evidence that a real, flesh-and-blood human being lived there.

Truth was she'd never slowed down long enough to collect all that dust. She'd hardly ever slept, or stopped to think, or done a single thing for herself. That was how she lived her afterlife. Back when I was alive, I'd spent whole weeks of my life sitting in my bedroom giggling into a bong shaped like a Buddha. Not Max. She was a rolling stone, and I don't mean the wrinkly British guys.

I sat at the foot of her bed. It was hard, like a bed of nails, a good resting place for someone hoping to remember the pain she'd suffered even as she tried to get past it. Me, I just wanted a good night's sleep for a change, some honest-to-God peace.

The tramcar swung wildly and sent me sliding up against a chick[49] with a hairdo that looked like an angry crow was perched on her head. Smacking hips doesn't exactly make you look friendly, and the girl gave me a look that would have boiled water. Creaking and squeaking, we twisted on the cable, feeling the high winds ripple up the cliffs and rumble along the car floor. It was the longest trip I'd ever taken, and every time I looked out the foggy windows, I was reminded how far I'd come and how little I'd changed.

I wanted to find Max. She was my best friend, and she'd left me because I was worse than a coward. I was the coward who's such a pussy that when he's drowning, he grabs onto another drowning guy and uses him as a flotation device. Since I didn't have Violet to cling

---

[49] Yolanda Wild, 1967–2001: complications from asthma when trapped in an elevator with members of a boys' chorus.

to, I'd latched onto Max, and she didn't deserve to get dragged down to where I was probably headed.

I knew that the Fiendish Lot—plus one Bob Sumo—were scheduled to play a gig at some venue in the farthest-away city of the Afterlife, a place that had the unfortunate name of the Beaches of Acheron, which to me sounded like some kind of board game about wizards. If I could find them, and Max, maybe I could apologize, make my peace. It was the least I could do.

I took a look around me in the tramcar, at Kevin with his nose deep in a *Penthouse* like it was an actual book, and at a snuggling old couple[50, 51] who seemed to have dodged the whole lost-souls thing and were cuddling up happy as two shriveled-up clams, and then down at the never-ending scenery outside the window. The growing fog made it so you couldn't really see where we were going, and what I saw came at us too fast to prepare for.

---

[50] Harold Mills, 1952–2004: misinterpreted the signals of his high school sweetheart, proposed, and was unhappily married for thirty years, all the while too cowardly to do anything about it; killed in a taxicab collision in New York City.

[51] Amanda Mills, 1954–2004: killed in a taxicab collision in New York City.

And as that crow-haired chick began to slide down low in her seat, face smashed into my shoulder, body going limp with sleepiness, I began to feel her dead-weight hanging on me, and I thought back to my grave sitting there alone in a patch of weeds, only a few months old and already forgotten.

When your mind gets used to the idea of giving up, you can't think of anything else. No more knocking your head against a world that doesn't seem to want you in it. No more "how you doings" or "see you laters." No more looking in the mirror and seeing the one person you'd hope to never see again: yourself. Once you imagine what it might be like to give up all that heartache, the whole idea begins to seem less crazy and eventually even makes a bit of sense. I was starting to realize that never having to try again was the best thing I could strive for. Because I was tired, and I did not want to keep on keeping on if it meant I had to do it as me, Jo-Jo Dyas.

The tramcar arrived at the station and wobbled back and forth on its wires. A voice said something in static over the loudspeakers, and everyone around me groaned and got to their feet. I stood up, holding onto a handle for support. When I let go, my fingers left a dark wet handprint on the metal, the sign of a lost sol.

With a *ding* the doors opened, the people filed out, and I followed.

Now, I'd been to a lot of strange places in my afterlife. This was the exact opposite of my old life, in which the one time I'd ever left the county was to meet a drug dealer in a Food Lion just over the Pennsylvania border. But ever since that morning when I came to in a wriggling pit full of slimy arms and legs, I'd become Indiana freaking Jones. I'd seen the world—a city up on stilts, like it was trying to walk around without getting its feet dirty, and one that never stopped burning and smelled like a holiday cookout gone real wrong.

But the Beaches of Acheron was different. You knew it the second you felt the moist wind sweep in through the tram windows. It was less like a sea breeze than a genuine ocean tide, rolling in to drag you away in the undertow.

If the Afterlife had put out a yearbook with those little labels in the back pages, like the ones that say, "Most Likely to Get Real Chubby," or, "Best Sideburns," the Beaches would have won the "Most Mysterious" label, because as hard as you stared and as much as you saw, you never quite knew what you were looking at. The entire town seemed to flash in and out of a speedy cloak of fog that swirled around our heads in dizzy spirals and smelled faintly of a blown fuse. The ground was nothing but wet, gray sand, and it was a bitch to hike through. Clumps of it kept getting trapped in my shoes, like crushed ice.

There really wasn't much in the way of a city once you left the station, only half-assed shantytowns strewn along low sand dunes, like the squatters' villages that had risen up under some of the overpasses back home. That's where the lost sols congregated, where they outnumbered the regular folks a good three to one. Looking at the endless sand and the eerie white light shining far away over the dunes, I half expected people to be screaming, "Spring break!" But the air was as cool as ever, and the mist clung to your skin like an eerie layer of sweat, and you knew right away that the Beaches of Acheron was where folks came to die.

"What do you think?" I asked as we left the tramway station and nearly got run down by a stampede of lost sols moving off together in one direction.

"I think I understand why no one ever comes down here," said Kevin.

"You think Max is here?" I asked.

"Probably," he said. "But if she knew what was good for her, she would stay in Avernus. At least there the fog doesn't eat you."

Off in the distance, several tall black smokestacks burped out a trickle of red smoke, which blended right in with the rest of the smog. If hell was real, it probably looked something like that, except hotter, bigger, and with a lot more pitchforks.

"What's that all about?" I asked Kevin, who usually seemed to have the answers.

"Object-rendering plants, I'd guess," he said. "Like power plants."

"Keep an eye out," I said, trying to hold my bead on him as the fog made my walking a near stumble. "We're looking for a place called Green Pastures. I think it's a bar or a hotel or something."

"Comforting," he said, and grabbed hold of my shoulder to steady himself. And we took off at a shuffle, the blind leading the blind.

Green Pastures was actually pretty tough to miss, even with its white rectangular billboard buried under a tidal wave of sand that had blown in from the Edges. It was like a huge old East Coast beach hotel you saw on postcards at flea markets, places that had long since been bulldozed to make way for condos. It stood high on a rise near the outskirts of town where the haze was thickest and where its pointy towers looked like they were dissolving in the polluted murkiness of the low-hanging clouds.

We passed the last few empty buildings, a small shack called "Big Al's Last Stop Shop," and then came across the wide front steps leading up to the house. Our feet made no noise as we climbed, and when we reached the wraparound deck, we found the front door hanging open and a small silver luggage cart with nothing on it waiting by the welcome mat. The place filled me with chills, and not the usual kind you get from being dead. Behind the long, curving deck rail clicked a line of rocking chairs, all moving all together like a crowd doing the wave at a baseball game. Faded bodies filled the seats, sputtering with weakening lights. It was pretty, *too* pretty, like some kind of trap. We went inside.

432

The main lobby was as high and hollow as a church. Tall picture windows along the back wall gazed out over the fog as if it was a view of something, which it wasn't. Nobody stood at the front desk, but there was a single cigarette petering out in an ashtray. A small silver bell sat quiet on a back counter below a group of hanging mailboxes that looked like a tic-tac-toe game. Kevin tapped it, and then we waited as its shiny sound jumped out like an alarm.

Nothing happened. Off to one side of the counter was a cardboard standee. It showed a drawing of clouds and seagulls and read: "Welcome to Green Pastures, a resting place for those about to move on." And the fine print: "Our goal is to provide a peaceful, relaxing environment in which people can come to terms with their existence and make informed choices. So relax, enjoy, and take a load off. You've earned it."

"They make it sound like you're buying a mattress," Kevin said after reading.

Poking around behind the desk, we found a pair of patio doors that opened out onto a gigantic garden with nothing in it but dried fountains, empty flowerpots, and a crooked set of risers that leaned dangerously to one side. The rest of the marble patio was open space and coated knee high with fog.

As soon as we set foot outside, there was a shout from across the cloudy openness, a "Hey!" and then someone clapping. I saw a hand waving back and forth. "Hey, the prodigal moron returns!" The voice sounded miles away, farther than it should have. It was Ed. He walked toward me, pretending to swim through the rolling waves of mist. On any other day it would have been a riot.

Getting closer, I saw the band's equipment piled up behind the risers, a tepee of guitar cases leaning against a tower of drums. Coolers of sunshine had already been raided and left empty, their pried bottle caps dotting the marble. I shook hands with Ed, who smacked me on the back, a little too hard, actually.

"Hey," he said, and then, "Whoa! You're freezing!"

"We were hoping you'd show up!" yelled a second person. I turned around and saw Wes sitting in an oversized Adirondack chair wearing a winter hat with earflaps on either side and a ball on top. He wore little else. Beside him sat the band's part-time drummer, the ponytailed Bob Sumo. He slouched there practicing

434

his autograph on a napkin.

"Is Max with you?" I asked.

Ed scratched his neck. "Well, unless she got real ugly and real dumb and became my brother, then no, she's not here."

"Don't listen to him," shouted Wes, snuggling into his chair, his dark body standing out on the white chair like a shadow. "She's inside looking for a sweater."

"Wes doesn't need sweaters," added Ed. "He stores-like fat for the winter."

Wes yawned. "Hilarious. Ha. Ha."

"Max is here?" asked Kevin.

Ed eyed him. "Why should I tell you?" he asked. "Aren't you her uncle or something?"

"I'm her cousin," said Kevin, "and I'm guessing that you guys are Max's band. I'm delighted to say I've never seen a show."

"I'm hurt-like," said Ed as he took Kevin's hand and shook it politely. "And if you don't mind, these goobers are *my* band not Max's. Please don't make that mistake again."

"If only that were true," said Max. The outside door slammed, barely making a sound and sending a curl of fog breaking over the rest of us. Carrying a steaming mug with both hands, she carefully crossed the marble, trying not to spill a drop of whatever she was drinking. Whatever it was, it gave off a warmish glow that turned her snowy face a California-suntanned gold.

Max looked like she was dressed for the holidays at a ski resort, with a multicolored sweater that was now a linty gray and a pair of tight jeans that had been sucked of their blues by the Afterlife's unholy acid wash. On her feet she wore a high pair of winter boots with white fur lining the tops. Penny came out behind her looking like he'd just woken up, even though I knew the guy hadn't slept in years.

"Is that Jo-Jo?" he asked, giving a weak salute. "What brings you down to the edge of the world, mama?"

"He followed me," said Max. "It's what he does." Her words pricked like icicles.

I walked toward them, but as I did, Max veered out of my path and made a wide arc around me, balancing that mug so nothing spilled. "Listen," I started, "I'm sorry, really. I know I screwed up. I understand now."

She extended one chubby little hand to stiff-arm me. "You don't understand anything," she said. "After everything I've done for you."

Reaching the chair with Bob Sumo's ass planted in it, she glared at him in a way that only worsened that nip in the air. "Get the hell out of my seat, *Bob*." And damn if that little creep didn't pop up off that chair as if he'd been sprawled on a spring.

I stood to one side. "You were right," I told her. "I can't be alone."

"You're *not* alone, you idiot," she said.

"I think I know what I need to do," I said. "And you helped me figure it out."

With a flick of a thumb, she showed me the door, or, in this case, the fog, which hid a door in there somewhere. "Tomorrow, you're gone," she said. "Your ass is out of here."

Concerned, Wes sat up, which he only ever did for a real good reason or because a girl was taking off her top. "Wow, Max," he said, "isn't that kind of harsh-like?"

Max looked at me, and it seemed as if she was trying to make me leave right there and then, with nothing but the meaty strength of that stare. "No," she said. "I've put up with him long enough."

"You're right," I said. "You have."

"Tomorrow, you're gone."

I nodded, feeling a familiar freedom wash over me. I wasn't afraid no more. "You're probably right," I said. "Tomorrow, I'll be gone."

"Probably nothing," she said. "This is your last night with the Fiendish Lot. So enjoy it." Then she cocked her head and gave me the sassiest, bitchiest, and sexiest smirk I'd ever seen on a girl that wasn't a porn star. If I'd still been a dumb ass, I might have fallen for her all over again. But I wasn't in love. If I knew nothing else, I knew that.

Ed rubbed his chin and sat down on the risers. The whole stage gave a loud groan and dropped a few inches, which knocked a snare drum loose and sent it rolling down the rickety steps and off into the mists of the underworld.

He looked at Penny, Wes, and then Kevin. "Does anyone have any idea what they're talking about?"

"They must have hooked up or something," said Bob Sumo, and for once, no one told him to shut the hell up.

14

On the morning of the final show of the Fiendish Lot's last tour, the group of us got up pretty much like we had every other day before that one, kicking off the day with a single bottle of sunshine that got passed down the line, starting with Penny and ending with me. Once I finished my one long, warming swallow, Wes serenaded us with a burped chorus of Bon Jovi's "Livin' on a Prayer." That, too, was a ritual.

But no matter how on-key Wes's burps were that particular morning, a dark cloud hung over the dressing room of Green Pastures Resort and Sol Spa. I rolled off the couch, restless, knowing I was back where I'd started.

I'd never been good at much. Not once did I really put any effort into anything, schoolwork or work of any kind, really. My ma had wanted me to take piano lessons, but she died long before that ever happened.

Once I had an English teacher who said I had promise, who offered to tutor me after school. I never took her up on it and spent my afternoons huffing adhesive and throwing rocks through the windows of an abandoned warehouse. My life, the living part of it, had been one long series of screwups. The only stuff I'd ever had a talent for were giving up, and doing nothing.

So deciding to walk off the end of the world like I was walking the plank, well, it wasn't too tough, not when I'd already tried to off myself once. If a guy can't find a reason to go on living when he's alive, I don't know why he'd suddenly find a reason to when he's dead.

That chilly, wet morning near the Edges, the Fiendish Lot got up off their sheets and went to pee but didn't really seem to know what to do after that. They sat in a little circle in the middle of the dressing room, which was already totally trashed even though they'd only showed up at the hotel a day before. Hardly anybody talked, and if they did, it wasn't to me. We spent most of our early moments staring at each other, which wasn't that fun since every one of us was an ugly cuss.

As I sat on a stool in the small dressing room watching the fog move slowly over the balcony and through the open windows, like a river overflowing its banks, Penny, Ed, and Wes surprised me by starting to clean up the place. I was pretty positive that those ratty bastards had never cleaned up a day in their afterlives, yet there they were, sporting brooms instead of guitars and tidying up like a bona-fide cleaning service. It was such a job that I grabbed a broom from a closet full of old hand soaps and little Star of David napkins from some past Hanukkah party, and I got my hands dirty too.

No one said much as we swept and shined and collected bottles from under tables and along windowsills. I didn't have a clue what brought this on. I wanted to think the guys were bummed I'd been banished from the group, but I knew it was more mysterious than that, like one of those complicated math problems where two guys are riding on two trains in two different directions and two different speeds, and you're supposed to know at one point they're going to intersect, but the only answer you ever come up with is more of a question in itself: "Why didn't they just pick up the phone?"

Max stood near the door to the balcony, alone. She hadn't said a word to me all morning. Down on one knee, she cinched up her fat duffel bag, which had been mostly emptied and become all droopy.

I walked over to her and waited. I didn't really know what to say, except sorry.

"What do you want?" She hadn't lost any of her anger overnight. I was hoping she had. I was always hoping for second chances.

"I screwed up, and I want to apologize," I said.

"Me too," she said.

"I wish I could take back kissing you," I said. "But I can't."

"I know."

I stuck my hands in my pockets. "For what it's worth, you were right, about me relying on other people and all, wasting my life. I let a lot of people down."

"Who doesn't?" she said.

"It won't happen again," I promised her.

"Well, at least you learned something, bunny," she said, and turned away.

I guess that was good-bye.

A knock at the dressing-room door interrupted me and gave Max an opportunity to walk away, leaving me wanting to say more, though I didn't know what.

I walked across the room and opened the door to find some little kid[52] waiting on the other side.

He came up past my knees, but only if he stood on his tiptoes, which is what he was doing when I caught him. By God, he was funny-looking. His eyes were so big that they almost crashed together in the open spot above his nose. And he had one of them 1980s helmet haircuts, all black, like he was sporting the shell of a weird crab on his melon.

He was also about as see-through as they come. Even though he was a foot or so away from me, I could still feel that strong zap of cold he was giving off, and the voice when he talked was thin and distant-sounding, a transmission from some other galaxy. No matter how goofy he looked, that kid had my pity the second I saw him.

"What do you want, kid?" I asked, face in the crack of the door.

"Is this where the Finnish Lot is playing?" asked the kid.

"The *what*?" I asked. "Man, you messed that up real bad."

---

[52] Gideon Wright, 1996–2004: no record.

"The guy said the Finnish Lot is going to be playing here."

"It's the Fiendish Lot," I said. "And what guy? Don't you know better than to listen to some guy?"

"Everybody's saying it," said the kid, creepy eyes growing big and white. "They're talking about the feeling you get when you hear the music."

"Yeah, well, they ain't lying," I said. All those fading spirits would probably burst into flame, like when Penny got lost in the music and went atomic.

"Well, is this the place?" asked the kid. He couldn't have been more than six or seven, but he had the back-talk of a ten-year-old.

"Sure," I said. "Come back later."

He cocked his head and gave me the hard stare. "Are you in the band?"

"Sort of."

"What instrument do you play?"

"I don't."

"Then how are you in the band?"

"I just am."

Those beady little squints aimed right at me. "You can't be in a band unless you play an instrument," he

444

said. "That's what bands *are*."

"Shut up," I said, and pushed the door shut in his face.

But the kid had a point. Behind me, the band had tidied up real good and had started croaking out short sentences to each other, like a bunch of babies learning to talk using single words to express what they wanted. "Girls?" said Ed, hitching up his drooping pants. "Okay," muttered Wes. "Cool," Penny added, nodding. "Great," Ed said. They hung around by the big picture window, their bright sols beaming through the tails of fog that snaked along the floor. I was going to miss them. They were a lot like some of the sons of bitches I'd known back in the day, but they were also a lot different.

I didn't play anything, so I didn't belong. The only place I'd ever fit in had been with my girlfriend, who I wasn't allowed to be with. All I had left of her were the memories, and even those seemed to be fading.

When the band's backs were turned, I headed out the door and into the fog, hoping I'd at least get to see the edge of the world before I walked off it.

15

When it happened, I was sitting at my kitchen table eating a bowl of Lucky Charms. I'd always been partial to the marshmallows—red hearts, yellow stars, green clovers—probably the reason why my teeth were shot to hell. Between bites, the phone rang. My sister handed me the receiver without saying who was on the other end. She knew it was your grandma by the voice but didn't know the voice well enough to catch the fright underneath the words, the tremble.

But it became clear just like that. I didn't catch the first few words—she was stuttering, coughing—but I knew enough to shut up and listen as closely as I could. Somehow I was up from my chair, one hand on the table and one hand in the air, telling Carrie to stop what she was doing and not make a move, not make a sound lest I miss something. She'd never been so loud in all her stupid life, every footstep a rumble.

Your grandmother told me what you said, the message you wanted to pass along to me, things that I carried forever. I kept them to myself, always.

They were great things, really. They helped me get through the days I looked at the razors, and then down at my wrists, and contemplated making that easy cut. They got me through the night I opened my window and walked to the gutter's edge and saw my shadow twenty feet below on the concrete. It was huge. They got me through all the ordinary nights when I didn't consider anything nutty, but felt like the only person on Earth, as if some disease had turned everybody around me into dust, leaving me alone in my bed. Your words were almost all I needed to survive without you.

Almost.

I don't remember much after our conversation, but I remember howling. Making that noise I never made again afterward, I turned over the kitchen table and I tore down the pot rack and kicked in the glass of the oven door, and all the while the baby was screaming with those powerful baby lungs of his, and Carrie was shrinking back into the corner with her hands over her face, not even bothering to throw herself in front of the kid for its protection. Typical.

And when I was done punching holes in the drywall, I started beating my brain, sinking to the floor in the middle of the spilt milk and all those unlucky charms, wishing it was me who'd been calling you. Wishing it was me who'd been dying.

Because after those words I was as good as dead. My life was over.

As unbelievable as it sounds, you really can find someone by following their footsteps. That is, if there are hundreds of them headed in one direction. Searching for a needle in a haystack, it ain't.

Lost sols leave really shallow tracks, but the ones I found were still plenty deep to trace away from the rendering plant and up the nearest dune, where I lost the trail in a pile of rubble that had broken off the side of a nearby cliff and fallen to block the road. Luckily, I picked it up again a dozen or so feet later, where the mess of prints shuffled off the road, up the shoulder, and then trickled off into the distant mist. That's where I stopped again, to stare, mostly. Far ahead, the world had been gobbled up by a thick blanket of fog that hugged the ground, like an endless sheet of pillow stuffing.

A line of razor wire stretched along the side of the road where I stood. It was old and saggy, vanishing under the sand like a fishing line twisting its way underwater. You've never seen so much sand outside the Sahara.

Ten feet past the wire, I found the body of a man[53] lying where the tracks of his size-eleven loafers ended. There wasn't much man left, just man shape.

As I gawked, wondering what to do, that poor sucker began to flicker with light, and he made a sound that wasn't really happy or sad but just sort of worn out.

Think of a waterfall, where the streams of thundering, falling water hit the pool below and explode into a fine mist that jumps up and hangs over everything. You can walk right into that cloud and not feel much, only to come out again soaked to the bone. That's what happened. Splitting apart into a billion tiny bits of human confetti, that guy's body mixed right in with the fog like it was meant to be there, like they'd been saving him a place all along. His light went out, and within a few seconds I was breathing him in.

---

[53] Chen Duen Muk, 1975–2003: backed over by a tour bus trying to parallel park.

I should have been reminded of how the old man, Ben, had passed on, but those two ways to go couldn't have been more different. Ben had burned up surrounded by folks that loved him. This poor fool had sputtered out alone, face in the sand, ass in the air, in front of a kid who found the whole sight pretty damn depressing.

I hiked a few more paces until I came right up against a sign that read: "YOU ARE NOW ENTERING THE EDGES."

Just in case I didn't get what it was trying to say, there was a little picture:

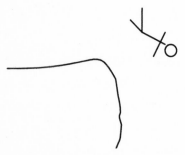

You wouldn't have even known you were going anywhere, if not for the ghouls that wandered out of the churning mist, weeping. They stumbled along not touching the ground, moving real fast toward something

I couldn't see but that had to be there. Smiles beamed from those phantom faces—wasted skeleton grins of haunted-house bliss. Every time I turned to watch them go, the bodies sank into the fog before I could get a good look.

The freakiest thing wasn't that you were never quite sure where you were headed, but that you didn't really care, because the farther you went, the sleepier you felt. It wasn't bad, kind of like being high, like tripping around with a stunned smile on your face looking for a gyro at three in the morning but not being too disappointed if you never found one. Being that empty and tingly again felt pretty damn good.

With that in mind, I began whistling Pink Floyd's "Comfortably Numb," first as a joke, but then for no other reason than to fill up the hollowness with a little music. Of course, I forgot it pretty quick, like I was forgetting everything.

Suddenly, far away, through the fog and haze behind me, the bounce of a bass line started up. A string was plucked once, twice, zipped up a loose riff, and then faded away into silence again. Somebody banged a drum—a military roll followed by a cymbal smash. It was the band starting their sound check for the show at Green Pastures. I don't know how the hell I heard it way out there in the Edges. I guess when there's nothing around to block the sound, it rings through loud and clear. Or maybe it was just that the Fiendish Lot was special.

Doubled over, hands on my knees, I climbed on up the dunes for what seemed like an hour, maybe. Far behind, the sounds of the Fiendish Lot colored the rolling puffs of smoke a real fiery-orange color, like tiny bombs were going off. Shadowy spirits filled the sand around me, scrabbling up the sand on all fours, just like I was doing, some hightailing it for the place where the world ended and, with it, the pain. Others headed back, toward the lights of my friends. I ignored the music and walked on.

Finally, I saw the top of the big dune, the last one. And past it was nothing.

I trudged up the incline, real slow, knowing it was the last time I'd drag those old legs anywhere. The fog swirled around me like I was in the eye of my own private hurricane, and I didn't feel no hurt. Whatever I'd lost couldn't reach me out there, not with sweet release waiting up one last hill and down the other side. All that was left was the climb.

I got to the top pretty quick, and when I did, I smiled. Turning in a circle, I took it all in. The view from up there was nice, a thousand blinking lights in the gloom, a desert of sols winking out for good, and that's when I saw the girl.

She was stubby, cute, and soft in all the right places, and she was just as beautiful as the day I'd met her. "Jo-Jo," she said, and I flinched. Like hearing my name was a bad thing. She stood at the bottom of the dune I'd just scaled, gazing up at me, scared.

When she didn't get a response, Max called again, louder, "Jo-Jo!" She was having trouble getting through the high sand as she swayed her way up to me, that big duffel bag shifting this way and that on her back.

"Go away," I said. My voice was gone now, a cartoon bubble with no words in it.

"I knew you'd come out here," she said, breathing hard even though she wasn't really working it.

I turned and watched her struggle the last few feet. "Why did you follow me?" I asked. It didn't seem like we were in the same place at all, and for a split second I wasn't even sure who she was. "Why do you care?"

"Because . . ." But she didn't finish.

"That's what I thought," I said. The longer I stood there, the more the mist pulled at me, tugging at my deepest pieces.

"Because . . . I wanted to see if you had the balls to do it," she finished at last.

If I'd been a gentleman, I'd have offered to help her up the last few feet. But it was too late for that now. "This isn't a joke," I said.

"I know," she said. "Do *you?*" Collapsing into the side of the dune, she ran a hand through her twisty hair to fix it and then pointed at me. "Look at your hands."

This took me by surprise, and I raised one hand to see what she meant. If I'd had a breath of air in those deflated lungs, it'd have gotten knocked right out of me.

My skin was crinkled and clear, like waxed paper. The ends, the very tips of my fingers, they weren't there no more, at least not like I was used to seeing them. They'd gotten blurry and seemed to shimmer like the passing smoke. If my hand was any indicator, I was on the verge of busting apart into a billion Jo-Jo pieces and

454

drifting away on a sigh. All Max would have left would be the taste of me on her tongue. Then that would vanish too.

"I have to do this," I said, raising my voice to blot out the fear.

"Do it, then," she said, crossing her arms, watching.

"I will," I said.

"Do it!" she shouted.

"I will!" I shouted back.

"Just do it, *do it now!*" She was on her feet marching toward me.

I didn't move, and when I raised my head to look in her face, Max slapped me hard across the cheek. The first time, her hand went clear through me, like I was some futuristic hologram. So she slapped me again. If I'd had any color, those hits surely would have left a mark. Then she grabbed me. She hugged me. She clung to my fading body like we were the last two sailors going down together on a sinking ship.

"There is no choice. Life is not a choice," she yelled, her voice a sob with a shriek wrapped around it. "You have it, or it's taken from you. You *never* give it away."

"Max," I said, feeling myself let go a little more every

second. The mist circled us. The stuff was like a school of sharks, waiting, biding its time until I was ready to give myself up and dive in.

Max slapped me again. "You don't get to give it away"—and her voice cracked, broke—"it's taken, ripped, and only over your dead body!"

In her words I saw the stiff body of my murdered girlfriend stretched across her kitchen floor, and the tended acres of headstones in Green Mount Cemetery, and the sight of the old man bursting into brilliance below his ivory sheets, a crazy tired grin on his ancient puckered face. None of them wanted to go, not really. They could have gone on living if they'd had the chance, the chance I had sitting right there in front of me.

"I can't. I can't do it," I said. It was the only thing I knew for sure.

"Because you don't want to," said Max. "You don't want to let go-like."

"Why would I?" I asked, the anger making me feel alive. "You of all people know what it's like to hold on. You carry a bag full of memories everywhere you go."

Without a word, Max dropped the duffel to the sand with a crash. The sound hardly made a dent in the muffled quiet. She gazed at me with dark, tired eyes, the kind that would have cried all night if they could have. "This isn't about stuff. It's not about what you can carry in some bag. It's about what you're carrying around inside, stupid." She laid a palm on her chest where her heart was. "Memories disappear," she said, "and if you aren't careful, they can take you with them."

"I love her," I said real loudly, as if someone were claiming I didn't.

"You always will," she said. "But Violet's going to leave whether you like it or not. It's how you learn to live with it that matters."

Max was right. I could have held everything Violet owned in my hands, every memory and every kiss, and she'd still be lost to me. After all I'd been through, I understood what I needed to do. And I did it for her, because it was what she would have wanted me to do.

Standing on the top of that dune, I closed my eyes. I felt Violet there. She wasn't with me, not really, but parts of her were, like words in a song you only half remember.

My memories of her pulled away from me, and so I let them go, all of them, once and for all.

first eye contact across the park, when she saw me standing there with a can of Coke and a hand in my pocket.

two hands touching, and I heard a name like a poem.

her hiccup, like a pop, like a bone coming out of its socket.

running, a whirlwind of bony arms and legs, and you could only stand back out of the way and laugh.

that sweet flip-flop *of worn heels in sandal soles, skipping, sprinting, and slipping off for a stroll in the grass.*

how she painted every toe but her big ones—never the big ones.

rubbing my cheek against the shrink-wrap smoothness of her wrists.

mornings in bed all rolled up together, our bodies a single sweaty shadow on the sheets.

her hand spread open across my stomach, dark fingers like continents on a map.

leaning in for a kiss, the crucifix around her neck ringing like a tiny golden bell.

the taste and smell of her skin on a hot afternoon, sweet mixed with salty.

the birdlike chirp of her whisper, every word crisp and hissed and musical.

the brush of her lips against my neck after a long restful night, a warm reminder that morning was coming.

Then I looked further and looked deeper, but nothing else was there.

I freed those sights and sounds and feelings, and once I did, they seemed to mingle with the fog, and a new sensation came over me. Like I was standing on my own two feet again, for the first time, planted. Violet wasn't gone, no, but what I remembered about her wasn't swallowing me whole with it into the emptiness and the dark.

With Max still pressed up against me, I stepped away from the edge, and as I did, a guitar chord sliced through the emptiness, echoing across the desert. It stung. It was like being pricked in the chest with a giant needle.

Max looked up at me, that wonderful round face growing clearer in the fog, little by little. I knew the worst was behind me as Wes twiddled on his bass strings and sent a ripple across the horizon.

I grabbed Max and pressed her to my chest. She didn't smack me again. She tried to hold me to the ground, even if a couple of seconds earlier my sol had wanted to be airborne. If I was going to turn into dust and light and whirl away into the smoke, then she planned to come with me.

"I'm okay," I said. It was true, for the first time in never.

"Are you sure?" she said.

I laughed. "I am right now."

"What about tomorrow?"

"Don't think too far into the future," I said. "That's what you told me. Tea leaves are for drinking."

She grunted. "I hate tea. It's weak."

"Not like you," I said, laughing some more, and feeling a bit like crying, too.

As if she'd been waiting to hear just those words for a long, long time, she slumped into me full bore, all hundred-and-something pounds of her, dense as a bag of cement. We rolled over backward onto the sand, spitting the grains as they coated our lips. "Good," she gasped, going all spread-eagle on her back, head on my belly, "because I'm tired-like, mama."

Lying there about to pass out, we heard the opening notes of the Fiendish Lot's set as it came alive and broke across the sand dunes. It was a pretty sweet song, whatever it was called. But even more than that, it was the sound of our friends reaching out and touching us way out there where the world fell away into nothingness. Even that endless march of fog couldn't keep them back.

"Bob Sumo is a shit drummer," said Max, taking my hand.

As the song rocked on, a wave of light spread across the sand, turning it the brownish gold it should have been, and every sol in the Edges lit up like a swarm of fireflies in a field.

It was a sight to see.

TRACK 6:
ENCORE

16

There comes a time in everybody's life when you got to take responsibility for the stuff you do.

I'd spent a good seventeen years coming apart real slow. A lot of people had their hand in my excuse for a life, but in the end I was the go-to guy for blame. When I popped up slimy and screaming in the Afterlife, there wasn't a single person for me to point my finger at. I'd been given a second chance, and damn it, I was going to go out in the end—whenever that came—with a party so big it'd be standing room only. My friends will be picking up the bottles for a week afterward. That's right, my friends.

I kicked back, reclining real easy-like in one of those fancy Adirondack chairs ringing the patio of Green Pastures. As far as I was concerned, I'd earned a nap.

The Fiendish Lot finished a song with a rip of Penny's guitar, and the ground suddenly stopped shaking, so fast that a few people near the back of the crowd lost their balance, swayed, and caught themselves just in time. They got to laughing—belly chuckles, a great thing to see for a bunch of saved sols. An hour or two earlier, falling down on their faces would have been the least of their problems.

Before the Lot had played, most of the audience had been aimlessly drifting away with the tides of fog sweeping in from the Edges. Now, though, the people looked positively rosy-cheeked. They'd come down the mountain to check in at the spa and then check out of the Afterlife. Of course, they hadn't counted on the Fiendish Lot reminding them what life was like above the clouds, even if you couldn't really call it "life."

Walking upstage, Penny was met with cheers. He raised his hands to quiet down the screaming, and then he waited. Thudding the bass drum a couple times, Max rolled the snare, and then Ed played a silly riff that sounded like what you might hear when a guy tripped on his shoelaces and tumbled down a set of steps—something goofy like that.

"Listen up," said Penny, straining his voice to be

heard. "Hey, listen!" The crowd obeyed, as they always did for him.

He stepped sideways so the towering drum kit was visible to everybody from the very front row to the peanut gallery in back where I was. "I want to welcome back our percussionist, Maxine Insco," he said, presenting her like he was a game-show host and she was a brand-new SUV with bucket seats and a sunroof. "Every band's got a heartbeat, and Max gives us ours. Without her we weren't the Fiendish Lot."

"What were you, then?" shouted someone in the front row.

Guitar neck bobbing with every heavy breath, Penny smiled and wiped away sweat he didn't even have—a habit, probably. It was so easy to forget you weren't alive, that everything didn't work the way you remembered. But when you really thought about it, there really wasn't much difference, was there? Living was living, no matter the backdrop.

"We were just three guys with guitars," said Penny, and he licked his lips.

"I play bass," shouted Wes.

"That *is* a guitar, knucklehead," Ed said.

"But we're not ones to dwell in the past," said Penny. Then he winked at Max and played the first three or four notes of "Stairway to Heaven," by Led Zeppelin. "Well, at least not anymore."

Like she was a cavewoman who'd just discovered that beating a stick against a rock made one hell of a sound, Max began to pound. It was a welcome sound, a beat that rattled the windows of the big old hotel and sent its useless weathervane sliding down the shingled roof and dropping to the ground. When Max hit a cymbal, its shimmer rang across the beaches. And I swear in the distance I saw more people following the sound, coming in from the cold.

The Fiendish Lot was back.

I turned to look at the guy sitting next to me, Bob Sumo, who nursed his bottle of sunshine with something like spite. The guy was grumbling down into his longneck. "Bitches," he mumbled.

"Oh, get over it, Bob," I said.

Before the big finale, which I knew was coming because I was probably the band's number-one fan, and groupies know that sort of shit, I had me a visitor.

I'd started to get used to sitting there on the patio alone—well, alone once Bob Sumo picked his ass up to go gripe in the lobby, where people who might care could hear him—when that little kid showed up and dropped onto the white cushions next to me. I didn't mind. I'd kind of been thinking about him, actually.

You didn't see many little dudes in the Afterlife, and if you did, they were kept real close to adults, as if smashing them up against a pants leg was going to protect them from dying young a second time. I could understand the desire to keep them safe, though. There were enough question marks in the world, enough "whys" without any answers. So it was scary to think what all those youngsters must have thought about it. Kids were the kings of "whys."

He bounced on the patio chair for a few seconds, sort of enjoying it, before settling down. I'd forgotten how creepy-looking he was, one of those horror-movie kids, the kind of little tyke they stick into stories just to scare the bejesus out of you without having to work too hard.

That oily black hair made a perfect bowl around his snowy-white face. Eyelids drooped halfway open, set deep in two little pits above his sharp cheekbones. Still, his look had improved since I'd seen him earlier, like most lost sols that had been lucky enough to find themselves within earshot of Penny and his magical mystery tour. The whole trip had been less like a concert and more like a traveling revival.

I watched the kid screw around, bouncing up and down until he'd about driven me so crazy I felt like popping him one.

"Why aren't you onstage with your band?" he asked, pointing to Penny, who was discussing something with Ed before launching into the last song.

"I'm not in the band," I said.

"No shit, Sherlock," he said.

I gave him the evil eye. I'd been practicing. I was going to try to carry on Max's grandpa's tradition of being an old coot, even if it was before my time. "You shouldn't cuss, man. That's not cool."

"What do you care?"

"I don't care," I said. "That's your parents' job."

"I don't have any parents," he said.

"Well, that explains the attitude," I said, leaning back and closing my eyes and taking a long drink of sunshine.

I could feel that little squirrel watching my every move. "What about you?" he asked. "Where are your parents?"

"I kind of been spending my time looking out for number one," I said, real bossy. "Besides, I'm too old for parents."

"Well, that explains the attitude," he said, real smart. I should have seen that one coming a mile away, the little dick.

We sat side by side, his tiny stick-figure self next to my big one. I relaxed, feeling the sunshine coat my insides and warm me up from the bones out.

"Can I have a drink of that?" the kid asked after a second.

"No can do," I said.

With a thunder of bass, the Fiendish Lot broke into the finale. I opened my eyes, and watched Ed go airborne, legs tucked behind him, chin to chest. His sol was blinding as he flew across the stage, laughing.

"Hey," I said to the kid. "Did you ever run into any girls out there?" I motioned toward the beaches where the mist hung heavy.

"I saw lots of girls," he said.

"What about a real pretty one with dark black skin and big eyes? She had really pink lips and crazy long fingernails?"

"This is a *girl*?" he asked, boggled.

"Yeah, her name was Violet," I said.

Shrugging to the beat of Max's tom-toms, that kid placed his hands behind his head like he was taking a nap on a real beach filled with real people, and like it was the light of the sun that was shining down on him, and not the light from some crazy Southern California kid who'd died when he'd fallen off a roof cleaning the gutters. "People come and go," he said.

It sounded funny. "They do," I agreed.

"So who was this Violet girl, anyway?"

It was a loaded question if ever there was one.

"She was this real special girl," I said. "She was my girlfriend."

"And she's dead, huh?" he asked, sitting up on the cushion, weight on his sharp little elbows.

"Yeah," I said. "But I'll never forget her."

He worked me over with those eyes again, thinking. Then he said something real strange. "I got nobody, and you got nobody, so why don't we got nobody together."

472

I didn't know what he meant, exactly, but he did look all pathetic and lonely sitting there on that giant cushion, the freaky little dwarf. He reminded me a little of me at that age, only uglier, if such a thing were possible. Besides, like I said, I was done looking out for number one. If there was ever a time to start making a difference and give folks a reason to care, it was now. No time like the present.

"Let me think about it," I told him. "Now clam up and listen."

Smiling, he wriggled into the chair next to me, hands under his chin like he was praying.

And we sat that way for a long time, watching the show, together.